MOON TOUCHED

ZODIAC WOLVES: THE LOST PACK #1

ELIZABETH BRIGGS

CHAPTER ONE

AS A ZODIAC WOLF, my fate was tied to the stars. Too bad my stars were more crossed than aligned. Being the outcast of the Cancer pack had taught me that all too well.

The sea lapped up to meet my bare feet like an eager puppy trying to gain its owner's affection. I dug my toes deeper into the cool sand and looked out over the water. It was beautiful, I couldn't deny that, but not in the way the rest of my pack said it was. Members of the Cancer pack talked about its call, like something deep inside of them being answered. For me it was a pretty picture, nothing more. I could photograph it all I wanted, but I never seemed to capture the essence of what they were talking about.

My only hope was the upcoming Convergence, which would unlock my wolf. If I could feel the connection to the sea that the rest of my pack did, maybe they would start to feel like my own people as well. Right now, they were no better than strangers. Sometimes, more like enemies.

I shoved the loneliness aside. It could easily consume me, if I let it. Instead, I focused on the dark ocean once more, trying to frame a shot. The moon just brushed the horizon, casting out reflections onto the water that shifted with every breath of the sea. It really was peaceful, and even if I didn't feel a pull to the sea, I did feel it toward the moon. That alone let me know that I belonged in the Cancer pack, even if nothing else did. Not that anyone else in my pack agreed with me.

I lifted my camera, deciding to try and snap a few pictures before the moon rose higher. I should have been home packing for the Convergence, but here I was, taking pictures instead. I'd use any excuse to get out of the house for a while.

I held my breath as I took the shot, trying to get it crystal clear. I snapped another one in quick succession, just to be sure, and lowered the camera so I could look at the tiny screen. Before I could decide which photo was better, a rustle from the bushes alerted me that I wasn't alone. I turned away from the water, trying to see what had caused the disturbance. For a moment, nothing moved and I figured it must have been an animal.

Something dark burst out of the brush, and I took an involuntary step back. A large gray wolf bounded toward me, and three more dark shapes joined it in a rush of fur and claws. *Damn.* It was too late for me to run, and I didn't have shoes on, besides. While it was fine to run around on the sand barefoot, I couldn't say the same about the sharp rocks above. If I wanted to make it to safety, I'd have to cross them.

The four wolves surrounded me like I was their prey before shifting back into their human forms. Their leader, Brad, was muscular and intimidating even when he wasn't in his wolf form. With blond hair and blue eyes, he would be handsome if he didn't look like he was always about to pick a fight with someone. The other two men were his thugs, Owen and Chase, and they sneered at me from their much less attractive faces. Brad's mate Lori made up the fourth member of their group since she always clung to him like a barnacle. They were all naked after their shift, but none of them were bothered by that, and they displayed their Cancer symbol proudly—their Zodiac pack marks. Brad had his mark on his chest, while the others had them on their arms. Then there was me—I didn't have one at all.

"Ayla," Brad said my name like a snarl. "What are you doing out here all alone?"

A pang of anxiety went through me. Brad was never friendly, and he wouldn't be talking to me at all if he didn't want something. Being the son of the Cancer beta, he looked down on me. I was technically above him in rank, but no one cared.

Lori giggled and tossed her perfect strawberry blond hair. She stood at Brad's shoulder, a possessive hand on his arm. As I tried to gauge my chances of escaping unscathed, Owen and Chase leered at me. They all ran in the same circle, the sons and daughters of the most influential Cancer pack members. I was the only one who wasn't invited, even though I should have been at the forefront, being the daughter of the alpha. Having human blood made me the outcast of the pack instead.

"I asked you a question, mutt," Brad snarled, kicking sand at me.

Swearing under my breath, I held my camera higher, trying to avoid getting sand onto the lens. Wesley had just bought this lens for me the last time he'd visited, and I couldn't let these idiots mess it up.

"I'm sorry," I snapped back. "I didn't realize your stupidity required answering. Anyone with two eyes and basic brain function can see what I'm doing. But you're obviously missing one of those. I'm still not sure which one."

Brad moved too quickly for me to counter, shoving me to the ground. I hit hard, my elbow taking the brunt of the trauma as I held my camera up in an attempt to save it. This was exactly why Mira told me to keep my mouth shut, I thought as I tried to roll away—and directly into Chase's foot. Shit. He kicked me hard in the stomach and pain shot through me as I instinctively curled in on myself.

"Where's your Cancer armor?" Chase asked as he kicked me again. "Oh right, you don't have any."

I gasped in air, trying to catch enough breath. "Thanks for the reminder, asshole," I managed to get out.

As he kicked me again, I curled around my camera, trying to protect it and the softest parts of myself. The others joined in, and I gritted my teeth and resigned myself to the beating. It wasn't any different than other beatings I'd endured. I closed my eyes and tried to breathe through the pain. Soon it would be over. They wouldn't kill me, no matter how much they hated me. For better or worse, I was still pack.

That plan was shattered the instant my camera was ripped out of my hands. My eyes flew open, and I struggled to my feet, pushing Chase and Owen away as Lori dangled the camera in front of me.

"You like taking pictures, don't you, little mutt?" she asked.

"No!" I yelled, reaching out for my camera, but she tugged it back and out of reach. "You can do whatever you want to me. Just let me have that back."

Lori dropped the camera into the sand. "I don't think so. The mutt needs to learn her place, once and for all."

A handful of blows from Brad came, hitting my back and sending me to my knees. I could only watch as Lori stomped on the camera with her shifter strength. The sounds of glass and plastic breaking were worse than the sounds of flesh on flesh.

Something inside of me broke. That camera was my only connection to the outside world, to a world where no one judged me for my half-breed heritage or for being born under the wrong stars. It was the only thing that brought me joy and gave me the smallest semblance of freedom.

I snarled, baring my teeth at the four of them, ready to fight. They must have sensed the change in my demeanor because they stepped back and fell into defensive positions. I couldn't take all of them—hell, without the Cancer crab armor they had, I could hardly take one. But the rage that boiled in my blood wouldn't let me just walk away from this like everything was okay. Something dark inside me woke up and rose to the surface, something wild and dangerous, just begging to be released. A power I'd felt before, that was always just out of reach. Maybe now was the time. Tension simmered in the air, snapping back and forth between all of us, waiting for the perfect moment to break.

"Hey!" The shout was distant but enough to distract all of us.

Lori turned away from where she still had her foot on the broken shards of my camera and snarled something unintelligible. My best friend Mira ran toward us, long black hair streaming behind her like a curtain. She had her bikini on as if she were coming to swim. *Really?* I couldn't help but think. *At a time like this?* I knew she loved swimming, but we were all getting ready for the Convergence.

"What the hell do you think you're doing?" Mira asked, coming to a stop beside me. Her eyes were on the other wolves, but I knew the question was for me.

"Stay out of it, Aquino," Brad snarled. "You'll walk away from this if you know what's good for you. We're teaching the mutt the lesson she's been begging for from the moment she was born."

"No way," Mira said. Stubborn, loyal Mira. She never knew when to back away from a fight, especially when I was involved. She had my back, even if she didn't agree with why we were fighting.

I was one to talk. I'd do the same for Mira under any circumstance. Still, she shouldn't have come here. This was my battle to fight, and she could get in serious trouble if she was seen standing up to the beta's son. She'd already been punished once by the alpha—she didn't need another mark against her.

"Mira," I said under my breath. She twitched, so I knew she'd heard me, but didn't turn to acknowledge me. "You need to go," I continued, though I knew she wouldn't listen to a word I said. "Please."

"If you have a problem with Ayla, you have a problem with me, too," Mira said, and dropped into her own defensive stance. She really wasn't going to let it go. I sighed and followed suit, raising my fists again.

Brad looked between us for a moment and laughed. "Neither of you would win. You don't even have your wolves yet."

"Yeah, but we'll still whoop your asses a little bit," I said, forcing the words out through the lingering pain with a wild grin. Then I let my eyes drop. "I bet at least one of us could get a knee to the balls, with yours just hanging out like that."

Brad growled at me and his hands shifted into claws. Mira glanced over at me like, *Really?* I shrugged. She was going to get on my case about being mouthy when she was almost as bad?

She rolled her eyes but then turned to Brad and added, "Do you really want to risk it right before the Convergence?"

Lori ground my camera into the sand a few more times before stepping back over to Brad. "It's not worth it," she murmured, just loud enough for me to hear. "I think she got the message."

Brad looked between the two of us, and then back at Lori. "You're right. She's not worth our time, and with any luck, she'll soon be some other pack's problem."

He shifted back into a wolf and the others followed him, then they sprinted back up to the rocks and into the bushes. Just like that, the tension bled from the air, leaving my entire body throbbing with pain, and a broken camera all I had to show for my smart mouth.

My shoulders sagged, and before I knew it, my knees were giving out. I searched around in the sand to examine the shattered pieces of my camera, but there was nothing salvageable. I let them all slip through my fingers as I blinked back angry tears.

Mira crouched beside me, resting her hand on my back. "Goodness," she muttered as she took in the bruises forming on my arms. "What did you say this time?"

"They just came out of nowhere," I said. "Even if I'd been nice they still would've gone after me for something."

"You know, if you didn't torment them, they'd probably leave you alone in the first place," Mira said. "I keep telling you this." She helped me stand, leaving her hand on my shoulder as I swayed, trying to catch my breath and balance.

"I can't help it." I wanted to pick up more pieces of my camera, but what would be the point? Lori had broken it beyond repair. "They say such stupid shit. They're practically begging for me to call them out on it."

"They shouldn't be talking about you like that. You're the alpha's daughter, and they need to answer for that."

"Yeah, right. You know my dad's even worse." I glanced

down at my arms. The new bruises only added to the fading ones from the alpha. As long as I could remember, he'd been making bruises all along my body. Never my face, though. He did have appearances to keep up, and beating your daughter didn't lend itself kindly to the gracious alpha persona he worked hard to protect. But everyone knew he treated me like an outcast, and he didn't care when people like Brad behaved the same. Mira was angry for me, but I'd long since accepted the fact that I'd never be the daughter he wanted. It was my lot in the world, and I tried to take it in stride.

I knew why he beat me, even though it didn't make any logical sense. *I* hadn't asked to be born half-human, but Dad loved to punish me for the affair he'd had with my mother, even though I'd had no say in the result. Everything about me was a constant reminder to him of his mistake. My birthday outside of the Cancer sign dates, my lack of Zodiac mark, and my absence of pack abilities made it easy for him to hate me.

His mate, Jackie, even seemed to find my red hair offensive. I fingered a strand of it, whipping around in the light breeze. It set me apart from everyone else in the family and served as a constant reminder that Dad had screwed up and gotten some human pregnant. I'd tried to say that one time, when I'd been angry and my mouth had—once again—taken over. All it had earned me was a shot to the face from Jackie.

Mira was still focused on the bruises, fretting over them like the mother I'd never had. "They should look better before the Convergence," she decided finally. "You're lucky that I decided to come have a swim before we leave tomorrow. Who knows what would have happened if they had their way with you."

"It doesn't matter," I said, shrugging and making my way back over to my shoes and jacket. "The bruises just prove that I'm not a true Cancer. I could call up the armor if I was." The crab armor was a Cancer ability all pack members had from birth, allowing them to protect themselves. All except me. I sighed. "At least once I get my wolf, I'll heal faster."

"Lots of things are going to change after the Convergence," Mira said softly.

The Convergence happened twice a year, at the summer and winter solstices, where all twelve Zodiac packs gathered to discuss issues, recognize new pack alphas, and bless newborn babies, among other things. This Convergence was at the summer solstice, the day before the start of Cancer season, and it would be in Montana, in the Sun Witches' territory.

Mira and I would finally get our wolves at the Convergence too, now that both of us were twenty-two and considered of age. We were the only Cancers getting our wolves at this Convergence—all the other pack members got theirs at the winter solstice. Except me, of course. I'd been born in March, another sign that I didn't belong in this pack.

As for Mira, she should have gotten her wolf at the winter solstice too, but she'd been forced to wait another six months, all because her father had challenged the alpha on something he didn't agree with. Mira hadn't been involved at all, but Dad knew punishing her was a blow to her entire family. It wasn't fair, but that's how our alpha worked. And when he gave an alpha command, we had to obey.

There was one other event at the Convergence too, the mating ritual, when anyone who had gained their wolf could try to find their fated mate. I hoped beyond hope that my mate—if I had one—would be from another pack. I'd do almost anything to get away from my dad and the rest of the Cancer shifters.

"I hope we'll get mates from the same pack," Mira said, her thoughts following the same vein that mine had. She'd said it so often that I almost expected it. I made a noise of affirmation but didn't say anything. I wanted to stay with her, of course. But if she ended up having a mate in the Cancer pack and I didn't, it wouldn't make me too sad. Getting out of here was top priority.

It was the one thing my father and I agreed upon. He wanted me gone just as much as I wanted to leave. "I hope you'll end up as some other pack's problem," he'd started saying the moment I'd turned twenty-two.

Thinking of my father sent my mood spiraling. I had to get back before he sent someone to get me. I turned to Mira and gave her what I hoped was a convincing smile. "Whatever happens at the Convergence, we'll always stay friends and never lose touch."

Mira hummed happily, taking my hand in hers and leading us back up the beach. I knew she meant well, but once she settled in with her mate, things would change. They always did. We'd drift apart, even if we did end up in the same pack, and the thought sent a shiver of wrongness through me.

I glanced back at the ocean and the scuffed sand where Brad and his gang had come after me. *Will I ever feel like I truly belong anywhere?*

CHAPTER TWO

I PACKED the last set of clothes I'd need for the Convergence and tied my bag shut. I looked around, trying to figure out if I'd left anything behind. I didn't have many possessions, and the fact that they could fit into this bag was pretty sad. I'd never had much of anything, too worried about Dad smashing my stuff in a fit of rage, and everything important was kept on digital files on my phone or in the cloud. I had all of my photography saved there, and that was what mattered most.

A knock came at my door, shaking me out of my thoughts. I went into instant panic, picking up my bag and getting ready to bolt the moment the door opened.

"Ayla?"

I smiled at the voice and relaxed. My brother Wesley was the only person in this family who wouldn't hurt me. "Come in."

As he stepped inside he grinned at me, his smile almost

exactly the same as I remembered from my childhood. He was four years older than me, but he'd always seemed so much bigger, even before he shot up during puberty and filled out with lithe muscle. He'd moved out to his own apartment a few months ago, and it felt like I never saw him anymore, even though he came back and visited fairly often. He had made growing up here better, and other than Mira, he was the only other person in the Cancer pack who gave a damn about me.

"Wesley!" I cried, launching myself into his arms. He hugged me tight, a bit too tight, and I hissed in a breath.

He pulled back, his face pulling down into a frown. "You've been beaten up again." He looked back toward the door. He hated how our father treated me, and always tried to be kind to me to make up for it. It was almost enough.

"Nothing I can't handle," I said, pulling at the string of my bag. My travel and photography books were sitting beside it, still waiting to go inside. I was hesitating on bringing them with me or leaving them here. They'd be heavy if I had to do any serious walking, but now that Wesley was here, I knew I'd have to bring them with me. There was no other option.

Photography had always been my passion. I loved being able to capture beauty in one still shot, to present it to the world through my own eyes, and Wesley had been sure to nurture that. Dad had always made it very clear I was an outcast, especially in my own house. It was a good year if he bought me new clothes—after I'd stopped growing, he'd sometimes go years without getting me anything new. Even when the seams were ripping and there were obvious holes, he kept forcing me to wear them. Food was kept to a bare minimum as well, and beyond that all the other luxuries I should have enjoyed were absent. No phone, no computer, not even when I'd needed it for school.

The moment I'd turned sixteen, he'd sent me to work at the grocery store in town, and had the entire paycheck funneled to him. Payment for putting up with me, he always said. Having him as a father and the alpha of my pack made it impossible for me to do anything else. I couldn't fend for myself or go behind his back, because he was the ultimate authority. All he had to do was use his alpha command, a unique power gifted to the alphas of every pack, and everyone had to do what he said. Including me.

Wesley had been the only one who had ever bought me anything nice. When I'd shown interest in photography at a young age, he'd sneaked me books on the subject. I'd pored over them, devouring each one voraciously. Oftentimes, he'd take the old ones back and bring me new ones, since having too many books would raise Dad's suspicion. But the ones I really liked, he let me keep. He'd even faked breaking his phone one time so he could give it to me, and when I'd told him that I wanted to go to the local community college, he'd bought me a camera and said, "Do it."

The only reason I'd been able to graduate with a degree was due to his help. He convinced Dad that it wouldn't do for the alpha's daughter not to go to school, and our father reluctantly allowed me to go. I got an earful all the time about what a waste of money my education was, but it was worth it in the long run. I ran a hand over the books, watching Wesley smile as he remembered bringing them to me.

"You pack your camera?" he asked.

"It got smashed." I looked down, sadness filling me. If I'd just kept my damn mouth shut, I'd probably still have it. I pushed the emotions down. I couldn't let anyone see how much Brad and the other bullies affected me, not even Wesley. I gave him a smile, trying to make it convincing. "At least I don't need it for school anymore. I can just use the phone camera, even if it's old."

"You would never have dropped it," Wesley said, frowning again. "Who broke it?"

"No one," I said, shrugging. I tried to play it off, overly casual, but Wesley had always been good at seeing through my lies.

"I know you're not going to tell me." He sighed and I relaxed, not wanting to try to evade the questions. It was still early, and I wasn't awake yet. "When I'm alpha of the Cancer pack, things are going to change. They'll be better, I promise."

I huffed and shook my head. "I'd like to believe it." I stuck the books into the pack and zipped it shut again. "Who knows when that'll be, though."

My only hope now was being mated at the Convergence. If it was with someone from another pack I would get to leave Cancer territory, but even if it was someone in this pack, I'd never have to return to this house. It had never felt like home, anyway.

I looked up at Wesley and gave him a crooked smile. "Hey, if I do get mated to someone from another pack, maybe I can buy a new phone so we can stay in touch. One that isn't cracked this time."

Wesley laughed, though it seemed more forced than usual. I knew he wanted me to stay here with him, but he just didn't understand. As kind as he was to me, it didn't make up for everyone else being total dicks all the time.

"You should do that." He paused, running a hand through his shiny brown hair. "I came up to get you. Mom and Dad are already in the car, and you know how they hate waiting."

Of course. They were probably already annoyed I was holding them up even though the sun had barely risen. I nodded and left my room without a backward glance. It had been a place to sleep and hide for the last twenty-two years, nothing more. I didn't have a home, not yet. Hopefully, I'd find one soon. Of course, with my luck, I'd probably be back here once the Convergence was over.

I locked the front door behind me as Wesley walked up to our parents, who were saying something I couldn't quite make out. Stepping off the front porch felt final, even though I didn't know for sure whether I'd be mated right when my wolf was unlocked. Some people had to wait years 'til their mate came of age, and a very small group of people never got mates at all. I prayed I wasn't in that category, but it wouldn't surprise me either.

When I approached the SUV, Dad was giving me a dark look, his mouth pressed into a scowl. I could almost hear him saying, *hurry up, you good for nothing half-breed.* I could feel Jackie's eyes on me as well, filled with hate as she waited for me to get into the car. I sighed. This was going to be a long ride.

I wished I could have ridden with Mira, but when I dared to ask last night, Dad growled and said I shouldn't be associating with her anyway. Her family was at the very bottom of pack hierarchy now, thanks to her father's actions. Besides, Dad needed me to ride with him, all to keep up appearances, of course.

There were other vehicles parked in our long driveway, all idling and ready to go at a moment's notice. Everyone really was waiting on me. I didn't realize so many of the Cancer pack were going with us this time. The beta and his family would be staying behind, so that meant no Brad to deal with at least, but there were several other people who would be hostile. At least I'd have Wesley and Mira with me, and the chance to meet several of the other packs.

"The drive's going to take about fifteen hours," Wesley said as I climbed into the backseat next to him. I'd been over-joyed to find that he was coming with us when he'd first texted me to let me know. Even though he'd gotten his wolf four years ago, he was coming for me.

"Have your bag?" Dad asked. His blue eyes met mine in the mirror. Though we shared them, I knew all he saw when he looked at me was his human mistake, not a daughter of his.

"Yes," I said.

"And you packed everything in it?" he continued,

curling his lip as if talking to me was bringing him physical discomfort.

"Yes," I repeated.

"Good. With any luck, you won't be coming back here. I can't wait to hand you off to some other poor sucker. Let you be their problem."

"Amen," Jackie muttered, just loud enough for me to hear. I couldn't see her, since she was sitting directly in front of me, but I didn't dare roll my eyes. She liked to punch, and she wasn't shy about hitting my face.

Wesley gave me a strained smile, but I looked away from him, and for once, I held my tongue. I'd never been to a Convergence before—Dad had never let me go, not even when Wesley came of age—and I could put up with their torment for a few more hours. With any luck, it would be the last long car ride with them.

As we drove, I reached for my camera just short of a dozen times before it really stuck in my brain that I didn't have it anymore. I wanted to capture the beauty of the land zooming by, and I soaked up all the sights from the trip, trying not to miss even a second of it. When we entered Seattle, I practically vibrated out of my seat trying to contain my excitement at being there. I'd never been anywhere but the Cancer pack territory on the coast north of Vancouver, and certainly never to the States. I'd spent my life reading about cities like Seattle, and I wished I could freeze this moment forever in a photo. I even snapped a few pictures with my phone, though the quality would never come close to that of my camera.

I'd always had the half-baked notion in the back of my mind that I'd run away to a big city in America to escape my life. It was a half-formed plan at best, but it was all I could do to make my existence bearable. I would daydream about coming to the States and hiding from the Cancer pack forever in one of the areas where there were no wolves. Now I knew it was only an escapist's fantasy, not logical in the slightest. The best I could hope for was a mate in another pack, and I'd still have to see the Cancer pack a lot of the time. I couldn't fully escape them, not really.

Soon the cities faded away, and we crossed into the more rugged areas of Montana. The sun was setting, and we were getting close now. Wesley had fallen asleep beside me, and I wanted to jab him with my elbow so he could share the anticipation as we drove down a small road through dense forest, the trees closing in over us. Suddenly we emerged into a huge clearing covered in tents, and my breath caught at the sight of all the shifters there.

We'd made it to the Convergence.

CHAPTER THREE

AS WE PARKED, I craned my neck to see over the rest of the cars, my legs aching from the long drive. I was eager to leave the car and escape the oppressive weight that filled it. Outside, there were tents everywhere, covering every spare inch of ground, and I'd never seen this many people before in one place outside of a city. Excitement thrummed through me, mixing with the anxiety that had been building up for weeks. My entire fate rested on what happened at the Convergence.

I got out of the car and stretched the travel strain out of my body, taking in the sights and scents of the Montana forest around the campground. It reminded me a little of Cancer territory, although the trees were different here and there was no smell of saltwater in the air. A couple of wolves bounded past me into the forest, and I caught sight of the Aquarius pack mark on them before they slipped away.

I left my bag behind since it was so heavy, planning to come back for it later, and followed Dad and Jackie through the parking lot with Wesley at my side. I caught his eye as we wound through the cars. He grinned at me, excitement pouring off him. It was infectious enough that it chased away most of the anxiety.

"Lighten up, Ayla," he said. "We're here now."

I nodded and relaxed a little. If he wasn't nervous, I didn't have to be, either. He'd been through this, and he'd be sure to pass on any important information to me. Besides, tomorrow I would finally get my wolf, allowing me to become my true self. There was no reason to be worried. Right?

"Don't do anything stupid," Jackie tossed over her shoulder. "All eyes will be on the alphas and their families. Especially Wesley, as the alpha heir."

"Yeah, we wouldn't want anyone to suspect we're not the perfect nuclear family," I said, sarcasm dripping off every word.

Dad spun around and lifted his hand like he was about to hit me, but then checked himself. He glanced around at all the people nearby, before speaking in a low growl. "Watch yourself, Ayla." He infused power into the words, giving me an alpha command that wrapped around my throat like a vice, forcing me to obey. "Or you'll regret it."

"Dad, stop," Wesley said, moving to stand at my shoulder. He couldn't officially challenge our father, not unless he wanted to fight for the role of alpha. Which would probably leave one of them dead. I touched Wesley's arm to show everything was okay—I couldn't bear the thought of possibly losing him. Someday he would be alpha, but until then, I could handle it.

We kept walking, pretending nothing was wrong, but there would be no relaxing as long as I was around my parents. I couldn't wait to get away from them. It was one of the perks of coming to the Convergence—I didn't have to always hang around my pack. I'd get a taste of how it would be to live among people who didn't hate my existence. Surely not every pack had the same toxic views toward half-human shifters. I knew I couldn't be the only one to exist. The more we mingled with humans, the more likely we were to interbreed with them.

The closer we got, the less like a random jumble the tents became, and a pattern began to emerge. Banners were stuck into the ground with Zodiac symbols on them to represent the different packs. The campground had been divided into quadrants representing the four elements, and we headed to join the other water signs.

Winding in between the tents were hundreds of shifters in both human and wolf forms, all here representing each of the twelve packs. Shifters of all ages mingled with other packs than their own, sharing meals, laughing together, and dancing under the sun like they were at a music festival. I'd never felt such camaraderie between different pack members, even the ones who were on good terms. The Convergence was neutral ground, and no one had to be worried about potential schemes or any attacks. Fighting was prohibited here, and the Sun Witches made sure everyone stayed in line.

Dad pulled aside a Pisces shifter and asked him where we should set up, but I was too focused on trying to take everything in to listen to the details of their conversation. The male pointed toward the northern side of the clearing, all the way to the back. Dad nodded and we began working our way through the Pisces and Scorpio tents to the Cancer area.

I recognized more people than I thought I would. Many of the different alphas had visited our house for as long as I could remember. There was always business to attend to, figuring out land disputes, negotiating alliances, and distributing resources. The Cancer pack was one of the largest ones, and we were allied with the Pisces, Capricorn, and Aquarius packs. We'd had a long-standing rivalry—or worse—with the other largest pack, the Leos, along with their allies, the Aries, Taurus, and Scorpio packs. The remaining Zodiac Wolves—the Gemini, Virgo, Libra, and Sagittarius packs—all remained neutral at the moment, but alliances were constantly shifting and changing. By the end of the Convergence, it might all be different again.

We passed by the Aquarius and Pisces alphas deep in conversation, and before I could recall the last time I'd seen them both, Mira came running over. I paused, letting the rest of my family pull forward a little bit to give us the semblance of privacy. It wouldn't do much, not with so many shifters around. Nonetheless, I'd never turn down an opportunity to distance myself from my parents.

"Ayla," she said, eyes shining as she danced around me, practically jumping out of her skin. "Can you believe how many shifters came this year?"

"No," I said, grinning back at her. Her good mood was infectious, and despite the torturous fifteen hours I'd just spent in the car with Dad and Jackie, I cheered up. "It's amazing. I knew there were a lot of shifters between the twelve packs, but seeing everyone together makes it feel like we could take on the whole world somehow."

Mira lowered her voice and pulled me in closer to her. "Have you seen all the hotties here?" she asked, eyeing a group of younger Scorpio pack males as they passed by us, none of them wearing shirts. "Mmm, delicious. *They've* certainly been training."

I laughed as one of them looked over and slanted a crooked grin at Mira. She glanced down demurely, but I could see the glee in her gaze. I opened my mouth to tell her that she wasn't being as sneaky as she thought she was but thought better of it. Why ruin the fun? Almost everyone here already had their wolves, and they would hear even the lowest whisper.

As if to prove my point, Wesley glanced back at us with a smirk. He'd continued on with Dad and Jackie, but none of them were far enough ahead for Mira's comment to have escaped them. Luckily, our parents were deep in conversation, but no such luck with my brother. Wesley rolled his eyes at me, but the grin on his face showed his amusement, and Mira's face flushed with embarrassment. I looked between her and Wesley with raised brows. I'd suspected that she'd been crushing on my brother for some time, and she'd just confirmed it.

I shook my head. It wasn't as if I could warn her off the scent. Wesley was a flirt, and everyone knew it. She'd have to deal with him on her own. He still hadn't found his mate and made the most of it. I wondered if she secretly hoped they'd be mated tomorrow. Of course, half the fun of the Convergence was wondering who you'd be paired with at the mating ceremony—if you were paired at all.

"Come on," I said. "Let's set up our tents."

Before I could move, someone shoved past me hard, nearly knocking me over. I stumbled forward, instincts kicking in just fast enough to stop me from falling. When I glanced up, a big, muscular guy with blond hair was walking past, along with his friends. He shot a look over his shoulder, and it was pure venom.

"Watch yourself," he said. "Or better yet, stay out of the way."

I gained my balance, rage sparking inside of me at the hateful tone like a Pavlovian response. I'd had more than enough of my own pack members talking to me like this my whole life. I'd come here to change that, to find the connection I'd been missing, and my first interaction with another pack member was someone who thought it was okay to treat me like the Cancer pack did. Fuck that.

"Watch where *you're* going," I snapped back. He'd already been walking away as if he didn't expect me to say anything back to him, but at my words, he paused and turned back fully, eyes smoldering.

Damn, he was attractive. I found myself checking him out, even though I doubted we'd get along if he talked to strangers like he had done to me. He was tall, muscular, and sun-kissed, with blond hair that was right on the verge of being long and wild. He obviously spent a lot of his time throwing his weight around outside.

He looked me up and down, and then peeled his lips back in a snarl. "You're the outcast in the Cancer pack, aren't you? I'd recognize Harrison's eyes anywhere, and you have your human mother's hair." He said the word *human* like it was dirty. Ah, yes, another reminder of home. Whichever pack he was a part of, I made a mental note to never associate with them.

I lifted my chin and faced him down. "And you're just another bully who thinks it's okay to pick on anyone you believe is beneath you. I don't need your name. Your actions speak loud enough."

Mira's hand caught mine and tightened at the words. It was a silent warning. *Careful.* I didn't want to be careful. Whoever this prick was, he could have a piece of my mind.

A low growl went through the group of males gathered around the guy, and the tension became palpable in the air. So much for keeping the peace. I'd managed to break it moments after stepping onto the campsite.

"Hey," Mira said, stepping in front of me holding her free hand out in supplication. "No fighting here, remember? We're on neutral ground."

The guy shook his head, disgust pouring off of him almost tangibly. "You're lucky we're at the Convergence. Anywhere else, and I would have given your half-human friend there the beating she deserved."

Something inside of me died at the words. I'd hoped that outside of the Cancer pack, my heritage wouldn't be as big of a deal, but here I was, dealing with the same prejudices I'd encountered on a daily basis. I was never going to escape this shit, was I?

The guy gave me one more disgusted once-over before walking away. The other males fell into line with him, almost as if he was commanding them. This male was high up in the ranks of his pack, and it irked me that dicks like him got to be in power so often. With a sigh, I pushed the encounter out of my mind. Hopefully, I wouldn't have to deal with him again.

Wesley jogged up to us, worry plain on his face. He put a hand on my shoulder and stared after the shifters. "What just happened?"

"Nothing," I grumbled, tugging Mira forward. "He was a prick, I told him to shove off. The asshole didn't know how to say 'excuse me' instead of 'move out of my way'."

"You shouldn't mess with him." Wesley's hand tightened on my shoulder, going from comforting to a warning. When I glanced over at him, his eyes were serious. "That's Jordan from the Leo pack."

As I watched the retreating group, they turned off of the main path where the Leo banner was planted into the ground, an instant confirmation of Wesley's words.

"Well, Jordan from the Leo pack needs to learn some manners," I grumbled, turning away. "No matter how much he doesn't like me, I'm still the daughter of an alpha. I get that Leos and Cancers hate each other, but this is the Convergence. We're all supposed to be getting along. Trust a Leo to try to bring our clan rivalry into this."

"You don't get it," Wesley said, his brow furrowed. "That's Jordan *Marsten*. Next in line to be the alpha of the Leo pack. He's not someone you want to fuck with. Stay away from him."

That explained how he'd known exactly who I was. I shrugged Wesley's hand off. "I'll stay away as long as he leaves me alone. I want nothing to do with the Leos."

When I was just a baby, the Cancer pack and the Leo pack had waged a war against each other until the other packs intervened and made them call a truce. There wasn't a clear victor, and because of that, there was never any concrete resolution. The animosity still hung around between our packs like a dark cloud.

I'd spent my childhood listening to Dad rant about the Leo pack and its alpha. Apparently, Dixon Marsten was constantly plotting ways to undermine us, or better yet, take over our pack entirely. I didn't know if it was fact or just Dad being paranoid. Both alphas refused to let the past go, always blaming anything bad that happened on the rival pack, and it perpetuated the old hatred. Dad was always scheming, half of his energy devoted to trying to deal with the Leo pack, once and for all. Almost every meeting he had at the house had something to do with gaining allies against the Leo pack or trying to get the neutral packs to join us. There were other rivalries among the rest of the twelve Zodiac packs, but no one had as many reasons to hate each other as Leo and Cancer did. Even the elements were natural enemies—fire and water.

I shook my head. I hadn't been old enough to remember the worst of the war, so I didn't understand the dynamic as well as other pack members did. I'd never seen the Leos actually do anything to us in years, but the scheming and manipulating and hatred continued. Maybe it was because I was an outcast of the pack, but I'd never understood why bygones couldn't be bygones.

I followed Mira and Wesley to the Cancer banner. People were setting up tents almost everywhere we walked. The Convergence started tomorrow, during the summer solstice, and most people had arrived already, though some would trickle in during the night. We were lucky that the Convergence was relatively close to Cancer territory this year. To make it fair, the Sun Witches changed locations every time, rotating between six different spots so they didn't show favoritism among the packs. At the previous winter solstice, the Cancer pack had to leave an entire day early just to make it on time, and they'd driven through the night.

As if thinking about the Sun Witches had conjured them into being, I watched as six women in flowing robes walked past. Shifters melted out of the way for them, falling silent and bowing their heads in respect. I could almost taste the difference in the air as they glided by. I sneaked glances at them as they passed, though it would have been better to just keep my eyes on the ground.

All the packs worshiped the sun god Helios and the moon goddess Selene, and the witches were concrete evidence of a connection to the divine. I'd never seen one in the flesh, but I'd been raised on tales of their astounding power as everyone had. They were allied with the Zodiac Wolves, unlike the Moon Witches, and it was terrifying to think what would happen if they *weren't*.

One of the witches turned to look at me as she passed, her eyes such a pale color they seemed to absorb hues from the very air around her. My breath lodged in my throat, pulse pounding wildly. I couldn't break her gaze. Something twisted inside of me, trying desperately to get out. It felt as if I'd been caught doing something wrong and my body was compelling me to shout it from the rooftops.

The moment passed, her eyes sliding over me almost as if I wasn't there. My breathing eased, and the strange feeling vanished. I glanced over at Mira, who didn't seem to be affected the same way I was. Maybe it was because I was half human? I shook my head and tried to put the weird feeling out of my mind. Maybe I was just being paranoid.

I sent a silent prayer after the witches anyway. They had a better connection to the gods than I could ever hope for and thus could twist fate around to their bidding. *Whatever god might hear me, please let me be mated with someone in a pack that will treat me well. I just want my life to be better.* It was a simple thing, so simple. Couldn't I have this lucky break after years of being stuck in my own personal hell?

And if I didn't get a mate... Well, at least I'd have my wolf and would be able to defend myself better. I'd become stronger and quicker, and if I was stuck in the Cancer pack, I could outrun and outsmart everyone who wanted to hurt me.

It would have to be good enough.

CHAPTER FOUR

I WOKE to Wesley shaking me. I hadn't even remembered falling asleep the night before. We'd all been up late setting up tents and getting everyone settled, and then Mira and I had watched the other shifters for hours, before finally crawling into our tents and passing out.

"You said you wanted to see the Sun Witches bless the babies," Wesley said when I groaned in protest. "It's almost time."

"I didn't realize it would be this early," I grumbled as I dragged myself out of my sleeping bag. I was so not a morning person, even on the best of days. If it were up to me, I'd stay up all night and sleep the day away.

Wesley had helpfully let me know that the food tents were close to where the Sun Witches performed the rituals, and I was curious about the blessings since I'd never seen magic in action before. I met Mira outside, who looked almost as sleepy as I did, her dark eyes still clouded and missing their usual spark. Despite her tiredness, she had a grin at the ready, and I couldn't help but match it. Today was the Convergence, and everything would change.

It could only go up from here, right?

The smell of cooking bacon and eggs wafted from the food tents, and the low murmur of conversation let us know we were headed in the right direction. I grabbed Mira's arm, excitement overtaking any apprehension, and before either of us knew it, we were lined up to get some breakfast along with dozens of other shifters I didn't recognize.

I didn't even pay attention to the food I was grabbing, too focused on the line of people bringing their newborns one at a time to the group of silent Sun Witches, all dressed in warm-hued robes as they stood in the bright morning sunlight.

Mira and I found a spot on the grass nearby while a Taurus female stepped forward. I paused, a piece of toast raised halfway to my lips, as the Sun Witch pulled the baby into her arms, cradling it gently. It fussed for a few moments, but the Sun Witch softly hushed it, putting her first two fingers on its forehead. She closed her eyes and murmured something, too quiet for anyone to hear. There was a slight shift in the air, like something settling, and a soft glow surrounded them both, like a beam of sunlight falling upon them.

If the Sun Witch didn't bless the child, it would fall prey to the Moon Witch curse and turn feral at full moons. It was important that every baby was blessed, or they'd spend the rest of their lives in agony, going mad at the full moons, waking up without remembering what they'd done while they were shifted. This way, once our wolves were unlocked, we'd remain in control the whole time, without the Moon Curse turning us into the rabid monsters of myth.

Three more babies were blessed, that shift happening every time in the air. It wasn't the fiery hands and sparks flying out that I'd imagined in my daydreams, but this subtle magic was almost as awe-inspiring. The female shifter would take back her child each time, smile down at it, and walk away with a dreamy expression on her face.

Mira nudged me. "Come on. We've seen enough. I think one of them is giving us dirty looks."

I glanced over at Mira, and then followed the jerk of her chin. It was the same Sun Witch I'd noticed looking at me yesterday, her colorless eyes caught directly on me. I swallowed, throat suddenly dry, and got up quickly, brushing the grass off my jeans. The same, panicked feeling followed me as we headed back to the food tents to throw away our paper plates.

"What are your plans for today?" I asked. I hoped she'd want to go exploring with me, but Mira was always more social and liked spending time with other shifters, rather than in the woods. I was wary of other shifters, always worried they'd accost me rather than befriend me—and I was almost always right. Mira was a full-blooded shifter, had her Cancer powers, and didn't have the same smart mouth that I did. She could worm her way into anyone's heart with her easy smile.

One option was to stay and listen to the trade talks and

watch packs squabble over things, but I had no interest in that. Mira didn't either. She'd never been involved in pack politics, and I didn't see her suddenly finding a long-lost interest in it. That was practically what I listened to on a daily basis living in the alpha's house, and it sounded like a huge headache. I was thankful that the title of alpha was never going to fall on my shoulders. It wouldn't fit me well at all, and Wesley was better suited to the job. He could keep a clear head during arguments, and that was essential to making it as an alpha.

"We could go explore," I said, motioning to the forest. I'd read up on the site of the Convergence weeks before we were headed here, planning out hikes in my head. There was a set of falls I was excited to see and wanted someone to share the view with. "The forest is beautiful out here."

Mira wrinkled her nose. "But there's no ocean. You know I only like nature when it's next to the water. I think I'll stay here, try to make friends." She leaned in and whispered to me conspiratorially. "Who knows, maybe I'll meet my mate."

I couldn't help but laugh, even as I rolled my eyes. "Out of the hundreds of people here? That would really be lucky."

"Well, it is the Convergence. All sorts of strange things might happen."

With that, she flounced off, leaving me standing by myself near the food tents. I quickly tossed my plate, noting the strange looks from some of the other shifters. I didn't want to draw any more attention than I already had, and I knew if anyone said something rude to me, there would be trouble. I remembered the tight grip Dad had on my arm a few days ago as he hissed the words into my ear.

If you cause any trouble at the Convergence, I'll cast you out of the Cancer pack myself. And he had the power to do that, which was the worst part of the threat. I didn't know if he actually meant it or if it was just empty words to keep me in line, but I wasn't about to find out.

I quickly walked back over to my tent, nodding to everyone I made eye contact with. Most of them I didn't know, but the Virgo alpha sent me a smile that bolstered my mood. Maybe everyone didn't hate me here. Maybe there was a chance I wouldn't remain an outcast for the rest of my life.

I pulled on my worn-out hiking boots that Wesley had gotten me for my last birthday, the second-best present I'd ever gotten, the first being my camera. I grabbed my phone to take some photos too, cursing Brad and Lori under my breath again, before stepping outside.

Dad was walking toward the tent, deep in conversation with the Pisces alpha, gesturing around as if he was plotting something out, and I quickly slipped away. I made my way back toward the cars, checking over my shoulder just to be sure he hadn't caught sight of me. He was focused on everything else right now, but it would be my luck that he'd catch me at the wrong moment and force me to stay by his side. I didn't want him to ask me where I was going because he'd say it was important that I stay here in case he needed me. *For what, his own personal punching bag?* I thought as I shook my head and continued walking quickly. If he'd had it his way, he probably would have confined me to the tent. No one would note my absence though. I knew that much. He spent so much of his time talking about Wesley that most packs forgot he also had a daughter, and a half-human one at that. It was an impressive feat he'd managed, almost completely erasing me from the minds of the other packs.

I found the trail head without a problem, and as the noise of the Convergence faded away, my shoulders relaxed. Out here in nature, I could be myself without any fear of repercussions. I could take pictures and hike, and no one would yell at me for simply existing.

I pulled out Wesley's old, cracked phone and took a picture of the way the sunlight filtered through the leaves. It was a beautiful day, not a single cloud in the sky, and I wanted to take advantage of it. There wouldn't be anyone out here except me. Everyone else was conversing with their friends from other packs, and humans were warded off by a spell the Sun Witches had cast across their lands. I could finally *relax*.

The further I hiked, the more at home I felt in this strange forest. It wrapped around me, comforting in its embrace, and I found myself smiling as I walked. The sound of rushing water grew louder, and before I knew it, I was crossing the stream. I was almost at the falls.

A few minutes later the falls came in view, the water feeding into an almost perfectly round turquoise pool. The sight took my breath away, and I felt the absence of my camera even more than I had on our drive here. I'd never be able to justify the sight with a phone camera, no matter how much editing I did.

I was so taken aback by the beauty of the waterfall that I didn't notice the large, naked man crouched at the bank until he moved. I took a step back, shocked to see another person out this far away from the Convergence. The graceful way he moved screamed *shifter,* but I couldn't see a pack mark anywhere on his exposed skin, and it was *all* exposed. His clothes were a pile at his feet, and his big, muscular body was fully on display. He was turned away from me, giving me a full view of a back corded with muscle and an ass so firm it begged to be slapped. Not to mention arms and thighs so thick they put the trees around us to shame.

I watched, unable to look away from his hands sluicing water over his hard body. His hair was dark, and water trickled down it onto his broad shoulders like a caress. Every inch of him was tan, and he looked like he spent more time away from civilization than in it, and was right at home in the forest. If I'd seen him in a city, he would have stuck out like a sore thumb.

Realizing I was staring like some kind of creep, I tore my gaze away with a ragged breath. As quietly as possible, I stepped behind a tree and wondered what I should do. It would be hard to hike back down without making any noise, and even the smallest crackle of leaves or snap of a branch would alert his wolf senses. It was a miracle I hadn't stepped on any on the way up.

As I tried to slink away, a twig snapped under my foot

and my theory was confirmed as he turned, eyes narrowed, searching me out. Definitely a shifter, and now he knew I was here. He lifted his head as if trying to catch my scent. I chewed on my lip, trying to figure out my next step. From where I was it looked like I was hiding, or even spying on him. I huffed in frustration. There was no good way out of this.

Before I could decide, he shifted. It was so easy, so smooth that I almost missed it. A huge black wolf with brilliant blue, intelligent eyes prowled directly toward me. There was no way I could outrun him on foot, not when he was in his wolf form. I stepped out from behind the trees, holding my hands up to show I wasn't carrying any weapons.

A low growl overpowered the thunder of the falls, and he crouched down, heavy muscles bunching as if he was preparing to attack.

"Dammit," I muttered. Without any Cancer armor, I didn't stand a chance against his wolf's teeth, and since I didn't have my own wolf yet—*really poor timing, Ayla*—I'd have to depend on his mercy alone. "I didn't mean to disturb you. I'm just hiking—"

The huge wolf lunged toward me, and I let out a startled cry as he rammed into me and knocked me to the forest floor. I tried to wriggle away from his sharp fangs and claws, but then he shifted back. Now a hard and very naked human body had me pinned beneath him. His knees dug into my thighs, and he captured each of my wrists with his hands. His tanned face was close enough that I could see that his eyes were just as blue as when he was a wolf, and he had some rugged scruff along his jaw that only made him sexier.

Stop it, I told my brain. *You shouldn't be noticing how hot he is, you're seconds away from getting your throat ripped out if you say the wrong thing.*

But as our eyes met, something passed between us, something that made my heart race faster and my breathing catch. Something that tugged on my soul and said *this one.* Desire and yearning like I'd never known before flared inside me, and I wondered if he felt it too.

"What are you doing out here?" His eyes dropped to my lips like he couldn't help himself, and then his face lowered, his nose slowly brushing against my neck, sending a shiver through me. I thought he might press his lips there next, but then he pulled back. "Cancer pack?" he snarled it like an insult. "You should be down with the others."

"I'm hiking, not lost," I said again, trying not to let the words tremble like my body was doing, while the pulse at my throat beat rapidly. I was all too aware that he was completely naked, and I kept my gaze pinned on his face, not daring to look down. He'd notice, and I didn't know if I could look away from his body if I broke his gaze. He radiated heat and it soaked all the way into my bones from where we touched. Even though I was terrified, I couldn't stop the rush of warmth pooling between my thighs from the feel of his hard body on top of mine.

"Hiking?" he asked as if he didn't believe me.

"Before the ritual tonight I wanted to take some time by

myself. That's allowed, isn't it?" I felt a little braver, and my smart mouth was back online. "This is all neutral land."

"Yes, but surely you have pack members who are missing you."

I wanted to roll my eyes. *Right.* Mira was too busy chasing after anything that smiled at her and Wesley was probably lapping up Dad's praise. "No one would miss me."

"Funny." His tone was patronizing, as was the slight smirk on his face as he took the rest of me in. His eyes lingered, and if I didn't know any better, I'd think he was checking me out. "And here I thought the Cancer pack was pretty tight-knit."

I snorted at that, unable to help myself. "You obviously don't know anything about me."

The man's face darkened. "And I don't want to. If you know what's good for you, you'll forget you ever saw me."

"Or what? You'll kill me? Please, go ahead. I'd like to see you explain how you killed someone in Sun Witch territory during the Convergence. I'll laugh at you from the afterlife."

His gaze darkened further, his blue eyes going almost black. "You have a death wish, little wolf."

Somehow that rankled more than *mutt* or *half-breed.* He couldn't have been much older than I was. "No, I've just got nothing to lose."

He curled his lips back in another snarl. He looked ready to say something else, but his attention suddenly shifted elsewhere, his piercing blue eyes focusing on the brush a few feet back.

I heard it a moment later than he did, the rustle of something moving within them, something obviously human. I tensed immediately. I'd been in enough fights to know that the arrival of someone else wasn't always a good thing. Especially this far out from my own pack. It would more than likely be someone from his pack, whichever one that was.

"Let me go," I said, squirming in his hold once more, trying to get the heavy press of his body to give. No such luck, and all it did was rub me against every naked, hard inch of him. And oh god, he was definitely hard. And big too. Lust flared inside me like a bonfire sparking to life. I'd never felt anything like it before, and it made me gasp. He glanced down at me, lips ghosting up into a dark smile like he knew exactly what I was thinking about, before pushing himself away from me.

"Get out of here, little wolf," he said. "And forget you ever saw us."

Before I could look him over further, he shifted back into his wolf and greeted the other two males who melted out of the brush with a soft *chuff*. I scrambled to my feet, stepping back toward the trail. Another low growl resonated from his wolf's lips, warning me away. The two males looked between him and me, but I didn't recognize either of them. It was likely I just hadn't seen them before, but something about this whole situation set my teeth on edge. What were they all doing so far away from the Convergence?

Now that his body wasn't on top of mine, a semblance of reason returned to my stupid head. Without looking back, I turned tail and fled, sprinting back down the way I'd come, trying to put as much distance between us as I could. It was only after I'd slowed to a slow trot that I stopped to wonder which pack they'd been from. The man had smelled like the forest, woodsy and heady, but I couldn't yet recognize scents like full shifters could. I cursed my lack of wolf for the second time. If I'd been able to shift, I could have unpinned myself, and my keener senses would have alerted me to his presence before I'd stumbled upon him in the first place.

The strange sensation stayed with me the whole way down. There was something odd about that wolf and the two males who had been with him.

Something my gut told me was trouble.

CHAPTER FIVE

IT WAS NEARLY dark by the time I emerged from the woods. I'd had to slow down for a lot of the trail. Once the adrenaline had worn off, I'd been tired and kept stumbling. I'd almost twisted my ankle a few times. The edges of the camp were all but deserted, and I hurried through them toward the dull roar of voices. The area where the babies were blessed this morning had been widened, the food tents pushed out of the way, and the place thronged with shifters. The twelve packs were all arranged in a circle facing inward, where the ritual would be performed.

I searched out my family, finding Wesley seated beside our dad. At my arrival, Dad looked up and his eyes flashed, and I realized that I'd made a mistake showing up after everyone was already gathered.

"Where have you been?" he asked.

I sucked in a breath. Surely he'd keep his voice down? "I was walking through the forest."

"You didn't embarrass me in front of anyone, did you?" He still hadn't lowered his voice, and the nearby packs were going silent, most looking at us. Usually he made it a point to keep up the act in front of everyone, but I realized this was an exercise in humiliation. I hadn't followed orders, and he was punishing me for it. Showing how tough he was as an alpha.

"No," I said. "I didn't talk to anyone at all." *Anyone except a hot male I can't stop thinking about.*

Dad raised his eyebrows. "So you were being antisocial then. You're representing our pack tonight, even if you aren't really a Cancer. You disappoint me constantly, Ayla."

"You make sure of that." The words slipped out as I looked up at him defiantly. He just had to make sure everyone knew I was an outcast. "If you hadn't screwed around with a human, maybe you'd have a daughter you could be proud of."

Dad's eyes flashed, and for a moment I thought he'd hit me right in front of everyone. But no. That would admit that I'd gotten to him. He'd never show that kind of weakness in front of this many shifters. He simply sneered at me and gave me another alpha command, just because he liked to see me bend to his will. "You'd better sit down now before you inconvenience us more."

I gritted my teeth and sat next to Wesley. When I chanced a glance up at him, his lips were pressed together in a tight line, but he didn't dare to speak up against an alpha command, especially in front of everyone. I wouldn't get any help from him. Jackie was ignoring us entirely, staring into the fire in the center that illuminated the clearing. Probably for the best.

As true night fell and the moon peeked out of the clouds, the silence dragged on, and I felt all eyes on me. I burned with shame, even though I hadn't actually done anything wrong. I wished I could sink into the ground and cease to exist. But no, that would give them all too much satisfaction.

I kept my chin held high as I glanced between the different packs, refusing to let them cower me. It was probably the one and only time I'd ever see them all gathered like this anyway, and I was curious. I spotted the Gemini pack, with their twin alphas—they always ruled in pairs—and the Virgo alpha, who was female and unmated. Unlike the rest of the packs, the Virgos were matriarchal and their women made all the decisions. I often secretly hoped I'd end up in their pack.

Finally, after what seemed like hours, the Sun Witches arrived. They walked through the crowd, shifters moving out of the way for them. I relaxed a little as they passed by, and the rest of the attention was taken off of me.

One woman stood out from the cluster of warm-colored clothes. She was the only one in bright red robes and was practically dripping with gold jewelry. She was beautiful, platinum blonde, and pale, but she didn't look human. It didn't take extra senses to feel the power radiating off her. My teeth buzzed as I looked at her, and I found myself focusing on the other women around her, unable to keep staring at her for too long.

"Greetings," the woman intoned as the other witches fanned out around her. "For those who are new, I am Evanora, the High Priestess of the Sun Witches, and it is my honor to lead this Convergence. This morning we welcomed the newest members of the packs, and tonight we will take those who have come of age and unlock their full potential."

As she continued in her smooth, sonorous voice, I found myself looking around. I knew what would happen already —I'd been preparing and reading about it for years. The others were all enraptured by her voice, but I found my mind elsewhere. Where was the male I'd seen in the forest? He wasn't with any of the alphas, and as I scanned faces, I didn't see him or the other men he was with either. The strange feeling roiling in my gut intensified. There was something off about tonight.

"Once you've gained your wolf, there is the potential to meet your mate tonight," Evanora said, and I felt her gaze heavy on me. A chill went through me as we locked eyes. Everything in me screamed to look down, to show my submission, but I froze in place, fighting the urge. Before I could look away, she moved on, her gaze finding the others who would be part of the ritual tonight. I drew in a breath. Maybe she hadn't been singling me out, as I'd originally thought, just doing whatever it was that Sun Witches did to make us feel their power.

A gasp went through the crowd, and for a moment, I thought it was because they were reacting to what she said. It didn't make sense, everyone knew of the ritual to meet their mate. It was what many of us looked forward to most at the Convergence, as much as unlocking our full powers.

Then I saw the movement. It came from the back, and I craned my neck to see what was happening. Evanora's smooth voice cut off as she noticed, and the whispers increased.

The front line broke to allow four people through. My jaw dropped as I recognized the large, rugged male from the falls, along with the others I'd seen right before I'd turned tail and fled. There was a female with him as well, one that I didn't recognize.

He was dressed this time, at least partially. No shirt, just dark ripped jeans, and the heavy muscles of his shoulders and chest looked even starker in the firelight than they had under the light of the sun. Now that he wasn't pinning me to the ground, I saw that his pack mark was on his upper chest. All three of the wolves with him bore the same symbol—a 'U' shape with a snake running through it. It didn't look like any of the twelve Zodiac signs I'd been surrounded by since birth, but it was a pack mark all the same.

Whispers rose up, replacing the stunned silence. I heard the word, "snake," muttered over and over again, and I wondered if they were talking about the tattoo on the man's upper arm, which twined around his skin as if it was a real animal, and not just ink. But no, they were looking at all of the new arrivals, not just him.

The other three hung back from the Sun Witches, but the man, who must have been their alpha, stepped right up toward Evanora. He took his time, looking around the gathered packs until his gaze stopped on me and lingered. My breath caught. Out of everyone in the crowd, somehow he'd found me. Had he been looking for me? I felt a bolt of fear go through me, and something else too—something like *need*. Another whisper went through the ranks of shifters gathered, but I couldn't move under his piercing gaze, like he was holding me down in the forest all over again.

Then, just as quickly as he'd found me, he looked away. Evanora was radiating hatred, and I felt the tension rise in the shifters around us, caught on the precipice of action.

"The Ophiuchus pack demands to be recognized," the man said, his voice carrying over everyone.

Shock spilled out, replacing the anticipation. The word Ophiuchus echoed inside my head, digging at old memories that I'd half-forgotten, folktales that I'd learned as a child and abandoned with age and maturity. Ophiuchus was the lost thirteenth Zodiac pack. They were legendary, known as the "snake bearers," and said to be vicious traitors who had no sense of obligation or loyalty. They lived outside of normal society and didn't interact with anyone if they could help it.

They were also supposed to be myths. I couldn't remember ever hearing of anyone seeing a member of the Ophiuchus pack in my lifetime. The only time they'd been mentioned was when we'd been children. *Be good,* the adults had told us, *or the Ophiuchus pack will come to take you away.* They'd been the bogeymen of our childhoods, always the shadowy figures that had grown less threatening the older I'd gotten.

Now they were here.

The fear I'd felt as a kid was visceral, and it returned as I looked at these strange shifters, outside of any pack I recognized. And the alpha who had pinned me down in the forest? He was the nightmares from my childhood come to life.

"Moon Witch lovers," someone muttered, and I remembered the other part of the tale. The Ophiuchus pack had been part of the Zodiac Wolves once, but they began interbreeding with the Moon Witches, who had cursed us all those years ago. As a result, the Ophiuchus pack was banished from the Zodiac Wolves. No one had heard anything from them since.

Until now. They stood in front of us in the flesh, standing toe-to-toe with the most powerful Sun Witch. I wondered if any of the stories were true, and they did have Moon Witch magic running through their veins. Could this alpha take on the High Priestess?

Evanora was the first to speak into the stunned silence, loud enough for all of us to hear. "You aren't welcome here," she said and pointed at the alpha. It didn't seem to have the effect she wanted, as he simply waited, shoulders drawn back, meeting her gaze. "If this wasn't the Convergence, and bloodshed was allowed, I would have cut you down myself already."

The alpha drew his lips back in a parody of a smile—all the right motions, but none of the humor. "I'm not here to fight," he said, and his posture went from threatening to neutral in the blink of an eye. I remembered the graceful way he'd shifted and moved in the forest. This was an alpha who had utter control of his body, who commanded each muscle. "But it's time that you allow us to rejoin the Zodiac Wolves."

"Never," Evanora hissed.

"I will discuss it with the alphas, Sun Witch," the alpha said, his growl rumbling low in his chest. "We may be on your turf, but this is wolf business. Even you couldn't hold back the force of all thirteen packs if we decided to turn."

"You'll never be one of us, snakes," someone called. I recognized the voice and found the alpha of the Leo pack standing. Dixon Marsten looked like a Viking warrior of old with long blond hair and a thick beard, and I could see people shrinking back from the intimidating bellow of his voice. Beside him stood his son, Jordan, who had his arms crossed. He shot me a look that practically burned off my skin before he jerked his chin back to the events unfolding in front of us.

"For once, we agree on something," Dad said, standing as well. "Get out of here, before we change our minds about the no bloodshed rule." It was an empty threat, but it got the rest of the packs nodding and making noise. I heard more than one jeer come from the Cancer pack before it was picked up by other packs and passed along.

The Ophiuchus alpha glared at Dixon with such seething hatred it felt like waves of rolling heat. "If you won't allow us to become your allies, then we will become your enemies." His voice was so deep, it was practically a growl. The hair at the back of my neck stood at that noise, and the threat contained within it. "And you really don't want me as your enemy."

Dixon actually laughed, throwing his head back and letting the booming sound free. It echoed across the clearing, not joined by anyone. "What can one little outcast pack do against the might of the twelve Zodiac packs? You're nothing. Leave this place before we tear you apart."

Many of the other alphas nodded, and a couple of them added in their own taunts. I'd never seen so many alphas agreeing on something. The only ones who weren't participating were the Sagittarius shifters. They kept silent, watching without participating, some of them with nervous eyes.

Even though so many seemed to agree, I couldn't shake the sense that there was more that the alpha wasn't saying. I'd felt the power contained in the alpha's grip as he'd pinned me to the forest floor. If half of his pack was as strong as he was, we'd be in for a fair fight.

The set of the alpha's jaw confirmed my feelings. He had a villainous gleam in his eyes that set my teeth on edge. *We should listen to him,* I thought. *We don't need another war.* But no one would hear me, especially after the public humiliation Dad had subjected me to. They'd scoff at me, just as they scoffed at this obviously powerful alpha.

"I see you've chosen to be enemies then," the alpha rumbled, and his voice cut through all of the noise somehow. "Prepare yourselves for war."

He jerked his head at his pack mates, and they melted back into the crowd. There were a few more jeers thrown their way, and I watched until they'd left the light of the fire and vanished into the darkness.

The moment they'd left the clearing, the mood relaxed and people sat back down. Evanora looked shaken but plastered a serene look over her face once more. As everyone quieted down it almost felt as if it hadn't happened at all, as if I'd only imagined the lost pack shifters arriving at our ceremony and disrupting things. Evanora called for order, and the wolves around me went back to listening intently as if everything was normal. When I looked around, no one seemed anxious like I was, and I had to bite back a scream. Of course they weren't taking this seriously. Why would they?

I alone seemed to be on edge, and I tried to stuff down the sense of unease as I waited to see what would happen next.

CHAPTER SIX

EVANORA RAISED her hands and everyone quieted, waiting to see what she would do. "Despite the unfortunate interference, we will continue with the ceremony."

Wow, they were really going to continue on as if nothing had happened. Surely they should at least talk this over, push the ceremony back a bit. But no one seemed to share my sentiment, all eager to move on from the incident and pretend it never occurred at all.

"All shifters who have come of age since the last solstice, please undress and step forward," she continued.

My anxiety spiked. I knew getting naked was part of the ceremony, but that didn't make it any easier. To a shifter, nudity was a way of life. Shifting didn't allow for us to keep our clothes, and it was said the more one shifted, the more comfortable being naked they were.

It would be different if I had access to Cancer's powers to protect myself. As I reluctantly slipped out of my clothes and laid them by my seat, I felt like every bruise and scar was glowing, marking me as weak and an outcast. *Not one of us,* they screamed. No one was paying attention, but I felt like a bug under a microscope anyway.

Mira stepped up to join me, and the panic rising in my throat abated. She was here with me, and we would get through this together. She smiled at me, giving me the strength I was lacking.

One of the witches, the one I'd seen looking at me earlier today with her strange eyes, stepped up and motioned us forward. She passed me a blanket and I took it gratefully, wrapping it around my shoulders. I was glad they offered us this semblance of decency.

Another witch picked up a sconce of incense and began circling the gathered pack members. The smell tickled my nose, heavy and cloying. Three times she circled us, and then she stepped back, blending into the rest of the Sun Witches as they came forward, forming up around us.

Evanora stood inside of the circle with us, and she looked at each of us in turn, her gaze penetrating. I could have sworn I saw contempt in her eyes as she locked her gaze with mine, but the fire was casting strange shadows over everyone. Surely, she wouldn't hate me too?

"This first shift is going to hurt," Evanora said, her voice solemn. "It's going to be the worst one, and you will have to get through it. Survive this, and you will come into your power. Do not disappoint us."

There were nods all around, and I sucked in a deep breath in preparation. I glanced up at the moon, begging for

Selene to give me the strength I was lacking, and then the chanting began. The Sun Witches raised their arms in unison, and the spell settled over me, more oppressive than the blanket.

For a moment I thought that would be the worst of it, but then a bolt of blinding pain went through me. I staggered, and I heard a few in-drawn breaths around me. This was bearable still. I breathed through it, just like I'd been told.

Evanora joined the chanting, and then all I knew was pain. I'd never felt such agony, not in any beating I'd endured, or any fall I'd taken. I'd broken my arm once, and that was the worst pain I'd felt up until now. This was ten times worse than that. My vision went red from the intensity of it. Every single bone was breaking simultaneously, all of my joints popping out of their sockets, before reforming into those of an animal. Even my *hair* hurt as it retracted back into my skull.

How could anyone breathe through this? That was the only thought that crossed my mind as I fought not to scream. I probably couldn't, not with the changes happening in my body. I'd never heard a wolf scream, but I was about to test that theory.

It probably only took a couple of minutes, but in my mind, each moment of agony stretched into an eternity. It lifted as quickly as it had come upon me, and then I looked at the world through new eyes. I stood on all fours, lower to the ground, and everything was sharper than it had been mere moments ago. I could make out the distant tree line as if it was lit by daylight, but my sight wasn't anything compared to smell or sound. Each was enhanced to such an insane level that I swayed. I could smell *everything*. The incense had seemed bad before, but now it almost overwhelmed me. I sneezed. Underneath that was the smell of the fire, of the wolves surrounding me. I could even smell Mira next to me. Sounds were enhanced, too, and I realized that I'd been spending the last twenty-two years speaking much too loudly. I could hear everyone in the crowd talking, the hushed whispers carrying like Evanora's voice had earlier.

I looked down, trying to come to terms with everything I was sensing. It was almost too much. What I saw was enough to distract me though. My paws were pure white, and with my enhanced sight, it was almost as if they were glowing. *Wait, what?* I turned and looked at my body. White. I was pure white. *Well, that's a surprise.* I'd thought that with my red hair, I'd be one of the russet-colored wolves. I swished my tail experimentally, and it felt like just another limb, not weird in the slightest.

Something nudged me, and I turned to look at the wolf beside me. Mira had kept her coloring, a comforting dark brown, with eyes that still looked like her own. She smelled of the sea, salt and sand, along with something uniquely *her*, and I knew how wolves scented each other so easily now.

Mira rammed her head into my side, just hard enough to get my attention. I opened my mouth to laugh, before remembering that I couldn't do that as a wolf. I nuzzled her head, trying to convey the overwhelming affection I felt toward her. She'd stuck with me this whole time, and now that we both had our wolves, we'd be set. It didn't matter what life threw at us, we'd be better, and stronger.

Mira growled playfully and bowled me over. I let her, reveling in my ability to respond so easily to the play attacks. My wolf body was stronger than my human body could ever hope to be, and for once I felt like I could keep up with the full-blooded wolves.

We tussled for a few moments before settling, and I took the time to look around at the rest of the shifters. The glee was palpable, and I couldn't help but get caught up in it. I felt as if some part of me had been asleep for my whole life, and it'd just been woken up. Of course, I'd heard that from everyone who had gone through the Convergence, but I'd figured they were romanticizing it.

Now I knew they hadn't been. This was the best I'd ever felt, the most like *me*. With my half-human blood, I wasn't sure what it would be like when I shifted, but there was no difference between me and the other wolves. I was even tempted to howl at the moon.

The witches began chanting again, and I felt the shift coming in my bones. It was an odd sensation, like being yanked by a cord right behind my naval. I scrambled to hold onto my wolf form with a soft whimper. I wanted to stay for a bit longer in this sense of *belonging*.

It didn't make a difference. No matter how much I wanted it, I couldn't hold my wolf when the spell was cast by the Sun Witches. It was just as painful turning back human as it had been to shift. Everything burned—my muscles, my bones, my skin. I knew each shift would get easier, but as I settled back into my human form, I almost vomited from the sheer amount of pain running through every inch of me.

"Apologies," Evanora said. "We would have more time for you to explore your wolf bodies, but the night grows long, and we must move onto the mating ritual."

I took a few deep breaths, trying to reconcile my human form. It was strange, how foreign it seemed now. I'd spent maybe ten minutes in my wolf body, but now my human body didn't really feel like *mine*. I reached down for the blanket that had fallen off me sometime when I'd been shifting and wrapped it back around my naked shoulders.

"You can return to your packs and dress," Evanora said, spreading her arms wide. She had a serene look on her face, and I let out a breath. I'd gotten through half of the night. Now at least I knew I could shift, and that my wolf form was just as strong as a full-blooded shifter. There was nothing marking me as half-human when I was a wolf. Thank the gods.

But the knot of anxiety in my stomach didn't ease. This next ritual was the one that would determine my fate.

I dressed slowly, trying to regain my breath. The two forced shifts had really taken it out of me, and after my hike, my body was ready to call it a day. Something felt different, underneath the bone-deep exhaustion. I flexed my fingers, testing the strength inside me. I'd have to try to pick something up or go for a run to be sure, but I was almost positive that I was stronger.

As my gaze traveled up my arm, I realized something else—my bruises were rapidly fading. Where they'd been vividly angry before, now they were hardly smudges. I tilted my arm so the light would catch it better just to be sure. *Yep.* As I watched, they faded away completely. The remaining aches and pains from the beating I'd received yesterday from Brad and his friends were also gone. I stretched, reveling in the way my body felt. *Now* I felt like I belonged, and even Dad's cruel words couldn't convince me otherwise. I was a shifter, and I had my wolf to prove it.

"Ayla!" Mira was beside me again, bouncing up and down. She'd also dressed, and had the same gleam in her eye as her wolf had. "Can you believe it? We shifted!" She launched into a detailed retelling of what happened, and I huffed out a breath. Typical Mira.

"I almost didn't even need to be there," I said to her as she wound down, ending with us shifting back. I made sure to keep my tone light. Mira rolled her eyes at me.

Wesley trotted up to us, grinning like a loon. "Mira giving you the replay?" he asked, and I didn't miss the way Mira blushed. He gave me a sympathetic smirk before his face softened and he grabbed me in a tight hug. "Your wolf is beautiful, Ayla."

"Thank you." I let out a relieved laugh as some of the tension left me. "I didn't expect it to be white."

"A rare color, but one considered lucky by the Cancer pack," Wesley said.

"I could use all the luck I can get for this next part." I glanced back at Dad and Jackie, but their faces were hard, and they didn't even give me a small nod. My heart sank at their lack of acknowledgment. I wasn't sure what I'd expected, but couldn't they have been the tiniest bit proud of me? And how could it still hurt so bad when my parents showed me for the hundredth time they didn't care?

Wesley put a hand on my shoulder. "No matter what happens with the mating ritual, you'll always be my sister, Ayla. I'll always love you."

I blinked back tears and punched him in the arm. "I love you too. But you can't be getting all sappy on me right now. Do you want me to cry in front of everyone?" My emotions were still running high, and it took me a few breaths to avoid falling apart in front of everyone.

Wesley looked ready to respond, but before he could, Evanora's voice rang out again. "All unmated shifters, please come to the circle for the mating ritual." I stepped away from the rest of the Cancer pack, and Mira and Wesley followed me, along with all the other shifters who hadn't found their mates yet. Most were young like us, but there were a few that were much older.

We'd doubled in ranks with the unmated shifters in the circle now too. A blond head caught my eye and I balked. Jordan, the Leo alpha's son, was among the unmated. It was unlikely that fate would gift me a powerful mate like that, especially since he was from a rival pack, but I sent another prayer up to the moon goddess anyway. *Not him, anyone but him.*

My mind turned back to the alpha from the lost pack

and the way my body had responded to him. *No.* That was even more impossible than Jordan.

Wesley parted ways with us to join the other males, after giving me one more squeeze to the shoulder and a tight smile. We stood, males and females facing each other, and Mira gripped my hand tight, before letting it go and stepping away. I wondered if her heart was racing as fast as mine.

I glanced over at her, and she smiled at me as well. It looked almost as strained as Wesley's had been. *Fingers crossed,* she mouthed, looking so innocent at that moment that my heart went out to her.

Fingers crossed, indeed. I straightened my back and prepared to meet my mate.

CHAPTER SEVEN

EVANORA CALLED out the name of a female shifter to come forward, and I watched with bated breath as the Sun Witches cast the mating spell. The other witches stood around the female shifter, chanting words I didn't recognize. Something like gold dust seemed to float from the sky down onto the shifter, and then the Sun Witches stepped back and quieted. At first, nothing happened, but then the female shifter locked eyes with a male from a different pack. I watched as both stepped toward each other, their movements jerky as if they weren't fully in control of their bodies. They met halfway, staring intently at the other, their expressions hungry. No one dared to try to distract them, and I doubted they'd be able to anyway. They only had eyes for each other.

Two alphas stepped into the circle to join the pair of shifters. The Capricorn alpha put his hand on the female shifter's shoulder with a nod, while the Aquarius alpha joined the male. The two alphas exchanged a few words, too quiet for anyone outside of the small group of people to hear, and then both alphas stepped back to allow Evanora to tie a ribbon around the two mated shifters' hands. The Sun Witches raised their arms and began chanting again. Bright light surrounded the couple and something in the air changed, like energy flowing around us that we couldn't see. I gasped as the Capricorn pack mark on the female shifter's arm shimmered, melted, and reformed into the Aquarius symbol. I'd never seen one change like that, but it made sense. Since her mate was an Aquarius, she would be an Aquarius now too and would gain all of their pack powers and lose her own. Only Virgo women stayed with their packs forever—their male mates joined them instead.

When I was a kid I once asked my Dad why the gods had so many of us change packs this way. He said it fostered peace between the different packs since shifters would have family ties in both their new and old packs, and it also prevented inbreeding. Then he told me not to question the gods and smacked me upside the head. That was around the time I learned to stop asking questions.

The newly mated shifters walked out of the circle to join the Aquarius pack, who parted ways to let them through while patting the male shifter on the back or greeting their new female member. Evanora watched them for a few moments, the barest hint of a smile on her face, before calling forward the next female shifter.

I had a feeling I'd be last, a knowing in my gut that didn't really make any logical sense, but one I felt all the same. Something unpleasant settled over me as I watched Evanora perform the ritual again. It would be just my luck to never get a mate, and thus never escape my current life or gain the powers of another pack.

The shifters paired off as Evanora drew them forward and cast the spell over them. Some even found mates within their own packs, while others didn't find a mate at all and would have to try again at the next solstice. I didn't feel quite so alone knowing that even if I didn't get my mate tonight, I wouldn't be the only one. I just hoped I wouldn't have to spend every Convergence standing in the circle, holding my breath and waiting for a mate to be chosen, only to be disappointed time and time again. *That* would be humiliating, and I'd feel like even more of an outcast.

My mind drifted back to the Ophiuchus pack as I waited. Everyone had seemingly put the encounter out of mind, not threatened in the least by the mysterious alpha or the other shifters, but I still wasn't convinced. I'd looked the lost pack's alpha in the eyes and seen more determination and strength there than in most of the other alphas here combined. If a single person would listen to me, I'd tell them they weren't taking that threat seriously enough. No one would, though. Even Wesley would just ruffle my hair and tell me I was being paranoid.

I pushed that thought away with a sigh, and my mind drifted back to the mating ceremony, wondering how the Ophiuchus got mates. Did their alpha have a mate already? Or did they not have mates at all, since they'd been cast out of the Zodiac Wolves?

Mira let out a noise that sounded suspiciously like a squeak next to me, and I yanked my mind back to the present, mentally chiding myself. I should be focusing on the mating ceremony, not thinking about the Ophiuchus pack. Or it's dark, dangerous alpha.

Mira gave me a wide-eyed look, and I flashed back what I hoped was a reassuring smile. She stepped forward into the circle of witches, and the spell was cast once more. I held my breath as the gold dust settled on her shoulders and seemed to be absorbed inside her. Then Mira looked around, seeking someone out. A handsome, muscular Pisces shifter with sandy hair stepped forward with a dreamy expression, and Mira stumbled toward him, her smile radiant on her face. He was exactly what she'd been hoping for, and I couldn't help but smile too as they took each other's hands.

Dad joined the Pisces alpha in the center, formally giving Mira over to her new pack. Although I would miss her terribly, I had to admit that Mira had lucked out. The Pisces pack was allied with Cancer, and they were located on the coast of Alaska. Her element would still be water, which I knew mattered a lot to her. She was so connected to the ocean that living somewhere landlocked would have been torture for her.

Mira and her new mate walked away from the center of the circle, and she shot me a glance as she joined the Pisces pack. I flashed her a genuinely happy smile and gave her a thumbs up. She returned it, something softening on her face like she'd worried what I thought of her new mate. I just wanted to see her happy, and the previous dread gnawing at my stomach dropped away at her success. Hope replaced it, making me giddy with the feeling. Maybe I would find my perfect match tonight too.

Several more shifters were mated before it was my turn. My gut feeling had been right. I was the last female shifter that remained unmated.

"Ayla Beros," Evanora intoned, her piercing gaze coming to rest on me. I stepped up to meet the Sun Witches and the unmated males, which included my brother. It looked like Wesley wasn't being mated tonight either, though he didn't seem upset about that. He shot me a big, reassuring grin, but as I glanced at the other males, I couldn't help but balk. There were only a few left, including Jordan, the Leo alpha heir. An instant wave of nausea went through me when our eyes met. *Anyone but him,* I prayed to the gods. Although at this point even the Leo prick would be better than no mate and having to go back to that house with my parents. I'd even take the tall lanky Scorpio shifter who looked like he hadn't fully grown into his height yet.

Evanora led me all the way to the center, but instead of starting the spell right away, something cruel shone in her eyes. "You're lucky that a half-breed mongrel like you is able to shift at all, let alone hope for a mate."

I stared at her, shocked and disappointed she'd be so rude and hateful too, but what else would I expect at this point? I lifted my chin and met her gaze. "I guess we'll see what the gods have planned for me."

"The gods?" She threw her head back and laughed. "Not even they can save you from what's coming."

While I wondered what the fuck *that* meant, she began chanting the spell, with the other witches joining in after a beat. My stomach twisted as the gold dust fell upon me and melted into my skin, the magic tugging at something deep inside me. For a second nothing happened, and I thought it hadn't worked and I would go home without a mate after all. Then my gut twisted and wrenched, like something was being yanked out of me, and I was filled with an over-whelming *need*. It drew me forward, my mind blank except for the irresistible pull toward my mate.

I stumbled toward the males, my eyes locking onto Jordan. *No,* I thought, panic rising in my throat. I turned back to look at Evanora, but her face remained cold and impassive. How was this possible? I knew that the gods chose the mates, but why would they pair me with such an incompatible match? They knew that the Leo and Cancer packs hated each other. Was this some sort of punishment for me?

I dug my heels in, trying to avoid the pull, but my feet kept taking me forward anyway. I couldn't resist the urge to go to my mate, even if my mind screamed that this wasn't what I wanted at all.

Jordan stumbled toward me too, with the same shocked and horrified expression on his face that was probably on mine. He broke my gaze, glancing back at his father with a grimace like he was physically pained by what was happening. He tried to resist the pull as much as I did, but the call was too strong. We took longer to get to each other than any other mated pair had, both fighting every single step. Even with the resistance, we stood before each other in a matter of moments. Only inches away, both of us breathing heavily, our eyes locked together.

That's when the pull changed to desire. Hunger. *Need.* I suddenly had to have this male, or every atom inside my body would be torn apart. He was mine, and I was his, and nothing could ever keep us apart from this day forward.

The rest of the world faded away. All I could see was how gorgeous Jordan was, all muscled and shades of gold, and I had the strongest urge to kiss him. Or tackle him to the ground and tear off his clothes with my new claws.

I wasn't the only one affected. As Jordan took me in, I saw his pupils dilate, and his eyes caught on my mouth and lingered as if he was thinking about kissing me too. As we each took a step closer, it felt as if something had slotted into place, something I'd been missing. *With a Leo?* my brain screamed at me, but I pushed it aside. The mating ritual had bound us together, despite our packs' animosity. If the gods wanted us to be together, how could we refuse?

Dad stepped forward, and when I managed to tear my gaze away from Jordan, I realized my father was *smiling.* I'd seen him smile before, of course, but it was always directed toward Jackie or Wesley, never me. But now he was giving me that same look, almost as if he was proud of me.

Hope swelled in my chest, a strange and new feeling I almost didn't recognize, and at that moment I saw a different path ahead of me. I could bridge the gap between the Cancer pack and the Leo pack, finally ending the years-long hatred that led us to squabble uselessly. That was my destiny.

Dad stepped so that he was standing directly next to me, while Dixon, the Leo alpha, took his spot beside Jordan. Dixon looked on edge as if he was still expecting my father to try something here at the Convergence. I had a lot of work ahead of me, I could tell.

"I give you my daughter, Ayla," Dad said, nodding his head to Dixon. *My daughter.* I don't think I'd ever heard him say those words without it being an insult. "The Cancer pack offers her to you and cuts all pack ties with her. She is one of yours now."

Dixon didn't say anything, and I watched as a muscle twitched in his jaw. He held Dad's gaze for a long moment, before turning toward his son. Evanora brought the ribbon, and I held my hand out so she could wrap it around our hands. Jordan was breathing heavily, staring at the ground and anywhere but me. When he did look up, it was toward his father, who shook his head with the slightest motion.

That was my first hint that something wasn't right.

Jordan yanked his hand away, breaking the ribbon binding us together. He stepped back, and my instinct was to follow, to take a step forward to replace the one he put between us, but I held myself back through sheer force of will. This time when Jordan met my eyes, it wasn't lust in them anymore, but anger. And worse—hatred.

"A half-breed Cancer wolf is no match for the son of the Leo alpha," Jordan snarled, low and intense. "I reject you as my mate."

He shoved me away from him, *hard*. I fell to my knees, as the bond between us was torn asunder, like a piece of paper being ripped in half. Pain seared across my vision as his words sank in. The agony was somehow worse than the forced shift had been, like someone was reaching into my chest and ripping my heart out. I let out a wheeze, unable to scream, unable to do anything but feel the pain coursing through me. I couldn't have held myself up, even if I wanted to.

A gasp went through the audience, the assembled shifters passing along the news. I heard the word *rejected* thrown around a few times, and it hit me like a bolt to the chest, knocking out all the air. Rejecting a mate was nearly unheard of—it went against everything we were taught our entire lives. It was like spitting in the faces of the gods and defying their plans for you. And worse, it meant that both shifters would remain unmated forever. Unable to join another pack. Unable to find love. Unable to have children.

That was the fate Jordan wanted for us.

Dad stepped forward, glaring at Jordan. "You *will* take Ayla as a mate," he said, every inch the commanding alpha again. When Dixon stepped between him and Jordan, a low growl went through both alphas. Dad broke Dixon's gaze first, turning to Evanora. "Make him accept her!"

I winced as I caught the tone. No one talked to the Sun Witches like that. Most of my focus was on Jordan though. I met his gaze, trying to beg him with my eyes to *take me*, to accept me. His face was cruel, unyielding, and he refused to even look at me. He'd made up his mind. He didn't want me, just like everyone else who was supposed to love me.

"It's out of my hands," I heard Evanora say, her voice resigned.

No. Surely this couldn't be the end of it? We were *mated,* chosen by the gods to be together. I hadn't wanted him at first either, but that didn't matter in the end. We were meant to be together. I'd felt it. Hadn't he?

"My son deserves better than a half-human mutt," Dixon said, his tone so condescending it almost sent another wave of physical pain through me. "We don't want her in our pack."

There really wouldn't be a change in my fate. Everyone would always hate me for my half-human heritage—and I would never have a pack to call home.

"Your son is a halfwit who should take what he can get," Dad snarled. "Ayla's better than *nothing,* and that's what he'll have if you don't let them be mated."

The Leo alpha roared in response. "You dare to insult my son?"

"Calm yourselves," Evanora said, her commanding tone cutting through the night. But no one listened.

Movement around me made me look up. Members of the Cancer pack formed up behind us, some in human and some in wolf form, supporting our alpha. The tension was shifting, roiling, and becoming even more dangerous. I watched Wesley step away from the group of remaining unmated males and take his place next to Dad, though he looked pained by what was happening. Jackie joined them too, standing proud as the alpha female of our pack. Wolves from the Leo pack responded, facing off on two sides of the circle, while growls resonated through the air.

As the two alphas started yelling, a few of the other packs began shuffling back, fleeing the conflict. Mira looked at me, eyes wide and dark, but before she could open her mouth to say anything, her mate dragged her away, their hands still bound by ribbon. She cast a helpless look over her shoulder before she vanished into the woods with the rest of the Pisces pack.

"You have insulted me for the last time," Dixon said. Then he threw back his head and unleashed his Leo lion roar—his pack's Zodiac power. The sound was horrible, sending true terror down my spine, and everyone around us either fled or cowered in fear. I covered my ears and felt like my eyes might bulge out of my face, my body unable to move as the roar echoed through me.

Even Dad was forced to freeze, and that gave Dixon just enough time to shift into a giant red wolf and leap forward. With a snarl, he ripped my father's throat out with his fangs. Blood sprayed, landing on me, and I let out the scream I'd been holding back for far too long. It happened so fast, Dad didn't even have time to shift or use his crab armor.

Then Dixon tore apart my father in front of me.

CHAPTER EIGHT

ALL I HEARD WAS SCREAMING. It was the only thing I could do as I watched in helpless horror as the Leo pack converged on my father's body and tore him to pieces.

I wasn't the only one screaming though. As I scrambled back, trying to get as far away from the blood and sinew, Jackie rushed forward, screaming and snarling at the death of her mate. It was too late though—Dad was gone, and she was taken next. I tore my gaze away as the Leos descended on her, my terror quickly turning to a desperate need to escape and survive. The Leo alpha's roar was finally wearing off, or maybe it was the shock of the rejection, but I could finally move again.

As I struggled to my feet, the world around me turned to chaos. Everyone was running, screaming, and shifting. The Sun Witches were gone, and both the Leo and Cancer packs were fighting in the middle of the clearing where we'd just had the mating ritual. I couldn't understand how things had turned so fast, or how I went from getting a mate to being an orphan in seconds. All I knew was I had to find Wesley and get the fuck out of here.

Aries, Scorpio, and Taurus pack members joined the fray, slaughtering members of the Cancer pack all around me under the command of the Leos. Where were our Cancer allies? They'd abandoned us the second they'd smelled trouble, showing just how little the packs cared for loyalty or honor. Now my pack—no, former pack—was outnumbered and being picked off one by one. While I wasn't overly fond of anyone in Cancer except my brother, that didn't mean I wanted to see them *dead*.

I yelled Wesley's name, trying to find him in the battle. I couldn't see him among the Cancer pack shifters falling left and right. I narrowly dodged an Aries wolf using their ram charge on a shifter who used to babysit me. The Cancer wolf fell to the ground, whimpering pitifully. I stuttered to a halt in front of her, trying to see if I could help somehow, and her dark eyes rolled up at me. They pleaded with me, though I wasn't sure if they were telling me to help—or to run.

The Aries shifter turned his gaze on me, snarling, and I quickly ducked out of the way as another one joined him. They pounced on the wolf I'd tried to help, and all I could do was turn and run before they got me too. I tripped over a dead wolf, nearly falling, but somehow managed to stay on my feet as tears streamed down my face. Other wolves were trying to flee too, but the Leos were taking them all down.

They didn't want any Cancer shifters escaping the massacre.

The Ophiuchus pack didn't even need to start a war. We'd done it ourselves.

Where were the Sun Witches during all of this? The Convergence was supposed to be neutral territory and fighting wasn't allowed, but they weren't protecting us or doing anything to try to stop this madness. *They* had betrayed us, just as much as the other packs had.

"Wesley!" I screamed, trying to crane my neck above the fighters. I scanned the crowd for his familiar face, praying and hoping that he had somehow escaped the initial violence. I hadn't seen him go down, but that didn't mean anything. It had all happened so fast, I could have missed it.

Then I saw him.

"Wesley!" I yelled again, charging toward him. I had no clue how I made it through that many frenzied shifters without getting a scratch on me, but somehow I reached his side. He looked half-crazed, blood splattered across half of his face—our father's blood. His hands had turned to claws, but otherwise, he was still in human form, barking out orders to the Cancer shifters fighting around him.

"Ayla!" He let out a relieved sigh, though his face remained grim. "You have to get out of here!"

"I'm not leaving you," I said, drawing up whatever remained of my strength. "You're all I have left."

As I said the words, movement caught at the corner of my eye, drawing my attention toward some approaching shifters. Scorpio wolves, extremely deadly with their pack's signature poison claws and tails. I wouldn't stand a chance against them without Cancer armor.

Wesley shoved me behind him as the Scorpios moved to surround us. "Go! I'll be right behind you!"

I stumbled back, then turned and ran, narrowly avoiding the slash of a Scorpio's poison claws. I thought Wesley was right at my heels, but when I glanced behind me, I saw him fighting the shifters, holding them at bay so I could escape. My chest tightened and a ragged cry escaped me as half a dozen Scorpio shifters converged on him at once, burying him under a sea of fur and fangs. I let out another broken scream as he fell beneath them, snarling all the way down.

"No!" I tried to rush forward to save him, even though it would probably mean my death too.

Suddenly pain exploded in my side, and I dropped to my knees, keeling over and landing hard in the dirt. I gasped in a breath and looked up to find Jordan standing over me, a snarl on his face. He'd punched me directly in the stomach, using his shifter strength and my own forward momentum to make it even worse.

"I can't kill you," he said, sneering down at me. "But I'm going to really enjoy making you suffer."

"What?" I managed to gasp out, my head spinning.

He looked at me with disgust, and I noticed his hands were bloody. "The bond. No matter how much I despise you, it's still there. Mates can't kill each other."

"But you rejected me." I'd thought he had broken the mate bond between us, but as I looked up at him, I realized he'd only torn it. Being near him again made the connection strengthen, and the pull I felt toward him returned. Everything in me wanted to stand up and draw him close to me, and my limbs actually trembled with the effort to resist the pull. It was fucking torture, and I hated that I still wanted him *this much*. He'd made it abundantly clear that the feeling wasn't mutual—and I would never be with him after what the Leos had done. "You killed my pack!"

"They're not your pack anymore," Jordan said, his voice cruel as he got that jab in.

"Why?" I asked, gesturing at the chaos around us. "Why do this? Just because I'm your mate?"

He lifted his chin. "We were already planning to take down the Cancer pack at the end of the Convergence. Our mating bond just sped up the timeline."

Rage boiled in me, knowing this had all been planned from the beginning. I tried to stand up, to defend my former pack, but Jordan was quick to knock me down again with his massive strength.

He put his knee on my chest, pinning me down. His face was downright psychotic as he leaned close and whispered in my ear, "I'll make you suffer for even thinking you could be good enough for me. For believing I'd ever take a half-human mutt as my mate."

His weight was heavy on my chest, and the words knocked out whatever breath remained in my lungs. Even though I hated him more than I'd hated anyone before, including all the bullies in my pack, the fucking mating bond still hummed inside me to the tune of *mine mine mine*.

I tried to shove him off, but he stood in one smooth

motion and kicked me in the ribs hard enough that I saw stars. I was no stranger to beatings like this, but it felt like every other person had been holding back until now, pulling their punches and softening their blows.

Not my mate though. He wanted me to suffer.

I gasped in another breath as I tried to get away from him. I could hardly see, eyes blurred with tears as I crawled toward the woods. The forest was within reach, and it gave me the last burst of strength my exhausted body needed to move forward.

"You really think you can escape?" Jordan asked, as his foot fell again. I heard the crunch of my bones, so loud it seemed to echo around the clearing, and I let out a ragged scream. My knee felt like it was on fire. I didn't know what exactly he'd done to it, but I suspected it wouldn't hold my weight. Not for very long anyway.

The pain cleared my head of any remaining pull toward Jordan, and it gave me the push I need to kick out with my good leg, catching him completely off guard. It wasn't strong enough to ground him, but it unbalanced him enough to give me a split second of extra time. That was all I needed.

With adrenaline fueling me, I pulled myself to my feet, pain lancing through my injured leg. It held me, barely, and I ground my teeth through the agony. I wasn't about to let this asshole win.

"Don't fucking touch me," I said, low and sure. Jordan looked almost surprised by my words as if he expected me to cower before him. He was just like the other bullies, but I always got up again.

With some effort, I shifted into my wolf form. I wasn't really sure how to do it on my own, but I let my instincts take over, and they told me I'd be better off on four legs than two. Once the white fur covered me, I snapped at Jordan, but instead of staying to fight like every cell in my body was screaming at me to do, I turned tail and ran. Or rather, limped away. I couldn't take him on, not injured like this, especially with the mate bond making everything so difficult. Which meant I had to escape.

I rushed toward the forest, hoping it would provide me some cover and safety. I'd hiked through it earlier, and I bet I knew it better than Jordan did. Four legs made it easier for me to ignore my injured knee, and once I succumbed to my animal instincts I started loping along at a decent pace. I could feel the healing power trying to mend my leg, but I was so exhausted, I knew it wouldn't be able to do much until after I'd rested. I was tapped out.

I reached the cover of the forest, but I wasn't fast enough. Jordan was right behind me, hot on my tail. He wasn't injured, and he would catch up to me easily. Something in my gut told me he wouldn't let me get away this time. I'd caught him off guard, and he wouldn't make the same mistake twice.

I glanced around, wolf's eyes taking in sharper details than my human ones could. The moon was high, casting enough light that the whole forest was practically illuminated to my enhanced senses. I heard the rustle of the wind in the trees and the distant sound of the waterfall. I'd need to hide somewhere, but *where?*

I headed deeper into the forest, intent on finding the perfect place. My wolf nose smelled something like an old fire, and I chased after it and found a cave. I was about to head inside when I realized Jordan would be able to smell it too—and probably me as well. Fuck. There was nowhere to hide.

I had to keep running.

With panic racing through my veins, I headed deeper into the forest, with no thought for anything except escape. Behind me, the screams, snarls, and moans from the clearing faded away, and I wondered if any of my former pack was still alive.

I glanced over my shoulder as I bounded up a set of boulders, almost missing a step with my injured leg. For a moment, I thought I'd finally escaped Jordan, but then a large red wolf burst through the brush with a growl and leaped into the air behind me.

I scrambled up, trying to outrun him, but he was faster, stronger, and had the advantage. He slammed into my side, knocking me clean off the rocks and back onto the forest floor. I fell on my back, breath leaving me in a huge *whuff*. I was stunned enough to not move for a few moments as Jordan leaped back down to me, his sharp fangs snapping at my neck.

In his wolf form, he was much larger than me, but I rolled out of the way at the last moment, defying those powerful jaws. He might have been strong, but I was quick, even when injured. And I'd had a lot of practice escaping bullies before.

When he turned on me again, he opened his jaws and used his Leo roar to make me cower. It was like my limbs defied my brain, making me crouch down, my head lowering in submission while I whimpered. In my mind, I was fighting as hard as I could to stand tall and fight, but my body refused to listen to me.

Jordan shifted back to his human form, and his naked, muscular body gleamed under the moonlight. "You can't even get away in your wolf form," he said, as he loomed over me. "Pitiful. This is why we don't breed with humans. You're Cancer's biggest failure, and trust me, the list is long."

My limbs unlocked, allowing me to stand once more on four legs and shake off some of his control. I was in full panic mode, heart pounding with the need to flee, but he was really pissing me off too, the way he was laying on the half-breed talk so thick I could choke on it. It wasn't my fault I'd been born half-human. All I'd ever wanted was a better life—and he'd taken that chance from me.

As I stepped back into a patch of moonlight, that darkness locked inside me awoke, coiling with my hatred for my mate and the entire Leo pack for what they'd done. Jordan strode toward me, his hands turning to claws as he prepared to attack me again, but I wasn't going to let him have the satisfaction. A flash of cold, dark power burst through me, washing away the pain and the exhaustion, filling me to the brim before spilling out into the forest.

Then the world *shifted*. I blinked and found myself twenty feet away from Jordan, whose back was to me now. My pure white paws illuminated in another patch of moonlight as I glanced around, wondering how I'd gotten here. Had I blacked out? Were my injuries that bad?

Jordan looked just as confused, swiveling his head around as he searched for me. Then he caught sight of me and his face changed, growing murderous once again. He shifted back into wolf form and bounded toward me at a speed I couldn't hope to match.

Panic filled me again, and I glanced up at the moon, praying to the goddess to help me. Power burst out of me just as Jordan pounced, and then I was standing someplace else, with the moon still shining down on my white fur.

Could it be? Somehow I was jumping between patches of moonlight without moving a muscle. I had no idea how or why, but when I looked up at the moon again for guidance, the magic took me away again, carrying me deep into the forest, away from Jordan. Soon I couldn't even smell my mate, and I realized I'd finally lost him for the first time since he'd attacked me in the clearing.

Just as quickly as it had come upon me, the strange power left in a rush. The extra strength it had provided me left me swaying on my feet, almost ready to collapse. I didn't dare shift back to my human form.

I glanced around but didn't recognize this part of the forest. I had no clue where to go, but knew I couldn't stay here either. Jordan would keep searching for me.

I limped along, still putting as little pressure on my injured knee as I could. It ground as I walked, awful noises that set my teeth on edge. I was almost ready to collapse and call it a night, right here in the middle of the forest with my enemy still stalking me, when a faint whiff of scent caught my attention. Even though I'd only smelled it once in wolf form, it was as familiar to me as my own. *Mira.* Thank goodness for my new wolf senses. I'd never have caught that with my human nose.

Mira was with the Pisces pack, and though they'd fled before the massacre started, they'd still be allied with Cancer. Hopefully. Going to them was a better alternative than staying here and praying that Jordan wouldn't catch up to me. My mind made up, with grim determination the only thing driving me, I bounded toward the scent.

CHAPTER NINE

I RAN through the forest as quickly as I could manage without the adrenaline assisting me. I knew Jordan was still out there, hunting me and tracking my scent, but he wasn't as present of a threat as he'd been only minutes ago. Somehow I'd gotten away from him, using some power I didn't understand, but I wasn't safe yet.

Mira's scent led me to a small clearing where several vehicles were parked. Pisces shifters ran back and forth, shouting terse orders at each other and quickly packing their things into their cars.

They must really be paranoid to park this far away. Though after what I'd witnessed tonight, maybe not. Or had they known about the impending attack all along? They'd certainly disappeared the second any conflict started, but I had a hard time believing they'd turn against the Cancer pack.

The air was thick with tension, and I swore I could smell

fear as I approached. As soon as I stepped into the clearing, I returned to my human form. My wolf had provided me with a little more strength, and my legs gave out the instant I was fully shifted back. I was completely naked, my clothes abandoned when I'd shifted, and covered in blood, both my own and others. My vision swam, and all I could hear was the blood rushing in my ears for several moments as I battled through the pain.

When I came back to my senses, holding onto consciousness by the barest thread, Mira was holding me up. "Ayla?" she was saying over and over as if I'd passed out.

I tried to smile at her, but the best I could manage was an unconvincing twitch of my lips, and then I was crushed to Mira's chest in a tight hug. I groaned as the motion jostled my hurt knee, looking over Mira's shoulder. Mira's new mate rushed over and brought me a blanket, which I gladly accepted to cover my naked body, and I saw the Pisces alpha approaching too. I felt a wave of relief rush through me. I was among allies, I reminded myself. They would help me.

"What happened?" Mira said, drawing me back and looking me over. Her eyes were wide, face ashen as she noted the odd angle of my leg. "Are you okay?"

I shook my head, unable to find the words to express how not okay I was. Now that I'd found a sliver of safety, tears filled my eyes at the thought of everything I'd seen. My father. My pack. My *brother*. All gone.

"What happened after we left?" Mira asked, more insistent this time. "I saw Jordan reject you and then the alphas were arguing, but then the Pisces alpha said we should go in case there was trouble. As we were running away, I heard screaming and I feared..." Her words died off like she couldn't say the rest out loud.

I wiped at my eyes and looked up at her. "Everything you feared is true. The Leos slaughtered our pack. Including my entire family."

Mira gasped, her face pale. "All of them? Even Wesley?"

I replayed the last moments I'd seen him alive, swarmed by Scorpio shifters. There was no way he could have survived that. "Dead," I whispered, grief flooding me at the memory.

Mira's lip wobbled. "My parents?"

My chest tightened. I'd forgotten they were there too. "I didn't see them. I'm sorry."

She covered her mouth with trembling hands as tears streamed down her face. "No, no, no. They can't be..."

We held each other, crying for everyone we had lost, but when she squeezed me too tight I yelped. She pulled back, wiped her eyes, and looked me over. "You're hurt."

"Jordan. He attacked me but I managed to escape." I pulled my leg in toward my chest, wincing at the awful crunching sound it made. "I'm pretty banged up, but I'll survive. I just need to get away from the Leos."

"You can come with us," Mira said. She glanced up at her new mate, who rubbed the back of his neck like he wasn't sure what to do in this situation. Then she turned to the Pisces alpha, who was watching us. "She can, right?"

The Pisces alpha's face drew down into a frown and he

crossed his arms as he looked at me. "I can't help you," he said. The words didn't penetrate my grief-addled brain at first, and I just stared at him, unable to believe what he'd said. "We're leaving immediately, but you can't come with us."

"Please," Mira said, glancing between me and the alpha. "Can't you see she needs our help?"

He shook his head. "She's not our problem. We can't afford to be at war with the Leos."

"But you were allied with the Cancers," I sputtered. "You were friends with my father!"

"And from what I hear, he *and* his heir are dead." His face turned grim. "I will grieve their loss, and pray to the gods for your soul, but I can't put my pack's safety on the line for you."

It was a punch to the gut. Surely, he wouldn't turn me away. He'd always seemed kind, whenever he came to visit. Kind and level-headed, unlike Dad. "No," I whispered, so quiet that it hardly came out at all. "Please, you don't understand, I have nowhere else to go."

"That's not our problem." His words were harsh, but I could see in the alpha's eyes that this was a struggle for him. He held strong though, unwilling to waver. "We're probably already next on the Leos' hit list, and having you with us will make them even more eager to tear us apart. We can't take losses like your pack can. The Pisces pack isn't even half as large as the Cancer pack is." He winced, and then amended, "Was."

Mira grabbed me tight and held me to her as if she could

keep me with her physically. "No! We can't just leave her here."

Her new mate grabbed her and tugged her away. "Come on. We need to go before the Leos find us. You don't owe her your allegiance anymore."

Mira reached out to me as he ripped us apart, sobbing. I stretched my hand out to meet her, tears running down my face as well. He shoved her into a car before we could even brush fingers, and I fell back to the ground, shaking.

The Pisces alpha looked down at me, his face hard. "I'm sorry, but I have to put my people first."

He turned and got in his Jeep, and the rest of the shifters got in their cars too. Then they drove away, leaving me in the dust. The only people who could help me, and they'd just driven away like I didn't matter at all. Like all the years of support from the Cancer pack meant nothing anymore. The second their loyalty was questioned, they turned their backs and ran.

Leaving me here. Alone. Naked.

Packless.

I glanced down at my arm, at the spot where I should have had a Leo pack symbol. That spot remained empty, showing every shifter I was an outcast. I wasn't a Cancer anymore, and the Leos wouldn't have me either. No one would take me in, not even the Cancer pack's closest allies. Where would I go?

Desperation drove me to my feet. I needed to get away from this place before Jordan found me. At the very least, I had to get out of this forest, and then I'd figure out my next plan. I had nothing with me except a blanket and sheer determination to not be a victim. All my belongings were back at the Cancer camp, and I certainly wasn't going there. Step one: find clothes and shoes.

I slowly headed in the direction the Pisces cars had gone, pain lancing through me with every step. Following them would get me back to civilization, where maybe I could find someone who could help me. To do what, I didn't know, but I had a lot of walking to do and a lot of time to think about it.

Everything hurt, and I had to move so slow I knew it would take me hours longer than it should have. I was limping, unable to put much weight onto my bad leg. At some point, my new shifter healing would help me, but I had to rest to get to that point. That wasn't an option. I even tried shifting back to wolf form, but that didn't work—I was probably too exhausted.

Every step brought me closer to collapse, and I realized I hadn't eaten or drank anything since the afternoon. As if in protest, my stomach growled. My ribs throbbed at the same time. I was pretty sure Jordan had cracked some of them when he kicked me. Every step only brought more pain to that area.

"What did I do in my past life to piss the gods off this much?" I grumbled to myself. "All I want is someone to actually *want* me, is that too much to ask?" Somewhere I could belong, with people who cared for me. A place where I wouldn't live in fear of hatred or the next beating I might get. A really hot mate wouldn't have hurt either.

Actually, no. I'd gotten a hot mate, but he'd turned out to be an asshole. Thanks but no thanks.

Jordan. The mixed feelings I had for him rose up in me, making me feel nauseous. I wanted to tear his throat out, but the mate bond also made me want to rip off his clothes and throw myself at his naked body. Would it be that way for the rest of my life? Or would the longing eventually subside if I got far enough away from him?

My mind turned instead to the alpha of the Ophiuchus pack once more, as it often did since he'd appeared on my hike. He was hot, hotter than Jordan actually. And dangerous too. I wondered who would win in a fight—him or Jordan? I'd seen them both naked, and they were both pretty damn impressive...

I shook my head. I was in the middle of an abandoned forest, talking to myself, comparing the physical qualities of two male shifters who I hoped to never see again. This really was the end for me. A deranged laugh bubbled up in my throat, threatening to escape. I was probably hours away from being brutally murdered by the Leo pack, and yet here I was, fantasizing about a male who wasn't my mate. I didn't even know his name, and I'd probably never see him again. Shit, I must be going into shock or something. If I made it out of this with my sanity intact, it would be a miracle.

I continued limping along, trying not to collapse, and entered a thicker area of brush. A twig snapped behind me and I froze, heartbeat fluttering as I looked around, eyes wide. Three dark wolves melted out of the forest, seemingly out of nowhere. I lifted my hands, trying to show I wasn't an enemy, but all three leaped at me in unison, knocking me over. They circled me, growling and snapping to make sure I wouldn't try to bolt.

I covered my head with my hands, tensing for the blows. They must be from the Leo pack, or maybe one of their allies, hunting me down on Jordan's behest. They'd likely beat me until I couldn't move, and then deliver me to Jordan to do whatever he wanted, like a gift-wrapped present. *Here's your mate, destroy her.*

But no blows came. The wolves threatened and surrounded me, but didn't touch me. I slowly lowered my hands, glancing between them. What were they playing at?

Then the alpha of the lost pack melted out of the forest in human form, while the other wolves parted for him. He was so light on his feet, I hadn't heard him coming. Like before, he wore no shirt, only jeans. My breath caught as he approached me, almost as if he'd been summoned by my thoughts of him, while the other wolves circled me so I didn't dare try to escape.

Like a dark angel come alive from one of my fantasies, he stood directly over me, his eyes cold and unreadable. "You're coming with us."

Before I could even open my mouth, one of the wolves sank their fangs into my arm. I started to cry out, but then exhaustion swept through me, so quickly it was impossible to fight. I struggled not to go under, but there was no stopping the call to sleep.

I could only stare at the dark alpha with defiance as my body gave out and everything went black.

CHAPTER TEN

I CAME TO SLOWLY, my mind so fuzzy it didn't occur to me that I was actually waking up until I blinked my eyes open. I lifted my head and glanced down at my body. I was lying on some sort of cot, covered with thin sheets, and I didn't feel any pain. I drew in a deep breath experimentally. Nothing, not even a twinge.

I lifted my knee, bending and straightening it. The crunching noise was gone, as was the pain. How long had I been out for my body to heal itself? Surely wounds that bad would have taken days. Maybe I was with the Virgo pack? They had healing abilities and weren't allied with the Leo pack.

I flung the sheets back, taking note of the too-big clothes I'd been changed into. Better than being naked at least. They hadn't given me shoes though. I looked around and noticed for the first time that I wasn't in a bedroom or infirmary. Iron bars formed a cage around me, sunk into the floor, and bolted to the ceiling. There was a small toilet in my cell, plus the cot, and nothing else. For a moment, all I felt was confusion. Had the Leo pack gotten me after all? Why was I healed if they planned to torture me?

Then my last few moments of consciousness returned to me. Cold, unreadable eyes looking down at me. I checked my arm, expecting to see a bite, but that had healed too.

Shit. I'd been taken by the Ophiuchus pack. The bogeymen of shifters, our worst nightmares as children, now back with a vengeance. I couldn't help but imagine all of the torture they were going to put me through, and that's if I was lucky. It could be worse than torture. Whatever the Leo pack would have done to me suddenly paled in comparison to what I suspected was ahead of me. I'd gone straight from one torment to another. Maybe I would have been better off alone in the woods.

"You sure like talking to yourself," a deep, gravelly male voice said.

I jumped, realizing I'd said all of that out loud...and that I wasn't alone. With bated breath, I turned toward the voice.

The lost pack's alpha stepped out of the shadows, arms crossed over his chest. His handsome face was severe, and he actually had a shirt on for once. *Pity,* my brain whispered. I shoved that thought far back. Now was not the time, and definitely not the place, to be thinking about how much of his skin I'd like to see on display.

"I didn't expect someone to be spying on me from the shadows like a perv," I let slip before clamping my mouth closed. *Shut up,* I told myself firmly. Mira had always warned me that my smart mouth would be the death of me, and I really didn't want that to be right here and now.

"You were talking to yourself when we found you too," he rumbled, uncrossing his arms. "What's your name, little wolf?"

I lifted my chin. Two could play this game, and if he planned to torture me to death, I at least wanted to know his name first. "What's yours?"

He gave me a hard look, his dark eyebrows drawing down. "Explain to me how you got away after the Leo pack attacked. You don't have any of the Cancer pack's abilities, and yet you are one of the only survivors. Possibly the only one. How?"

I opened my mouth but paused. I wasn't about to start answering his questions without getting some of my own answered first. "Why did you kidnap me?" I asked. "Planning some elaborate torture scheme?"

He set his large hands on the bars of my cell, fingers wrapping around them. The muscles in his forearms bulged as he squeezed tight, showing off his snake tattoo. "I don't think you understand how interrogations go, little wolf. Either you were hit on the head too many times, or you're always this dumb." He straightened, his face still hard and emotionless. "You will answer my questions if you want to stay alive."

"Will you let me go if I answer all of them?" I asked. "Or are you planning to keep me here forever, coming down to interrogate me anytime you need intel on the twelve packs?

I'm not a computer, and I'm certainly not inclined to answer to you."

"You just can't help running your mouth, can you?" The menace was clear in his voice, and I tensed, waiting for him to come inside and hurt me. Instead, he growled and tossed something into my cell.

I flinched as the object hit the floor, ready for whatever threat it posed, but then it bounced. It was a bottle of water, which was the absolute last thing I thought he'd throw in.

"Perhaps some time alone with your thoughts will loosen your tongue," he said. I almost laughed out loud. It wouldn't. "The bottle of water alone is probably enough to get you to answer anything. Maybe if you play nice enough, I'll feed you too."

My stomach growled again. How long had it been since I'd eaten? Suddenly answering a few questions seemed like a good idea. What could it hurt if he had my name? He already knew I was originally part of the Cancer pack, and it wasn't like there were many of them left. He could probably find my name out on his own if he tried—there weren't that many half-human mutts, after all. Still, I hesitated, all the things I'd been told as a child about the Ophiuchus pack echoing in my brain.

I was right on the verge of telling him my name when the alpha turned away with a huff. Then the bastard shut off the lights and locked the door behind him, leaving me in almost complete darkness.

I scrambled off the cot and dropped to the floor in front of the bottle of water. The cap snapped as I unsealed it, and

I let out a relieved breath. I wouldn't put it past them to try to slip something into my drink to drug me into delirium. That would be one surefire way to make certain they got answers from me. I took a long drink. I didn't know how long it had been since I'd had water, but I was *thirsty*. I didn't think I'd ever tasted better water.

I stopped myself, though I could have easily downed the whole thing. I needed to ration it. Who knew how long it would be before they'd give me anything else. In fact, they'd probably deprive me of any further water as a way to get me to talk. What did they want with me? Would they ever let me out of here?

Wait. The power I'd used to get away from Jordan. Maybe I could use that to escape.

There was a tiny patch of moonlight from the small window on one side of my cell. The window was higher than my head and only big enough to let a tiny bit of light in and nothing more, so there was no chance of escaping through it. I went over to it, straining up onto my tiptoes to see out while trying to use whatever that strange power had been.

I held my breath and reached out for the darkness, the moonlight, or whatever it was I'd used to teleport before. Nothing happened. I closed my eyes tighter and hoped and prayed that when I opened them, I'd be away from the cell and outside in another patch of moonlight.

No such luck. My shoulders dropped and I made my way back over to the cot. Maybe the patch of moonlight wasn't big enough, or maybe I was doing it wrong. I kicked at the legs of the cot for a moment, trying to think of another plan. The iron bars around me were sunk into the cement floor and drilled into the ceiling. There was no way I could shake one of them loose, not even with the assistance of my newfound strength. This cell had been made to hold a shifter. There was absolutely no way out.

I was well and truly trapped in the worst situation I'd been in yet, and there was nothing I could do to escape from it. The only thing that remained was to sit here and wait for the lost pack alpha to come back and interrogate me some more. Or maybe they had some other use for me. Whatever it was, it stank of foul things, and I didn't want to stick around long enough to find out more.

TO MY SURPRISE, I was able to fall asleep, even knowing I was surrounded by such dangerous shifters. This time I jerked awake, my bladder screaming at me. I hurried over to the toilet and relieved myself, and only when I was finished did I think to make sure I was alone.

Alone except for a bag of food. I didn't know how I could have slept through someone coming in and pushing it through the bars, but there it was. Then again, I'd had a very rough last twenty-four hours. Or was it longer? Forty-eight hours? There was no way for me to tell.

I walked over to the bag warily. It was plain, with no indication of where it had come from, but the smell emanating from it made my mouth water. I opened it and pressed the paper-wrapped food to my nose, breathing it in. I didn't care that it was cold, it smelled like heaven. I tore the paper open, finding a breakfast sandwich with sausage, eggs, and cheese. There were hash browns in the bag too.

My stomach grumbled and I groaned and dug in. It didn't even occur to me that I had no way of knowing if they'd drugged it until I'd plowed through half of it. I stopped mid-chew and sniffed the food again. Nothing to suggest there was anything unusual there, even with my new enhanced senses. Besides, if they'd wanted me dead, they would have killed me already.

I finished eating and found a bottle of water sitting beside the bag. I let out a laugh, unable to help myself. Here I was, being held captive by the worst of the worst, and they hadn't done anything more menacing than send their alpha to growl at me and ask me some questions. Shit, they'd fed me and hadn't beaten me yet. This was already two steps above my life in the Cancer pack.

Funny how things looked with a little perspective.

The door opened, and daylight streamed in. From the small window, I could tell it was day, but now I realized I'd slept through the night and probably well into morning.

The lost pack's alpha stepped into the small room and closed the door behind him. I couldn't help but notice the way he moved with both grace and power, somehow managing to command the room without even saying a word. His impressive body seemed to fill the space too, even while wearing clothes that hid all those muscles I'd seen in the woods.

He observed me for a few moments. "You're looking much better than when we found you."

"Well, I was practically on the verge of death," I replied. "You can't expect someone to look good after fleeing a massacre."

He walked the rest of the way into the room without answering and dragged a chair from the corner. He sat himself down outside of the door to my cell, chair backward.

"I'll get this out of the way for you," he said after he'd slung his legs over the chair and leaned his forearms against the metal bar at the top of the back. "My name is Kaden Shaw, and I'm the alpha of the Ophiuchus pack." His voice was low and sexy, and I found myself leaning forward into the words. "I need you to tell me what happened at the Convergence. How you got away."

I cocked my head at him. "Why the sudden sharing circle?"

"I'm hoping that if I share information, you'll be smart enough to return the favor," Kaden said. "I can't let you out until I know I can trust you."

"So you *do* plan to let me out?" I asked, hopeful.

"*If* you prove to be trustworthy. That remains to be seen."

I sighed. I supposed there wasn't anyone else who was showing me this level of kindness. "And you promise not to torture me?"

Kaden cocked his head to the side, copying my motion. "Do I look like I'm about to torture you?"

No. No, he lazed against the chair, legs spread wide,

hands carelessly flung over the back of it. He looked about as far away from torturing someone as he could get. And sexy as hell. I couldn't keep my eyes off his long legs or muscular arms.

"How do you know what happened at the Convergence?" I asked. "I thought you all left."

"We were watching from the forest and saw the whole thing. Including the fact that you're now mated to the next alpha of the Leo pack."

It was a slap to the face. I'd almost managed to forget. I jerked back, drawing in a breath. "My mate rejected me." There was no way I could keep emotion out of the words. "And since he helped kill my entire family and my pack, I don't want him either."

That wasn't completely true. The mating bond still hadn't totally faded, and I felt the pull toward him, though it wasn't as strong now. I tried to shove the feeling of longing away. Jordan didn't want me, and I didn't want him either. Except any time I thought of Jordan, I got jumbled up in the mess of emotions. My base instincts drove me to want him, but I couldn't come to terms with any of the things he'd done to me or my family.

"How did you escape?" Kaden asked.

"I don't know," I said.

In one smooth motion, Kaden stood, kicking the chair away with a burst of strength. "I told you not to lie to me," he growled, and the tension in the air sharpened. "I could kill you just as easily as release you."

Ah. There were the familiar threats. He was no different

than anyone in the Cancer pack, after all. "I'll tell you, but I want my own answers first."

He crossed his arms and raised his eyebrows. "Answers about what?"

"Where are we? What happened to my injuries? How did you knock me out? And who dressed me?"

He smirked at that. "I can't answer most of those. Not yet. But I will say...I'm the one who dressed you."

My eyes widened at that and my cheeks grew warm imagining those big hands of his all over my naked body. I picked at the enormous shirt. "You could have gotten me some clothes that fit me."

He gestured toward me, his eyes narrowing. "Your turn. Tell me how you escaped before my last bit of patience vanishes."

"I really don't know," I said, holding my hands out. "I stepped into the moonlight and then suddenly I was a few feet away. It happened a couple more times before I realized I was *moving* from one patch of moonlight to another. I have no idea how I did it, and when I tried to use that power again, I couldn't."

Kaden sat back down in his chair, looking almost intrigued. He was quiet for a few moments longer, and I thought he'd be interested in asking me more about that, but then his eyes moved up and down my body like he was appraising me. "You don't have a pack mark. I didn't see one on you when we first met either. Why is that?"

I ducked my head. *The fun questions now, apparently.*

"I've always been an outcast in my pack because I'm half-human. I never had a pack mark."

"Aren't you the alpha's daughter?" Kaden asked.

I looked up at him and gave him a wry smile that held no humor. "You'd think that would help, but it made it worse. I'm a result of his affair with a human. She abandoned me with the pack, and even my father couldn't turn me away. He raised me, but not as his own. The worst treatment came from him and my stepmother." I sucked in a breath, thinking of Wesley again. "The only one who ever showed me any love was my brother, Wesley. And now they're all dead and it doesn't matter."

I blinked away tears at the thought of my brother, turning my face away from Kaden. I didn't want him to see me like this. Any weakness, no matter how justified, could be used against me in the future. I drew in a shaky breath and continued. "I'd hoped that when I turned twenty-two and came to the Convergence I'd get a mate in a different pack. One who would treat me better." I let out a bitter laugh. "You saw how well that went."

Kaden was quiet for a beat longer, tension still thick in the air. "Do you feel any ties to the Leo pack or your mate?" he asked, instead of the million other things he could have said. "Do you want to go back to them?"

I whipped my head around to glare at him. "Fuck no. I want them all to die for what they've cost me." Then I hesitated. I could lie, but what was the point? "But yes, I still feel the mating bond with Jordan, though I wish I couldn't."

Kaden smiled, but it wasn't a nice smile. "I have good and bad news for you. Which do you want to hear first?"

"I don't care," I said. "It's all news."

"Good news first, then. You've become useful to me, so I won't kill you. Yet."

The implied threat may have cowed me, just a day ago. Now, I just stared at him blankly. "And the bad news?"

"You're going to use your bond with your Leo mate to set a trap for the Leos. You're going to be our bait."

I laughed, the sound dragged out of me. "You can fuck right off with that plan. I'm not going to be anyone's bait."

Kaden's lip drew up in a snarl. He moved so fast I didn't see him get out of the chair. It crashed to the floor behind him, and I jumped, despite my bravado.

"You're alive because I allow it. You will follow my orders if you want to remain that way." His hands tightened around the bars, thick muscles in his forearms flexing. Kaden's voice dropped so low, it was practically a growl. "And if you ever disrespect me again, I'll tear your throat out with my teeth."

The threat was very, very real. I'd just watched an alpha do it to my father, only hours before. Something cold slithered through my veins. No matter how well they were treating me, they still weren't my friends. I kept my face blank, not allowing him to see my fear. He could probably smell it, but I raised my chin anyway and met his eyes.

Kaden pushed away from the bars and walked to the door. "I thought you'd want revenge on the Leo pack for what they've done to you." He stopped and glanced back over his shoulder. "I can give that to you. No one else will have the guts to stand against them. Think about it. It's the only offer you'll get from me."

With that, he turned and left me with nothing but my thoughts and half a bottle of water to keep me company, while his parting words echoed in my skull.

CHAPTER ELEVEN

ANOTHER DAY PASSED, with meals being discreetly left inside my cell as if by an invisible visitor. But the next morning, as I got up, I noticed something else. Whoever left the food had also given me a change of clothes. I reached for them and then glanced around. I couldn't help the feeling of being watched, as if Kaden's heavy gaze was on me constantly. It was a ridiculous notion, and shifters accepted nudity as a way of life, but I still hesitated to get undressed in the middle of my cell.

Stop being pathetic, I told myself, then yanked off the oversized clothes. If he was watching, it wouldn't be anything he hadn't seen already. And maybe, just maybe, a small part of me that I didn't want to acknowledge actually liked the idea of him watching.

I'd been given a pale blue t-shirt with some anime character on it and some black sweatpants, and this time they actually fit me. A peace offering from Kaden, perhaps?

I was grateful to have the clothes, but what I really needed was a shower. I *reeked,* and when I reached up a hand to run it through my hair, I grimaced. There was still blood in it. It could have been mine, or my father's, or someone else's. I didn't know, and I didn't care to either.

I sat back down on my cot and devoured the food—this time, a burger and fries, plus an apple. Once I finished, there wasn't anything else to do except think and pace, and I wasn't about to give the invisible Kaden surveilling me the satisfaction of showing my nerves. I could see how people went insane from periods of long capture. I was just about over it and I'd been here for maybe a couple of days if the feeding times were anything to go by.

I tugged my mind away from that. It would be best not to dwell on it, or I'd find myself slipping into something bad. I needed to stay focused, and luckily, Kaden had given me exactly the thing to mull over.

The idea of getting revenge on the Leo pack intrigued me. The thought of knocking off the smug snarl on Jordan's face played through my mind several times before I snapped myself back to reality. They deserved to pay for what they'd done to my pack, and to my family. My throat clenched at the memory of Wesley being taken down. For his death, I would burn the entire Leo pack to the ground.

The unpleasant part was being the bait. I didn't want that, any more than I wanted to go back to the Cancer pack, whatever remained of it anyway. But what option did I have? The Ophiuchus pack was terrifying, and from what

I'd seen of Kaden he was dangerous and unpredictable. But maybe that was exactly what I needed right now.

I had no pack to call my own, not anymore. No one would take me in and shelter me. There was nowhere else for me to go. The Ophiuchus pack might be the only ones who could keep me safe from the Leos, and if they were offering me revenge on the people who killed my brother and stole my future from me, I would take it.

But why did Kaden want to take down the Leos? The Ophiuchus pack had come to the Convergence and asked to be made part of the Zodiac Wolves again but were turned down. The Leo alpha had been an asshole about it, but so had many of the other alphas. Was there another reason Kaden wanted vengeance on the Leos in particular?

Before I could ponder it further, the door opened again. This time, Kaden wasn't alone. Two big, muscular male shifters appeared on either side of him, staring at me blankly. I looked between the three of them, my pulse skyrocketing. *Shit, shit, shit,* I thought but kept my voice even. "Is this where the torture starts?" I asked. "Did I not make my mind up fast enough for you?"

Kaden gave me a sharp look, then gestured to the other two shifters to stay back. He walked up to my cell, and I tried to hold perfectly still. He went from playing my friend to threatening to kill me from one moment to the next, and it was impossible to read him. I didn't know him well enough, but I had the feeling that even if I'd known him my whole life, he'd continue to surprise me.

"Have you thought about what we discussed last time?" he asked.

"Are you serious about helping me get revenge?" I had several smartass remarks available, but I wanted a straight answer from him.

"I am." He looked me dead in the eye. I tried to find any deceit in those blue depths, but they were a mystery.

"What's in it for you?" I asked.

"I have a score to settle with the Leos personally. But it's not just them." A villainous smile crossed his lips. "I want all the Zodiac packs dead or defeated. The Leos took out the Cancer pack for us, but we still have eleven to take care of." The words sent a chill through me. All twelve packs, defeated? What could he possibly have against every single pack?

"Why?"

"It's time the Ophiuchus pack was recognized. I tried to play nice with the other packs, give them a chance to let us back into the fold. They turned us away like unwanted puppies." He drew himself up, eyes going dark. "The thirteenth pack is done being outcasts. Now we're going to rule, and anyone who doesn't bow down to me as alpha will burn."

On some level, I understood. I'd been an outcast my whole life, rejected by those who were meant to help me and keep me safe. I felt no remorse over the loss of the Cancer pack, except for a few people like Mira's parents who had always been kind to me. Once the initial shock of Dad and Jackie being killed in front of me had worn off, I didn't feel sadness, only a strange loss at what might have been. It was only Wesley's death that truly gutted me.

Thinking of my brother brought back the hatred of the Leo pack and the deep pain of loss in equal measures. I was almost bowled over by the intensity. I hadn't had time to properly grieve, and I didn't know when I would. I had to be safe first, and it wasn't happening in a cell.

As for the rest of the packs? They'd either sided with the Leos or run away like cowards, leaving the Cancer pack to their fate. Even the Pisces pack hadn't helped me, after years of camaraderie with the Cancer pack. Maybe they *should* all burn. There was obviously something wrong with the Zodiac packs, something festering from within, and perhaps it was time for a complete overhaul.

I'd make sure that Mira was safe, but everyone else could go to hell, for all I cared.

"I can hear your heart racing from over here," Kaden said. "Have you come to a decision? I do hope it's the right one." He leaned against the cell bars casually, but there was menace in his voice. "You can either join us in taking down the other packs, or I'll send you back to the Leos in a gift-wrapped box. You can be their problem, not ours. I don't have time to torture you, anyway."

I pushed away his cruel words and glared at him with defiance. "As long as you help me get vengeance on the Leo pack for killing my brother, I'm in. I don't care about the rest of them."

"Good," Kaden rumbled, the word sounding like more of a growl than anything else. "Put these on."

He threw some shoes at me, and I quickly slipped them on my dirty feet. Then he opened the door of the cell and stepped back. Just like that. I blinked at him, hesitant that he'd try to punch me in the gut the moment I stepped out. Kaden made a frustrated noise, jerking his head for me to come out.

I stepped out of the cell, bracing for an attack. It didn't come. I glanced up at Kaden. His face still revealed nothing. The other two shifters didn't move either.

I stopped in the doorway, squinting in the sunlight. It felt like ages since I'd looked up at the sun, and I had to hold my hand in front of my eyes, blocking most of the light for several moments before I could even take a few stumbling steps forward. I was still missing most of my strength, apparently. Everything that had happened the night of the Convergence had been healed, but my body needed more time to recover from it. My soul, on the other hand, might never recover.

I took in my surroundings as my eyes adjusted. The sounds of a small town rushed in, replacing the overwhelming sensation of being outside again. I could see a few stores and what must have been the town's version of a main street, along with rustic houses in neat little rows, surrounded by tall trees on every side. It looked picturesque, like something I'd find on a postcard depicting a woodland town couples visited for romantic weekend trips. I could hardly believe the most feared pack lived *here*, of all places.

What was most surprising was the smell of the forest all around me. I took a deep breath in, noting how pure the air was. I closed my eyes, soaking in the summer sun and the fresh air.

When I opened them, Kaden was watching me, looking almost smug. "Welcome to the Ophiuchus pack lands."

* * *

KADEN and the other two shifters I'd nearly forgotten about all but herded me to a large house on the edge of town that looked like a lodge in the middle of the woods. It was all dark wood and natural stone, very masculine, yet inviting and warm too. The kind of place you'd want to stay in during a snowstorm, sitting by the fire with a cup of hot cocoa. The border of the forest crept around the edges of the house as if trying to subtly suck it back into it, making it disappear forever.

As I was looking up at it, Kaden came to stand beside me, and I tensed. He'd said he wouldn't kill me, but that didn't mean we were friends, and I certainly didn't trust him any further than I could throw him.

He either didn't notice or chose to ignore my response. "This is where you'll stay for now."

"For now?" I asked.

"Until you either prove yourself useful to me, or I decide to get rid of you."

"Right." I resisted the urge to roll my eyes.

"You'll have a roommate since space is always an issue for the pack, but she's about your age. Try to get along with her."

I nodded and bit my tongue before I could say anything back. No need to antagonize him and make him tear out my throat. There weren't any bars keeping him from launching himself at me now.

"The pantry is well-stocked, and you're free to go anywhere in town. Clayton or Jack will have to be with you, of course," he said, jerking his head to the two males who stood behind us. "Don't try to leave town."

"I'm not quite that stupid," I couldn't help but quip. Before Kaden could growl something at me, I quickly asked, "Where are we? Canada, or the United States?"

"You don't get that piece of information yet," Kaden said, and I fought the swell of frustration in me. "You'll have to become a full member of the pack for that to happen."

My mind shuddered to a halt. *Wait, what?* "Are you serious?" I asked, looking over at him, trying to find any hint of a joke on his way too handsome face. "Is that even possible? I thought the only way to join a pack was to be born into it or mated to someone in it."

"The Ophiuchus pack has taken in other rejects before," Kaden said. "After all, we're the outcast pack. Most of us know what it's like to be rejected and unwanted."

I certainly knew how *that* felt. Hope began to rise within me. I couldn't help it. Was this the answer to my silent plea to the moon goddess? I looked away as we continued walking closer to the house until we stood right next to the porch steps. Could this lost pack provide me with the home I'd been searching for my whole life? A place where I would feel accepted, not shunned for being different? "How do I join?"

"If you want to be a part of this pack, you'll have to follow my orders and prove yourself to me. Loyalty is earned, not given." He crossed his arms. "Your training starts tomorrow, and every day you will prove your usefulness to the pack by cleaning a building I assign to you." He smirked as if it brought him joy. "From now on, you'll be the pack janitor."

And just like that, I was back to being the outcast, the lowest of the low, a position all too familiar to me. They were no different from the other packs, and fuck, I was so tired of being treated like trash.

I glared up at him. "So it's not enough that you want me to risk my life for you as bait? Now I have to do your dirty work too?"

Anger flared in his eyes as he moved toward me with a clear threat. I stumbled back until I hit the wall behind me, my breath leaving me in a rush. He pressed his hands on either side of the wall beside my head, effectively trapping me so I couldn't slip out from under his arms, and leaned in close. *Very* close.

His body was hot and hard and only inches away from mine. Now I couldn't catch my breath for an entirely different reason. Despite his awful personality, I couldn't help the rush of desire that ran through me, especially when I breathed in his scent. It drove my inner wolf wild, and though I was terrified of him, I wanted him too. Even with the guilt tearing me up inside, reminding me he wasn't my mate, that I belonged to someone else—even if that someone else wanted nothing to do with me.

"Let me make one thing crystal clear," Kaden said in my ear, lips so close I could feel the warm air as he spoke. "I'm the alpha. This is my pack. My family."

I shivered at the possessiveness in his voice. What would it be like to have an alpha who cared about me that much? Or a mate, for that matter?

"I'm giving you a chance," he continued. "If you prove your loyalty, you will never be mistreated or abused, only welcomed as family. But if you do anything—*anything*—to betray or hurt my pack in any way..." He trailed off and inhaled deeply. Probably smelling my fear and my desire, mixed together. "You won't live long enough to regret it."

"More threats," I said, unable to help myself. Being so close to him made me feel reckless. "But would you really go through with them? Or is your bark worse than your bite?"

He took my chin in his hand, forcing me to meet his eyes. "If you keep challenging me, you'll find out soon enough."

As we stared at each other, the heat between us became undeniable. My chest rose and fell as I looked into those hard blue eyes, and then my gaze fell to his mouth. Was it bad I secretly wanted to know what his bite was like? I licked my lips, a knee-jerk reaction, and his fingers tightened on my chin in response. For a second I thought he'd lean in, either to nip at my lips or kiss me hard, and it surprised me how much I wanted that. I held my breath, staying completely still as I waited for him to make his move. I must have made some small noise because his eyes left my lips, and when he met my gaze again, his face turned hard once more. He let me go and stepped back, crossing his arms as he waited for my answer.

I stood up straighter and tried to regulate my breathing. "Fine, I'll be your janitor. Anything else?"

"Just get inside," he growled. Then he turned away and stalked into the forest without another word.

CHAPTER TWELVE

I WATCHED as the trees swallowed Kaden up, and then I was alone with my two bodyguards, who were conveniently looking everywhere but me.

"Is he always like that?" I asked, trying to diffuse the strange tension that still lingered in the air. I thought they'd both ignore me, but the smaller one cracked a grin.

"Pretty much," he said.

"Shut up, Jack," the bigger one growled, lightly shoving the smaller male's shoulder.

"He's always so dramatic," a female voice said, and I turned back to the house, startled by the sound. Only another shifter could have moved so quietly. A young woman with shoulder-length dark hair stood on the porch, an easy grin on her face. "Don't let him scare you too much," she said. "Once you get to know him, Kaden's a big softie."

"Somehow I find that hard to believe," I muttered.

She grinned wider at that. "I'm Stella."

"Ayla," I replied. "How do you know Kaden?"

"Oh, he's my brother."

Brother? The thought of Kaden having a sister who could smile and joke seemed impossible. It stood to reason that with an attitude that bad, he'd inherited it. Looking over her once more, I could see the resemblance. If Kaden smiled more, he'd probably look strikingly similar to her.

Stella jerked her head toward the house. "Come inside."

She opened the door and motioned me through. I stopped in the entrance, taking in the dark wood and vaulted ceiling, along with the huge windows that let an exceptional amount of natural light in. The house was huge but somehow still felt cozy, and looked like a fancy ski lodge from one of the photography books Wesley had gotten me. The forest was visible on all sides, making it feel as if the house was part of nature, instead of a shelter from it.

Stella gave me a quick tour, through a large kitchen that had been remodeled recently, featuring dark oak cabinets mixed with stainless steel appliances. The attached family room was huge, with overstuffed chairs and a large leather couch circled around a huge wood-burning fireplace. A sliding door led out onto a huge deck with some outdoor furniture, a fire pit, and a grill. I felt a pang go through my chest. This was a home for a *family*.

"We're going to be roommates," Stella said, grinning at me.

"Do you live here alone?" I asked, remembering what Kaden had said about *limited pack space*.

Stella laughed. "No. It's Kaden's house. We live here together."

Shit. Just when I thought I'd get a break from him, I found out I'd be living in his freaking house. I pictured myself waking up to find him sulking in the kitchen, snarling at me as I tried to get my morning coffee. *Kill me now.*

I opened my mouth to say something—to protest or ask if there was somewhere else I could stay, I didn't know—but Stella cut me off before I could say anything.

"I'll show you to your room." She motioned me to follow her up the stairs to the second floor, which had at least five bedrooms. She gestured toward the first door. "This one's mine. We share a bathroom, but you'll have your own space."

Stella opened the second door and stepped back to let me go inside. The room was clean and cute, but plain. There were no personal touches to speak of, just a queen bed shoved into the corner, a plain wood dresser in another corner, and an empty desk placed under the window, which looked out over the forest where Kaden had disappeared.

"This was one of our guest rooms, but it's yours now," Stella said. "Feel free to make yourself at home."

I ran my fingers across the dark wood of the desk, feeling something tighten in my throat. For the first time in days, I felt...safe. Here, among the pack I always assumed were monsters. "It's perfect. Thank you."

She nodded and left me alone in the room. After she was gone, it hit me that I didn't have any way to make myself at home. I didn't have anything to unpack. All of my belongings had been left behind during the attack. Even the clothes I'd worn at the Convergence were gone, torn apart and abandoned when I'd shifted.

My phone. I patted my pockets uselessly. Of course it wasn't there. I'd lost it somewhere when I'd fled from Jordan, and it was probably smashed in the forest in the middle of Montana. Or worse—in the hands of the Leos. I shuddered as I pictured Jordan thumbing through my phone, looking at the photos I'd snapped and the texts I'd sent. I was suddenly fiercely glad that my camera had been destroyed before I'd left home. If I'd lost that at the Convergence too, it would have destroyed me.

I checked the small closet, but it was empty. I didn't have any clothes other than the ones I was wearing, and no toothbrush or shampoo either. I grimaced and headed to the bathroom to see if there was anything in there I could use.

The bathroom was modern, done in soft sand tones, and smelled like jasmine. A towel was rolled up on the counter, with shampoo, conditioner, and a new bar of soap set beside them. They weren't anything fancy, but I sighed in relief when I saw them. Now I could get the blood out of my hair, and stop smelling like a barnyard animal.

I hopped into the shower eagerly, standing under the spray of the warm water for a long time and letting it run from red, to pink, to clear. I took my time, luxuriating in the feeling of cleaning myself off, while I let my thoughts go blissfully blank. When I stepped out, I felt so much better, and a lot more like myself again.

I still didn't have a change of clothes, but the ones that

had been provided to me were relatively fresh. I threw them back on and headed downstairs to investigate. I walked down the stairs slowly, trying to listen for any movement. Someone was shuffling around in the kitchen, making noise, and I hoped it was Stella and not Kaden.

When I entered the kitchen, Stella turned, a sandwich on a plate and a smile on her face. "For you," she said, handing it to me.

I looked up at her, eyes wide. "Thank you."

I tried to be polite as I dug in, but after the first bite, I couldn't help myself. I wolfed it down like I hadn't eaten in days. Stella watched, a slight smile on her face. I froze mid-bite and ducked my head.

"It's really good." Even though it was just a ham and cheese, it was delicious.

"We're going to need more food," Stella said, her smile turning into a grin. She turned and rifled through a cabinet, pulling out a bag of chips. "You must be starving. Here, have this as well. And sit down, you'll get crumbs on the floor."

Stella motioned me over to the island, and I sank onto the stool gratefully as I tore into the chips. She didn't even know me, but she was being so nice to me anyway. I spotted the Ophiuchus pack mark on her upper arm as she turned, and wondered if everything I'd been told about them was a lie. Kaden certainly lived up to their dangerous reputation, but his sister was another story entirely.

"I need to go to the store," Stella said, and I cocked my head at her. "You should come with me. I can show you around the town and you can get whatever you need."

I shook my head. "I don't have any money."

She waved my worries away. "Kaden will pay for whatever you need."

I nearly choked on one of my chips. "I don't want his charity."

"He's the alpha, and he takes care of us," she said like it was a simple fact. "That includes a visitor like you."

"Visitor?" I snorted. "More like a captive."

She gave a little shrug. "Kaden just wants to make sure you can be trusted. He's not so bad. You'll see."

She'd lived an entirely different life than I had, I realized suddenly. I'd never seen someone look so content with their alpha before. I wished, not for the first time, that I'd been born someone else. I'd had the thought so often as a kid that it was practically a mantra in the back of my head. I'd spent twenty-two years yearning for a pack like this, to the point I'd believed it wasn't possible. But Kaden, despite his growly nature toward me, obviously took good care of his pack. Even Dad had been a sub-par alpha at best, I realized now. I knew many of the Cancer members had been disgruntled with his leadership, but they'd never been able to do anything about it. Wesley had been our only hope for the future of the pack, but he was gone.

A pang of sadness went through me at the thought of Wesley, and of what might have been. Tears threatened to fill my eyes, but I blinked them back, keeping the emotions in check. I would grieve later when I was alone. And someday I would have my revenge.

Stella noticed the look on my face. "What's wrong?"

I shook my head. "Nothing. Let's go."

Stella led me outside. I noticed that the two males Kaden had said were my guards hadn't moved from where we'd left them on the porch. Stella noticed me eyeing them, despite my attempts to make it subtle.

"Clayton is the beta of the pack," she said, motioning to the taller of the two. "He and Jack are Kaden's friends."

Friends? Hard to believe he had any. And why would he put his friends on guard detail, when he so clearly held me in such low esteem? Surely they had better things to do.

I didn't have long to dwell on it. We walked into the town, and I found myself occupied with looking around and taking it all in. The buildings were well-maintained, the houses recently painted, and the shops welcoming. It looked like a well-preserved historical town, and my hand itched toward my camera. I didn't like architecture as much as nature, but there were exceptions.

"This is Coronis," Stella said, standing in the middle of the road on the main street, and spread her arms like she was presenting it to me. I couldn't help but smile and shake my head. She and Kaden really were like day and night. She'd offered the information without any prompting, whereas Kaden had withheld it and gotten gruff with me when I'd asked about anything.

"What?" Stella asked.

"Nothing," I said, shaking my head. "Continue."

She pointed out various buildings as we passed them. Everything was centered around a big grassy area with a few community buildings on one side, including the school, with the shops on the other. I noticed that everyone we passed was a shifter bearing the Ophiuchus mark somewhere on them. It was still hard for me to believe I was really here, amongst the lost pack.

"You have to try the bakery's pastries," Stella said, grinning as she pointed out the coffee shop. "They're divine. Although what you really need are some new clothes. Follow me."

CHAPTER THIRTEEN

STELLA GUIDED us into the town's only women's clothing store. It wasn't large, but it had a pretty decent selection of things, and I hesitated before the racks. With all of the different selections available, it felt overwhelming.

"Is something wrong?" Stella asked. "Don't worry about the prices. As I said, Kaden will cover it."

"It's not that." I ducked my head, feeling foolish. "At home, I just got hand-me-downs or whatever I could find in a thrift store. My Dad...he didn't let me buy new things." I tried to keep the bitterness out of my voice but knew I failed. There was so much pent up over the last twenty-two years.

Stella's face softened, and she nodded. "I can help you if you'd like?"

I nodded, relieved. "That would be great."

Stella clapped her hands together, grinning. "This is going to be fun. Let's see. You have gorgeous hair. We should take advantage of the color, really bring it out."

I winced. My hair had always marked me as something *other,* something *less than.* I couldn't imagine wanting to bring attention to it, but then again, I wasn't in the Cancer pack anymore. I trailed Stella as she wound around the racks, tossing clothes back to me until we made it to a fitting room.

"In you go," she said. "Feel free to ditch anything you don't like."

I smiled at her and stepped inside. She'd given me way too many clothes. What would I even do with more shirts than days of the week? But as I tried each one on, I found that Stella had an impeccable eye for color. The clothes she chose for me brought out my eyes and made my hair stand out in a way I actually liked. They also somehow made my curves look like something desirable, instead of something I should hide. It was like truly seeing myself in the mirror for the first time in my life.

Then I looked at the vast quantity of clothes. There was no way I'd need all of these, but when I brought them out, Stella wouldn't let me put anything back.

"It's a good basic wardrobe," she said. "You'll need more eventually, but this will do for now."

More? "I thought we spent most of our time nude."

Stella grinned over at me. "That doesn't mean we can't look hot the rest of the time."

She also made sure I had some underwear, bras, and socks, then handed the clerk her credit card. I shoved aside any guilt I felt. It was Kaden's money, and for locking me up and his bad attitude, I should make him buy me this whole store.

I reached out to pick up the bags, but Stella tutted at me, shooing me away. She jerked her head toward Clayton and Jack, who had followed us into the store. They exchanged a glance but came forward anyway.

"Make yourselves useful," Stella said, shoving the bags toward them. I opened my mouth to protest but stopped at the grimaces on their faces.

I hid a smile. The exchange reminded me of how Mira would interact with the Cancer pack. Stella was a lot like Mira, at least in character. Physically, they looked nothing alike, but something made me feel at home with Stella.

Thinking of Mira brought a pang of loneliness. I wondered if there was a way to get word to her that I was safe, and that I hadn't been brutally murdered by Jordan or the Leos. She must be worried sick, even as she adjusted to her new life in the Pisces pack. I imagined her reaction to me telling her I'd been taken in by the lost pack—she'd never believe it.

"Ayla?" Stella said, and when I glanced over at her, the look on her face said it wasn't the first time she'd tried to get my attention.

"Sorry."

"It's all right, you looked a million miles away. What were you thinking about?"

"Just someone I knew," I said. "A friend in the Pisces pack. She last saw me half-dead at the Convergence and I'm sure she's worried sick about me. Is there any chance I could send her a message?"

"No, sorry." Stella's face was somehow both sympathetic and unwavering. "We can't let you contact anyone outside the pack. For our own safety, you understand."

Damn. I'd suspected that would be the case, but I had to try. "So I guess a new phone is out of the question too?"

"After you join the pack, you can have one. Until then, we can't risk it."

Back outside, a small bundle of motion ran past my feet, and I jumped out of the way automatically. Then I gaped as several wolf pups ran past and tumbled over one another in the grass, growling and nipping playfully at each other. Wolf pups? How was it possible?

"Boys!" Stella said, almost sternly, as if this was completely commonplace to see young wolves running around. "They're some of my students," she added, noting my look and misunderstanding it completely. "I'm the kindergarten teacher in Coronis."

I couldn't seem to pick my jaw up off the floor as I watched them play. "It's not that. How did they get their wolves so early? I've never seen shifter wolf pups before."

"Oh, right. I forgot you grew up in the Zodiac Wolves." Stella gave me a slightly pitying look. "We don't need the Convergence to get our wolf forms. Or our mates, for that matter."

"How do you get them?"

"It happens naturally," she said with a shrug. As if it was

just that easy, as if I hadn't been hoping and praying for it ever since I knew what it meant to *have* a wolf. "Most of us shift the first time when we're toddlers."

"That's incredible. The years of training you must have..." I trailed off. "And mates? How do you find one without the Sun Witch spell?"

"When we become adults, we can sense if someone is our mate when they're nearby, as long as we're both shifted. Or so I'm told, anyway. I don't have a mate yet."

I couldn't believe it. I'd wondered how the Ophiuchus pack found their mates, but I'd never imagined it was all so...simple. What made them so different from the rest of the Zodiac Wolves, that they didn't need the help of the Sun Witches?

That train of thought led me to another. "What about the Moon Curse?"

"The what?" Stella asked.

For a moment I thought she must be messing with me, and I looked at her face, trying to find a hint of humor or any indication that she wasn't being truthful. All I saw was vague confusion.

"The curse that makes shifters go mad at the full moon?" I asked slowly. "The Sun Witches have to bless us at birth to make sure that won't happen."

The confusion became a full-on frown. "That sounds like some sort of fairy-tale. Who's telling you these sorts of things?"

"It's what we're taught our entire lives," I said, my voice a little shaky. "The Sun Witches bless us as babies, and then they unlock our wolves and help us find our mates when we turn twenty-two."

Stella spread her hands. "I'm sorry. I don't know about any of that. Maybe all of that happened after our pack was kicked out of the Zodiac Wolves."

I nodded, wondering if that was all there was to it. Or maybe it had something to do with the rumors I'd heard that the Ophiuchus pack had bred with the Moon Witches long ago. I glanced over at Stella, trying to see some physical sign that she was more than shifter, but saw nothing unusual. If not for her Ophiuchus pack symbol, she could have been in any of the twelve Zodiac packs.

Before I knew it, we'd stopped in front of the grocery store, like my feet had simply followed wherever Stella had led me. I'd been so wrapped up in my thoughts, she could have led me right into the forest to the edge of a cliff, and I wouldn't even have noticed. Everything I'd known my entire life was slowly being uprooted in front of me. The lost pack was treating me more kindly than my own birth pack had, and apparently, they had access to their wolf powers and mates without the aid of the Sun Witches. What kind of alternate world was I living in?

"Here's the store," Stella said. She was either oblivious to my sudden turmoil or was doing her best to counteract it. "I'll get us some food, and I know you need some toiletries. Feel free to grab whatever you need, and meet me at the checkout." She motioned me over to the 'personal care' section and flounced off with a cart.

The guards stayed with me as I picked out what I

needed, and I observed them out of the corners of my eyes. Even when Stella was nearby, they never seemed to stray far behind. In fact, the only time they weren't within eyesight seemed to be inside of Kaden and Stella's house. What did they think I'd try to do? Run? As I glanced back at them once again, the shorter one—Jack—stared at me intently. I whipped back around and picked up a random tube of toothpaste.

I met Stella back at the checkout and she handed me some cold compress packs. "Here, you'll need these for tomorrow."

I took the packs and eyed them. They were the kind you threw in the freezer and used on injuries. "For what?"

"You're going to start your training tomorrow," Stella said. "Trust me, you'll need those for all your sore muscles. Even shifter healing won't help with that."

"Right, Kaden mentioning some training..."

Stella paid for our items at the checkout with a warm smile to the clerk working there, then turned back to me. "It's part of your trials to see if you can join the pack. You'll have both combat training and wolf training."

My heart rate quickened as I thought about being in wolf form again. This time I wouldn't be in mortal danger, and I could bask in the strength it gave me and learn how to use my new abilities. And combat training? I'd never been allowed to partake in that before with my pack. Dad hadn't wanted me to know how to fight back. "That sounds...fun."

Stella snorted. "Tell me that again tomorrow when you're done."

We headed outside with our groceries and my two guards followed us, close enough that it was just this side of uncomfortable. I lowered my voice, though I knew they'd still hear me. "Why did your brother assign these guards to me? I'm not going to run. Even if I wanted to, there's nowhere for me to go. I don't even know what part of the country we're in—or *which* country, for that matter. Are they just waiting for me to slip up and make a mistake so they can kill me?"

"Of course not. Kaden wouldn't have let you out of that cell if he wanted you dead." She looked over at me with a smile. "Kaden just wants to make sure you're not a threat to the pack. He's been burned too many times in his life to trust easily."

"I can understand that," I muttered as we kept walking. "But he captured me and brought me here against my will, to live with a pack I didn't even know was real a few days ago, then told me I can't leave and set guards to watch my every move. It's hard not to feel like a prisoner."

"I don't know what horrible things you've heard about our pack," Stella said. "But they're all wrong. Kaden *wants* to trust you. He brought you here, yes, but he also healed you. He hopes you'll pass the tests and join our pack. That's why he asked me to look out for you and help you with whatever you needed."

I frowned as we made our way back to the house. Stella's words seemed at odds with how Kaden had acted toward me. But then again, this pack wasn't anything like I'd expected. I was having all my assumptions challenged today.

Maybe there was more to the sexy alpha than I'd originally thought too.

CHAPTER FOURTEEN

KADEN WOKE me at the crack of dawn with a harsh knock on the door. "Time to get up, little wolf."

By the time I'd crawled out of bed and opened my door, he was nowhere in sight. It was hard to believe I was living in the same house as him, as I had yet to see him. Not when I'd gotten back with Stella with our groceries and helped put them away, nor when she and I had shared dinner that evening.

That changed quickly enough though. After I got ready and went down to the kitchen, he stood at the counter, arms crossed like he'd been waiting for me to come down. His dark hair was a bit rumpled from sleep, and the top button on his shirt was open, showing a tiny glimpse of all that hard muscle underneath. I tried not to let my eyes linger too long, even though they very much wanted to linger.

"Good morning," I said, mostly to see the scowl on his face deepen.

"Get something to eat, and then you can start cleaning," he said. "You're going to begin with my house. Every room except for my bedroom and bathroom. Don't go in there. Understand?"

"Loud and clear," I said, trying my best to not let the sarcasm show in my voice, but I must have done a pretty poor job because his frown became borderline murderous. I bit my tongue to stop myself from saying something else stupid.

"Cleaning supplies are under the sink," he threw over his shoulder as he left.

I sighed as I looked over the house. It wasn't filthy, so at least it wouldn't take a long time, but it was still much bigger than any house I'd cleaned before. It had been my duty to clean Dad's house, and Jackie always made sure to leave things around for me to do. *In case you get bored,* she'd say, tossing me unfolded laundry. At least here Kaden would likely ignore me, and I couldn't see Stella being petty like that.

I started in the kitchen after eating a light breakfast and made my way slowly around the house. Despite my resentment at being the pack's janitor, I made sure to clean everything thoroughly. Stella came down at one point, grabbed a blueberry muffin and some coffee, and then headed off to her job as a kindergarten teacher. It still amazed me that the kids here all had their wolves so young. I bet that made her job a lot harder, but probably more fun too.

I stopped outside of Kaden's room last. His was the only

door I hadn't seen open, and I had no intentions of breaking his rules. He'd no doubt smell that I'd been in there the moment he stepped inside. But I couldn't help but be curious what it looked like inside his room.

Instead, I went back downstairs. It had taken me the entire morning to clean this place, and I was ravenous. I ate lunch quickly, thinking about Stella's words to me at dinner. *Tomorrow afternoon is when you start training. Head to the clearing behind the house.*

My mood lifted as I stepped outside, breathing in the warm summer air. I'd get to shift today, and I was looking forward to that most of all. Even if I had to put up with Kaden's growling and glares. At least he was nice to look at.

There was a small path that led from the backyard into the forest, and I followed it, hoping I was heading in the right direction. I was instantly surrounded by the sights and smells from these woods, so much more noticeable now that I had my wolf senses. I couldn't wait to bound through these leaves and under the trees on four legs.

I eventually found the clearing, a huge open space big enough for dozens of shifters to move around without getting in each others' way. I was surprised to find it empty except for Kaden, who stood in the center, face tilted up to the sun as if he was trying to catch the scent of something. Light streamed across his features and my heart clenched at the sight, filling me with something a lot like longing.

He looked over as I approached, and when he pinned me with those intense eyes, I almost missed a step. His masculine presence seemed to fill this entire clearing, and even though he was intimidating as hell, I kept walking toward him without looking down.

"Where's everyone else?" I asked.

"I'll be overseeing your training personally," Kaden said. "I need to know what you know. How you fight, and how you'll handle yourself in a situation when you face a real enemy."

I arched my eyebrow at that. I wasn't sure if I should feel honored or terrified to have his complete attention on me during these sessions. "And here I thought you didn't want anything to do with me."

He scowled at that but chose to ignore my comment. "Have you been taught to fight?"

"No, my dad didn't want me to learn how. But I've been in plenty of fights, and I always made it out alive."

"The last fight you were in would have ended pretty differently if we hadn't rescued you."

I snorted. "That felt a lot more like a kidnapping than a rescue."

His tone turned hard. "Would you rather I'd left you in the middle of the woods for the Leos to find you?" When I shot him a sharp look, he gestured in front of us. "You'll start with stretching. I'll show you what to do."

He sat down on the ground and motioned for me to follow. Then he led me in a series of simple stretches, and my limbs burned as they woke up. It helped get rid of any lingering aches from the cleaning earlier today. I watched the toned muscles of his arms move as he hugged one knee to his chest and quickly looked away. *Focus.*

"You'll do this every day," he said as we finished up.

I nodded, still looking at the ground. "I can do that."

"Even if we don't train," he added. "You need to be agile enough to fight at any moment, and these exercises will help keep you limber."

Easy enough. It wasn't anything I hadn't done before, and he wasn't doing any crazy handstands or anything of the like. So far, it looked like training was going to be manageable. I wasn't arrogant enough to say that it would be a breeze though. I still had to see if I could fight. But this part, this small chunk, I had under control. It felt like a tiny accomplishment after everything I'd been through since the Convergence.

Kaden stood to his full height, making me look up at him. "Now, attack me."

I expected him to take some sort of fighting stance, but he just stood, hands loose at his sides. For all intents and purposes, he looked like he was relaxed, but I knew he was simply waiting for me to make my move.

I stood and observed him for a few moments, trying to think as a fighter would. It would be best to try to catch him off guard. I was smaller and weaker than him, and he had proven multiple times that he had the ability to pin me down without an issue. I stepped back a few feet and tried to read his expression. His eyes gave nothing away.

"We don't have all day," he snapped.

I launched myself at him, fists raised protectively in front of me, and darted around to his side, trying to get under his guard. The moment I sprang into action, he slid into a fighting stance. He moved out of the way as if he'd guessed exactly what I was doing. My fist met the air, and I overbalanced. He grabbed onto my outstretched arm and pulled me the rest of the way over, flinging me right past him and onto the ground. I hit with a *whuff*, and let myself collapse. Damn, he moved so fast.

"That was terrible," he said, sounding almost bored. "Trying to get past my defenses. You made it blatantly obvious you were going to do it, but at least you weren't stupid enough to try and attack me head-on. Get up and do it again."

I pushed myself to my feet, still trying to orient myself. This time, Kaden didn't let me duck past him, just caught me and pushed me back. I stumbled but didn't fall. A small swell of pride went through me. I wasn't perfect, but I wasn't awful, either. I could do this.

"Again," he said.

The more we fought, the more I realized how little I knew about *anything*. He would simply move out of the way and let my momentum carry me past him several times, or block my attacks and use them against me.

"How are you so fast?" I panted, as we circled each other.

"You're a shifter, Ayla. Use your wolf reflexes."

He darted at me, and I jumped back. It wasn't the smooth, physics-defying motion he would have used, but I'd escaped. We circled each other some more, and I breathed in deep, trying to focus my senses. It didn't help. I could see how quickly he was moving, then slow it down a bit so I could try to track his movements as I came closer, but I wasn't able to land a blow on him. Frustration built as he continued evading me.

"I get it," I said, as I tripped over his conveniently placed foot. "Can you actually teach me something now?" I looked up at him as he held his hand out to me. I reached up to take it but paused. "You're just going to use it to flip me over your back or something, aren't you?"

"Maybe. I wouldn't trust my own word." A slight hint of amusement played across his lips.

I glared at his hand and pushed myself up on my own. It was hard to focus on my anger when he rolled his shoulders, muscles rippling. *If you don't stop focusing on his muscles, you won't learn a damn thing,* I told myself sternly.

"I'll show you some basic moves," Kaden said. "It'll give you a good base to start with, something to build on over the next few days."

For the next hour, he went through some moves with me. It felt unnatural, trying to move my feet with my punches. Twice, I tripped over nothing but air. Each time, Kaden's face broadcasted, *seriously?* I couldn't help the blush that spread over my cheeks. I'd never been particularly clumsy, but there was something about training my body to do something different that made me feel like I'd never truly used my limbs before.

"You make this look so easy," I said when I paused to take a breath.

"I've taught you the moves correctly," Kaden said. "Your timing is just off, and you need to work on your body placement. It's sloppy. You're too worried about thinking about what you should be doing, and not letting your body do it." He paused, and I huffed out another breath. "Go into a forward roll, like you've just punched someone and then come out from under their return attack." He demonstrated the movement, making it look as easy as breathing.

I nodded and planted my feet, holding my hands up in the defensive position he taught me. "Start here, right?"

"Wider," Kaden said, and I sighed and widened my stance. It felt *wrong,* and even as I tucked down and launched myself forward as he'd taught me, I could tell my balance was off.

I didn't get fully over so much as I dove headfirst into the ground. I got my hands up in front of me in time, and rolled off to the side, pushing my momentum into *not* breaking my face. This was a lot harder to do than I thought it would be. Especially with how easy Kaden made it look. I had a feeling that the ground and I were going to be very well acquainted by the time training was over. When I glanced over at Kaden, he had his arms crossed over his chest, and I watched him let out a deep breath.

"We have a lot to work on," he said, shaking his head.

Next, I watched as he demonstrated how to fall properly without getting injured. Then, he started pushing and tripping me again. This my body took to like it was natural, and it was. I'd learned over the years that in order to survive a fight, I needed to be able to take a beating and find a way to escape. It was how I'd survived this long.

A few times I looked up to see Kaden nodding, as if almost impressed. From him, it was practically glowing praise.

"Are we done yet?" I asked, panting as I stared up at the sky after rolling out of one more trip.

"One more thing," he said. "Holds. You're weak, weaker than most shifters, and if one gets you in a hold, you'll have to be able to break it. Otherwise, you won't stand a chance."

Great, I thought as I pushed myself up off the ground again.

"We'll start with simple holds, like this one." He spun me around, and I didn't even have time to open my mouth to ask him what he was doing before he caged me in his grip, pinning my arms against my sides. My brain short-circuited as his body pressed against mine, his broad chest hard against my back. His breath stirred the loose hairs at the back of my neck, almost as if he was leaning down to kiss the exposed curve of skin.

I didn't even register that he was talking for several moments, his words coming to me as if they were slogging through molasses. "Use your arms, push mine up, and drop to the ground."

What? It was hard to remember what I was even doing, let alone why I should want him *away* from me.

"Break. This." He tightened his arms around me, fists pressing into my abdomen, just this side of painful.

I drew in a sharp breath. The pain snapped me out of

whatever the hell that had been, and I struggled in his grasp. His instructions registered a moment later, and I lifted my legs up, letting myself fall, and tried to push my arms out and up.

He let me go, and I fell to the ground. *What the hell?* I thought and scrambled away. How was I supposed to learn how to break out of holds like that when I couldn't even *think?* Why did he have this effect on me?

To my dawning horror, that wasn't the only hold we were going to practice. Kaden dug the heel of his boot in my back. "Up," he said, and I pushed myself to my feet again. "That was an easy one. Let's see if you can get out of this one."

We went through various holds, each one pressing his body closer than comfort to mine. They didn't catch me off guard like the first one had, but I was still disturbed by the way my body responded to him. He didn't show any signs of being as winded or sweaty as I was, and as I struggled against his holds, I half-expected him to just give up on me.

He hadn't yet, but I was pathetically weak at the holds, and it felt like just another defeat. It was clear I had a lot of work ahead of me, and I expected him to pass me off to another trainer. As I tapped out of yet another hold and Kaden sighed, I waited for those words exactly. Instead, he just said, "That's enough. Meet me here tomorrow after lunch and we'll continue."

"What?" I asked. "You're not tired of my incompetence yet?"

"You have a long way to go, but you're not entirely hopeless," Kaden said and headed toward the house without another word.

High praise indeed. I let out a long breath while my entire body ached, and I was glad Stella had gotten me those cold compress packs. I had a feeling I'd need them tonight.

CHAPTER FIFTEEN

I TRUDGED to the edge of the forest, surprised to find Kaden waiting outside the house with Stella. I'd expected him to melt into the forest itself and reappear when he was ready to glower or menace again, but he just nodded to me as if he hadn't just spent the last couple of hours watching me struggle to fight him.

"Stella is going to be taking over your wolf training," he said. "She's one of the best natural hunters and trackers in her wolf form that my pack has ever produced."

By the way Stella was bouncing on her heels like an excited child, I suspected she had practically forced Kaden to let her be my teacher. If their relationship was anything like mine and Wesley's, then Stella probably had Kaden wrapped around her finger. I started to smile before the grief hit me once again. It still hurt more than anything else knowing Wesley was gone. I spent most of my time trying to avoid thinking about it because it hurt enough that I had to stop and catch my breath.

I closed my eyes briefly, trying to breathe past the pain in my chest. One of the easiest ways to get past sadness was to transform it into anger. I shoved all of my hurt and pain into the thought of getting revenge on the Leos who took him away from me.

When I opened my eyes, I wasn't blinking back tears anymore. I was calm, collected, and I met Stella and Kaden's eyes without issue. Kaden nodded to me and walked away without saying goodbye. At this point, I wasn't even offended. Clearly, that was just how Kaden acted. No one else seemed to have a problem with it.

"Come on," Stella said, motioning me to another part of the forest behind their house. I followed her through the trees, looking around. I still wasn't sure where I was, and even Stella in her increasing kindness refused to tell me. I'd given up guessing and had resolved to wait until they trusted me enough to tell me. It wasn't like I needed to get back home or anything. My home probably no longer existed.

Stella stopped in a patch of forest that looked like the rest, with trees all around us. "This is where the pups come to learn how to be a wolf and pack hunt. But we'll be alone today."

"Because you don't trust me?" I asked dryly.

"No, because they're in school," Stella said, giving me an odd look. "I know Kaden comes off as a bit heavy-handed, but we are trying our best to make you feel welcome."

I nodded and ducked my head, feeling just a bit ashamed. Stella had been nothing but nice to me, and even Kaden hadn't threatened to kill me in a few hours. Though that might change at any moment.

"I'm going to stay in human form while you shift," Stella said. "We're not pack members yet, so I won't be able to communicate with you in wolf form. Now take your clothes off."

I hesitated just a second before stripping my clothes off. It wasn't as bad, being around one person, but I still angled my body away from view. Maybe someday I'd be able to just rip my clothes off and leave them in piles, but today wasn't that day.

"Shift now?" I asked Stella.

She nodded, and I closed my eyes, bracing myself for the pain. It wasn't as bad this time, but it seemed to take forever, each bone reshaping slowly enough that I felt like I was being pulled apart at the seams. Finally, after what felt like a few long minutes, I settled into my wolf form and swished my white tail back and forth experimentally.

Stella beamed at me. "Wow, look at your beautiful fur! So rare to see such a pure white color. I can tell you've only shifted a few times. Don't worry, it'll get easier and faster the more you do it. Never as fast as an alpha, though. They're the only ones who can do it instantly."

I'd seen how fast the alphas could shift, including Kaden, and I envied the ease with which they did it. Even so, my wolf form was pretty damn amazing. In fact, it was just about the best thing in the world, especially when I wasn't running for my life. I crouched down and sprang into action, sprinting around the trees. I wove through them as easily as if I'd trained for it for years, my wolf body responding much quicker than my human one would have. The clumsiness I'd felt with Kaden disappeared. Stella's laugh followed me as I circled her and then dove into the grass, rolling around. My body moved so easily, so quickly. It was incredible.

"You're like a three-year-old pup," Stella said, still laughing. I looked up at her and grinned as well as I could, still on my back in the grass. She shook her head at me and let me roll around for a few more minutes before she called me back over to her. "Time to start training," she said, and I cocked my head at her. "We're going to test those wolf senses of yours."

She pulled a few objects from their house from her bag and waved them in front of me. "I'm going to hide these, and you're going to track them by smell. Now close your eyes."

I dipped my head in acknowledgment and closed my eyes. I heard Stella walk away, and focused my ears on other things. It wasn't hard, since there were so many things to listen to all around me, enhanced by my wolf's hearing to the point it almost became overwhelming. I couldn't imagine being in a city in wolf form.

The wind whispered through the trees, shaking the leaves. I heard small animals skittering through the branches and along the ground, and larger ones plodding along further away. They must have smelled us and ran away, but the birds and squirrels paid us no mind as we traipsed through their forest. I twitched my ears backward, trying to see if I could hear anything from town. With glee, I detected a few voices and the sound of cars.

Stella's light footsteps sounded close to me. "You can open your eyes now," she said, and I blinked up at her. She had one hand on her hip and was smiling down at me. "I hid ten objects from the house. See if you can find them all."

I lifted my nose to the air. The previous concentration I'd had on the sounds of the forest vanished now that I was actively using my nose and eyes again. I caught a whiff of something familiar, something like bread, and followed it. My nose led me through the brush in the direction I'd heard Stella walking when she first left me. I tried to only focus on the familiar scent, but I kept getting distracted. I could smell other animals and plants, and when the wind shifted, I lost the correct trail for a second. I had to backtrack, and suddenly I caught scent of another object. I looked between the two, trying to decide which one to follow. The second one was stronger, as if Stella had gone back and forth several times, rather than the fainter, less pronounced first one.

As I tried to decide, a squirrel skittered across the ground before me, and my wolf instincts made me chase after it up a tree for a few seconds before I realized what I was doing. I put my nose to the ground and inhaled deeply, and decided to follow the second path. *Food*, my nose told me. *Meat*. The trail ended abruptly just a few feet later, and

I looked around, swiveling my head to try to find the object she'd hidden. Nothing.

I back-tracked and tried to find the first scent again, but it seemed to have disappeared. Frustrated, I made my way back to Stella and sniffed around to catch another scent. She stood, watching me with that twinkle in her eyes.

"It's overwhelming, isn't it?" she asked. "You'll get used to separating smells the longer you do it. Trust me, everyone is overwhelmed at first."

I shook my head at her, my tongue hanging out, and kept searching. Every time I smelled food, I went after it, growing more and more hungry. I always thought I was close to getting something but then I'd come up empty, the scent disappearing and no object in sight. I only managed to successfully track one thing, an old running shoe that looked like it belonged to Kaden. That stinky thing had been easy to track with my nose.

When I brought it back to Stella, she called a halt. "Good job. You can shift back now."

I felt weak, like I had after training with Kaden, and sat down on the forest floor. I barely managed to shift back and get dressed, and then I regretted it. My human senses seemed dull in comparison to the time I'd spent as a wolf, and I was even more hungry now.

"You used food for some of the objects, didn't you?" I asked. "But when I got there, they were already gone."

Stella laughed again, and it was almost a cackle. "I knew you'd go after the food first because that's what every wolf pup does. What fun would it be to make it easy?" She helped me up off the forest floor. "You did good, for a beginner."

I shook my head. "I only found one thing. I think you're just buttering me up because you're stuck with me."

She grinned. "You'll do just fine. Come on, let's go get some dinner."

Underneath the bone-deep tiredness, I felt gratitude. I was so thankful to be receiving this training, no matter how hard it was. If I'd still been with the Cancer pack, I wouldn't have learned any of this. It was up to family and close pack-mates to show others how to be a wolf, but Dad wouldn't have bothered. He'd left me to figure everything out by myself up to this point in life, so it wouldn't have been any different this time. And the Leo pack? I couldn't imagine they'd be much better to me.

I'd take this knowledge any way I could get it.

I felt something else stirring inside of me as we walked back to the house. I hadn't felt it for years, since I was a child. It took me a few moments to understand what it was. I wanted to make a good impression, to have Stella look at me and say *good job*. It was odd, feeling it after all this time. I used to feel that way with Dad before I realized that nothing I did would be good enough for him, and I'd stopped trying.

To a lesser degree, I even wanted that from Kaden. I still didn't like his shitty attitude or his harsh methods, but I could at least respect him as an alpha. It came down to one simple fact: he could help me get stronger. It didn't matter that he wasn't the kindest teacher, or that he seemed inca-pable of giving out praise. He could help me get revenge for

Wesley, and that was all I cared about. I had no problem putting up with his cocky, arrogant attitude if it meant I'd get the satisfaction of seeing the Leo pack on their knees, begging for their lives. Knowing this rejected wolf was the one to help bring them to their ruin.

I couldn't wait.

CHAPTER SIXTEEN

IT SURPRISED me more than anything when Kaden sat down with us at the large dining room table. When we'd come in and he'd been in the house, I'd half expected him to glare at me and go upstairs, but he'd sat at the island and cut vegetables for the pasta dish we were having. They sent me up to shower off the dirt and sweat from my training, while Stella ran an almost entirely one-sided conversation with Kaden as they cooked.

When the food was ready, Kaden took a seat at the head of the table. I stood, plate in hand, wondering if I was allowed to sit with them. Stella nudged me with her elbow and jerked her chin toward one of the middle chairs. I expected her to take the other end seat, but she sat across from me.

We ate in silence for a few minutes before Stella broke the quiet. "So, Ayla, tell me what it was like to grow up in the Cancer pack?"

I stopped, a bite halfway to my mouth. "It was..." I paused. I wouldn't lie. I'd been lying through my teeth about my treatment for years. "Awful," I finally said. Stella blinked as if it wasn't the answer she was expecting. "I was always shunned for being an outcast, and treated poorly by many of the other pack members."

"Weren't you the alpha's daughter?" She tried to share a look with Kaden, but he had his gaze focused on his plate, eating slowly but methodically.

"I was, but that didn't matter." I fingered a strand of my red hair. "My father had an affair with a human, and I looked too much like her for him to ever forget it. He made it clear that despite sharing blood, I was no daughter of his. Wesley, my brother and the alpha heir, he was the golden child. He was the only one who treated me kindly."

"Was?" Stella asked softly.

"He's dead now, thanks to the Leo pack and their allies." I couldn't keep the bitterness and pain out of my voice, but I did manage to blink back the rush of tears.

For a moment, I thought I'd killed the mood, as the quiet blanketed us once more. The clink of forks against plates was the only sound in the dining room. Maybe I shouldn't have said anything.

"The Leo pack killed our parents too," Stella said, and I glanced up at her. She looked sad, but the kind of sad that said that it had happened a long time ago. When I glanced over at Kaden, his hand had tightened around the fork, his knuckles bone-white.

That must be why he hates them so much, I thought.

That explained why he wanted to go after the Leo pack first. I nodded and ducked my head again, going back to eating. It was an excellent pasta dish, made with linguine in some kind of white sauce with vegetables and chicken. Stella clearly knew how to cook beyond basic survival skills.

Stella took a long sip of water before she continued. "Our parents were trying to meet with the other alphas to see if any of them would be willing to take our case to the rest of the packs and help us rejoin the Zodiac Wolves. But the other packs wouldn't have anything to do with us, and for a while, we thought nothing would ever change. Then our parents got an invitation to meet with the Leo pack. It was suspicious, but our father was so excited to finally meet with one of the packs that he didn't listen to anyone else's advice."

I sucked in a deep breath at the pain in Stella's voice. "And they betrayed you. Didn't they?"

Stella nodded. "The Leo alpha killed our parents and some of their closest friends and advisors. That was when Kaden became alpha."

I'd never heard about anything like this, even from the boastful Leos. Then again, they'd probably wanted to keep the truth about the Ophiuchus pack a secret. If anyone knew they were real, and not the monsters of myth, the lost pack might gain some sympathy among the Zodiac Wolves. "How long ago was this?"

"Ten years ago. Sometimes it seems like it happened just yesterday. It feels like it, in here." She put a hand over her heart. Her eyes burned with the same mix of rage and grief I felt, and suddenly I knew that ten years from now, I'd feel the same as I was right now. I didn't know if I could bear it. "Since then we've been waiting to get our revenge."

"Ten years is a long time to wait for revenge," I said. "The Leo pack has only grown bigger and stronger over the last ten years. Why wait until now?"

Kaden put his fork down, a little too hard. I jumped at the sudden noise. He looked up, eyes burning with hatred. "I spent every day of the last ten years preparing my pack for war, ever since I became alpha. Training all pack members to fight. Gathering weapons and resources. Studying the other packs' weaknesses. And now we're finally ready." He leaned forward, his voice low. "As long as you do what I say, we'll both get our revenge on the Leos."

I looked into those hate-filled eyes and believed it. He must have been young when he became alpha, and it was impressive that he'd been able to take control of a pack and prepare them for battle. I certainly wouldn't want to stand against him.

After that, the mood was well and truly killed, and we spent the rest of the dinner in silence. Kaden was the first to finish, and he washed his plate and put it in the dishwasher, before stalking upstairs. *That* was more of the dramatic exit I'd expected him to make before dinner.

"Don't mind him," Stella said as she stood up. "He had to grow up fast after he became alpha. He really does care about us under all of that grumpiness."

I believed it, for her at least. Me? I was still an outcast here.

I washed up and ran the dishwasher, before heading upstairs to spend the rest of my evening resting. Training had really taken it out of me, but as I laid in bed, I found that I couldn't relax. Last night I'd fallen asleep easily, between my exhaustion and grief, but it wasn't so easy tonight.

There were too many questions that needed answering. I glanced out my window and found puddles of moonlight on the ground outside. For one, I needed to understand the strange power I'd used to get away from Jordan back at the Convergence.

I got up and padded to my door, listening. The house was quiet. I opened it and stepped out into the hall. Kaden wasn't there, snarling at me, so I figured it was safe.

I crept down the hall and down the stairs. Still nothing. I relaxed as I made it to the back door and stepped out, relieved to be leaving the house without any of my guards. I made my way into the forest as quietly as I could. Not too far, but just far enough that if Kaden or Stella happened to look outside they wouldn't see me.

I stepped into a patch of moonlight and tilted my face up to the moon. It just seemed like light, nothing special about it. I didn't feel the strange tug in my gut or the way the world had shifted. I closed my eyes and concentrated.

Still nothing.

Had it been only a one-time thing? Some strange survival instinct that shifters had?

Then I remembered that I'd felt as if I was going to die, and tried to conjure up the same feeling of fear and panic. *I need to escape,* I thought. *I need to get away.* The urgency grew within me easily enough. It hadn't been too long ago that I'd been hunted like an animal, and the feeling was all too familiar.

I drew in a sharp breath and opened my eyes. I was ten feet away from where I'd been before. I nearly laughed, though it contained no humor. Whatever power I'd used before was still inside of me.

I closed my eyes and tried again. It was like shifting. The more I did it, the easier it became, like working out a muscle. I made a circle around a copse of trees using only patches of moonlight and then tried to skip over a patch. That didn't work so well, but at least I was beginning to know the limits of this strange power. When I paused to take a breath, I felt tired, like I'd been training or running.

Suddenly the feeling of being watched raised the hairs on the back of my neck. I swiveled my head around, trying to see who it was. Kaden leaned against a tree about twenty feet away, completely in shadow, but there was no mistaking him for anyone else. I'd know those broad shoulders anywhere.

"What are you doing?" I asked, hands on my hips. "How long have you been watching?"

He uncrossed his arms and stepped into the moonlight, letting it illuminate his way-too-handsome face. "I need to make sure you're not going to escape, since you decided to leave the house in the middle of the night, acting like you were sneaking out."

"I just wanted to figure out how this weird power works," I said. "I didn't have it before the Convergence, and

I haven't exactly had time to practice yet. You know, being locked in a cage and all."

I expected Kaden to snarl something at me, but he simply ignored my jab and stepped closer. I took an involuntary step back, but then stood my ground, lifting my chin. I wouldn't let him intimidate me.

"I know what you are," Kaden said. "I suspected it before, but after seeing you move in the moonlight, it's obvious now. You're Moon Touched."

"I'm what?" I'd never heard the term before.

"You've been given a special gift by the moon goddess, Selene," he elaborated, which didn't really clear anything up at all.

"Why would the moon goddess give me gifts?" I snorted. "I've never been anything special in my life." Dad had made it exceptionally clear that I wasn't anything to write home about.

Kaden's eyes raked up and down my body in a way that made me shiver. Instantly, I flushed with heat, but I shoved the feeling away. It irritated me to no end that my body responded to him like this.

"I have a theory," he said.

"Mind sharing with the class?" I asked.

He smirked at that. "Yes, I do. I think I'll hang onto it for a bit."

Asshole, I thought.

"How much do you know about the Ophiuchus pack and why we're outcasts from the rest of the Zodiac Wolves?" he asked before I could snipe back at him.

I shrugged. "About the same as any other shifter, I'd expect. We were raised on ghost stories about you. I didn't think your pack was real until I saw you." I tilted my head as I recalled some of the things I'd heard. "The legends say your pack interbred with the Moon Witches long ago to try to gain extra powers. They also say that you tried to take over once before, and all it got you was being kicked out of the Zodiac Packs."

"Partially true," Kaden said. "Long ago, the Moon and Sun Witches were allied, and they enslaved all wolf shifters to fight a war against the vampires."

I held up a hand to stop him. "Wait, hang on. Vampires? They're real?"

"Yes, although there are very few of them left, from what I've heard. They tend to live in Europe."

"How stereotypical," I muttered.

He shot me a look as he continued. "As I was saying... After the witches won the war, the shifters revolted and earned their freedom, with the help of the Moon Witches. The Sun Witches didn't take kindly to this betrayal, and the two groups became separate. The Ophiuchus pack remained on good terms with the Moon Witches and sometimes mated with them, but the other Zodiac packs didn't like our pack's growing power, and cast us out." He paused as if waiting for me to interrupt him, but I was just shocked by all this new information—and because I'd never heard him say so many words at once before. "The other twelve packs allied with the Sun Witches instead, which was a big mistake. The Sun Witches manipulated the twelve packs into thinking they were allies, but in reality, they're controlling them."

"That's not true," I said instantly. "The Sun Witches have protected us for as long as the Zodiac Wolves have existed. You must have it wrong."

"How exactly are they protecting you?"

I opened and closed my mouth a few times, but then said, "They stop us from getting the Moon Curse."

Kaden scoffed. "That? That's a lie. The Moon Witches removed the curse hundreds of years ago. It was wrong, inhumane, and they realized that. The Sun Witches are lying to you and all of the packs so that you *need* them."

"But why?" I asked, feeling as if I was very far away from my body. What Kaden was saying didn't make any sense, but the more he talked, the more I started to question everything. "It doesn't make any sense. They...they protect us. They help us get our wolves and our mates."

Kaden took a step toward me, his voice heated. "No, they keep your wolves locked away until you're twenty-two. You've seen the wolf pups here. Stella told me how shocked you were by them. But that's normal here, and it should be normal for all the other packs too."

I shook my head, unable to believe so much of my life was a lie. "I'm sure there's a good reason..."

"There is. The Sun Witches want to enslave all twelve packs again. They're slowly changing the amount of control they have over the Zodiac Wolves, so slowly that no one will notice or speak up about it until it's too late."

"Why would they want us enslaved? I don't believe you."

"I don't care what you believe," Kaden said, turning away abruptly. "And none of it will matter anyway, once the other packs are wiped out."

Back to being the same arrogant, prickly alpha. "What does any of this have to do with me?"

Kaden looked over his shoulder at me. "I suspect that your mother was a Moon Witch."

The words hit me like a punch. I started shaking my head before I could even fully comprehend them. "No. That's not possible. She was human." I took a step back from Kaden, his words ringing in my ears. "And even if that was true, there's no way for me to find out because my entire family is *dead*."

Kaden turned back and met my eyes, and I saw the slightest hint of humanity in them. "I'm sorry. I know what that's like."

I laughed, but it was bitter. "No, you don't. You have your sister and your pack. But me? I don't have anyone at all."

Something crossed his face, something that might have been pity, and I couldn't stand to look at him for another second. I had to get away from him and all the insane things he was saying. There was no way any of them were true.

I broke into a run, heading back to the house. He didn't call after me, and I didn't expect him to.

I didn't stop running until I was locked inside my room, gasping for breath.

CHAPTER SEVENTEEN

OVER THE NEXT FEW DAYS, my life settled into a routine. In the morning, I cleaned whatever place Kaden had assigned me to for the day. Then I had a quick lunch, before joining him outside for combat training, followed by wolf training with Stella.

My guards went everywhere with me during the day, tailing me close enough that it felt like they were always breathing down my neck. The only time they weren't around was when I was in the house, or training with Kaden and Stella. Clayton and Jack never hurt me though, and once I got used to being followed so closely, I found they weren't that bad. The only problem was that Kaden had told them not to answer any of my questions, much to my dismay.

Everyone else in the town was polite to me, although no one got too close either. It had been a few years since the Ophiuchus pack had gained a new member, Stella told me, so news of my arrival had spread fast. They all seemed to be waiting for their alpha to make a decision about me, but I wasn't called 'half-breed' or 'mutt' by these shifters, which was a nice change. I kept holding my breath and waiting for the other shoe to drop, or for the hatred to start, but after a week, I tentatively began relaxing around the pack.

The only person whose attitude remained frosty was Kaden's. I actively spent time trying to avoid him, but living with him made that difficult. Sometimes I ate meals with Stella, and other times I took my food up to my room so I could hide.

The routine kept my mind off of my brother and everything else, and it was only when I was alone in bed that the overwhelming grief swallowed me whole again. I cried for Wesley, for Mira's parents, for every person who had ever been kind to me in the Cancer pack. I cried not knowing what had become of the people who'd stayed home during the Convergence, and whether or not any of them were still alive. I cried for the future I might have had, if not for the Leos' betrayal.

And then, once I'd finally exhausted my grief and hoped I might be able to sleep, the mating bond thrummed to life again. It was always there, in the back of my mind, and when I was alone and quiet it was harder to ignore. The annoying tug turned to a desperate need, an aching for something—no, *someone*—along with the constant feeling of being unfulfilled. I'd toss and turn, desperate to put an end to the torment, but nothing worked. I even slid my hand between my thighs and tried to get myself off, hoping it would relieve the throbbing hunger in my pussy, but it was useless. Only Jordan could fix what was wrong with me.

Or Kaden, a voice whispered inside me. A voice I told to fuck right off. He wasn't my mate. Jordan was the one the gods had chosen for me, no matter how much I despised him.

I doubted Kaden would want me anyway. The man growled and glared at me anytime I had to spend any time with him. Even when he wasn't around, his presence seemed to follow me throughout my day.

In the morning, he left notes for me. *Clean the community center* was pinned on the fridge the morning after he'd confronted me in the forest like nothing had happened at all. I'd blinked at the note for several minutes before realizing that if I spent any more time being confused, I'd likely be late. Then the next day he sent me somewhere else, to act as that place's janitor too. Rinse and repeat.

Combat training with Kaden hadn't gotten any easier either. I did the stretching routine Kaden showed me, and I'd stopped face-planting every time I tried to do a basic move, but beyond that, I could tell he was frustrated with my lack of progress.

On the other hand, my afternoons with Stella were coming along nicely. Being in wolf form was natural to me, unlike hand-to-hand combat. With practice, I found it easier to shift, just like Stella had said, and it became almost painless over the course of the week. It was still harder to focus in wolf form, but even that was getting easier.

I thought of the freedom that my wolf form brought me,

how fast I could run, and how I could hear things so much clearer. I wanted to run for miles and miles until my wolf body couldn't handle it anymore, and then take a nap in a clearing, maybe by a little stream that would lull me into sleep—

"Stop daydreaming," Kaden snapped. I blinked and realized I'd been reaching for my toes for several minutes, far longer than I was supposed to. I got up and followed him to the center of the gym, which was empty except for us. He'd had me meet him here today, instead of the usual clearing, and now he led me to a punching bag.

"Show me a punch," he said, holding onto the bag.

"What, no instructions?" I asked.

"I need to see what I'm working with. If it's anything like the rest of this, I'll have to take you from the very beginning."

I bristled at his words. "It's not my fault that my pack didn't teach me this. My alpha never expected me to do much of anything."

"Well, I do. Now punch the bag." Kaden sounded almost bored, as he often did.

I hated when he acted like this. I knew he did it on purpose, probably to rile me up. *Getting mad makes you stupid,* he'd said once. *Keep your cool.* It was easier said than done, especially when he kept acting like an arrogant prick. I wound my fist back, ready to punch, imagining it was his face.

"Stop." Kaden let go of the bag suddenly and stepped back. I paused, muscles tensed to throw the punch. "Unless you want to dislocate your thumb. Get it out from under your fingers."

I complied, and Kaden held up his own hand to show me. I mirrored his clenched fist, leaving my thumb tucked alongside my fingers rather than underneath. Actually, that made a lot of sense, and I felt dumb. That was a common feeling while working with Kaden. It was as if he expected me to know everything already, and when I didn't he got frustrated. But how was that my fault? I was doing my best to learn. I punched the bag, but it didn't move like I'd expected it to, even with my shifter strength.

"You'll want to concentrate most of the punch in the first two knuckles," Kaden said, pointing to them on his own hand. Then, he drew his elbow back and punched. His breath came out in a sharp noise with the punch. "Always exhale on your punches. It tightens your core, which will give you better power. If you're going to punch someone, make sure you throw your entire body weight into it."

He guided me through the entire process, making sure to point out that I would be engaging my hips and legs too if I was doing it properly. Then he stepped back to the bag and held it. "Try again."

I nodded and planted my feet, then did what he'd shown me. This punch felt better, more solid, but the bag still didn't move.

"You're not using your hips." He slid away from the bag and moved directly behind me. "I'll show you."

My breath caught as Kaden pulled my body flush against his, one hand on my hip, and the other reaching out to encircle my wrist. What felt like an electric shock went through my whole body, rendering me useless. I moved, supple and pliant in his grasp as he twisted my hip back and extended my hand for me.

He was saying something, but the words didn't register. His hand felt hot enough to burn, just sitting there on my hip. Nothing he'd done had ever felt like this before. I could almost imagine that his hand would slide over my body, splaying flat on my stomach to hold me against him for an entirely different reason. His mouth wouldn't be telling me how to throw a punch but would brush my neck, moving slowly, surely. The hand circling my wrist would meet mine, intertwining with my fingers.

The image was so vivid, so real, that I staggered with the effect of it. I might have fallen if I hadn't been pressed so thoroughly against the hard line of Kaden's body. But then again, I wouldn't be in this situation at all if Kaden hadn't grabbed me like this.

Kaden's hand tightened around my wrist, as he drew my hand back and moved it through the right motion again. His hand *did* slide a little more onto my stomach, and I actually stopped breathing, wondering if I was going insane. I was certain Kaden could hear the way my heart thundered in my chest, or smell the lust from between my thighs. But if he noticed, he didn't say anything, and after a moment, he stepped back.

I swayed, still caught in the moment, wondering what would happen if I tilted my head back to encourage him to kiss me. I was caught halfway between reality and the fantasy, and it took a sharp, "Again," from Kaden to fully pull me out.

I shook my head and tried to remember what Kaden had said. I could still feel his hand on my hip, and I moved the way he'd moved it, making sure to exhale as I punched.

"Like that?" I asked, and if Kaden noticed that the tone was just this side of breathy, he didn't say a damn thing.

"Better. Again."

I punched the bag a few more times, making sure to engage my whole body each time. The strange spell that had been cast over me faded, and although Kaden was still distracting, at least he was distracting *over there* and not touching me.

"That's enough for today. Let's move on." Kaden let go of the bag and lifted his shirt over his head. He seemed to be allergic to wearing a decent amount of clothing, no matter the occasion. The number of times I'd wandered downstairs to find him standing in the kitchen in just sweats or jeans was bordering on ridiculous. I should have been desensitized by this point, but with a body like that, I doubted I'd get used to it anytime soon. And seriously, gray sweatpants? Was he *trying* to make me wet?

We moved into hand-to-hand combat next, which was my least favorite part of training because it felt so hopeless. Kaden was a true warrior, through and through, but that wasn't me. I was a scrappy survivor who somehow weaseled out of every bad situation, not a fighter. When things got bad, I ran. No amount of training would ever fix my true nature.

Kaden seemed to disagree though, or why else would he keep doing this? I could tell he was holding back though—probably good, or I'd end up getting punched in the nose—but I still couldn't land a blow on him.

It didn't help that I could still feel him pressed against me, holding me in such a casual, yet intimate way. My gaze slipped to his bare torso, and I soaked up the sight of all those muscles in all the right places. He'd been so *hot* against me, so hard. Like that day at the waterfall, when he'd been on top of me.

One of Kaden's blows glanced off of my temple, my instincts allowing me to pull my head away at the last second. Shit, I needed to focus or I was going to get knocked out.

"Good," Kaden said. "You're getting better."

Right as he said that, he shoved his hand flat against my sternum. The blow sent me sprawling on the ground. I tried to go into a tuck and roll to break the fall but didn't quite manage it. I still was able to avoid hurting myself, but it wasn't very graceful.

"You can't just say that, and then do that," I said, trying to catch my breath. It hadn't been hard enough to hurt, but it had taken the wind out of me.

"You seemed distracted." Kaden stepped up to me and held his hand out. I frowned at it, remembering the first day. *Right.* I took his hand, expecting him to fling me over his shoulder, but he simply lifted me up, arm muscles flexing.

Then he pulled me close and lightly touched my temple, his brow furrowed. Inspecting me to make sure he hadn't really injured me, I realized. Kaden's other hand still clutched mine tightly, and it had become hard to breathe, or move, or even think. Desire and longing made my chest tighten almost painfully, and I found myself reaching up to touch the soft, dark stubble on his jaw. But when my fingertips lightly brushed against him, he jerked back, like he'd been burned.

We stepped apart, and I pressed a hand to my chest, wishing I could calm my runaway heart. *He's not your mate,* I reminded myself. But my body wouldn't listen.

"Again," Kaden said, but his voice sounded a bit off.

I took a deep breath and tried to stay focused on the fight, not the fighter. We exchanged a few experimental jabs, and suddenly I saw an opening. I didn't know if it was purposeful, but he'd overextended in a punch, leaving his side vulnerable. I struck out quickly. He saw my fist coming for him and contorted, dancing out of range, but I felt my knuckles brush his ribs.

I let out a shocked laugh as I stepped back. "I almost hit you."

Kaden looked as surprised as I felt, but it faded from his eyes just as quickly. "You're becoming more confident in your body, in its instincts. The more you listen to it, the easier this will be. You keep getting in your head and second-guessing where your muscles want you to go. It's what trips you up the most."

We continued, and though I didn't come close to landing any more blows, the rest of the training session went without a hitch. Kaden continued to correct my positions, but he didn't pull me against him again. I shoved the disappointment down.

Finally, Kaden called a halt. I noticed I wasn't breathing quite as hard as I had been for the first few days. It was a small, but welcome improvement. Maybe soon I would go through this entire routine without breaking a sweat, like Kaden.

We cooled down, doing some light stretches. We usually did these in silence, so I was surprised when Kaden spoke up. "Stella says you're doing well with your wolf training."

I shrugged, ducking my head at the praise. "I'm still not that good at tracking, but I'm trying."

Kaden paused and appraised me. "The pack is going on a hunt tonight. Maybe you'd like to join us."

I froze, his words catching me completely off guard. Kaden was very protective of his pack, and I knew he didn't want me interacting with most of them until he felt I was trustworthy. This would put me in the thick of them, almost like a real member of their pack.

"I'd like that." Maybe if I spent more time interacting with the rest of the pack, Kaden would see I meant them no harm. I might even get him to trust me more.

Kaden nodded curtly and stood. "Be ready to leave at sunset. The deer are more active at night."

He left the gym without another word, abruptly ending our training session the same way he always did. I rolled my eyes and grabbed a towel to wipe off the sweat, then headed outside, where Jack and Clayton were waiting for me. Of course.

"Good session?" Jack asked, as they fell into step on either side of me. He was pretty handsome, with blond hair and a charming smile. "Seems like you worked up a sweat. It looks good on you."

Oh, and he was a total flirt, I was starting to realize. Everything he said was harmless though, and I had to admit it was nice to be flirted with instead of belittled or bullied all the time. "Yeah, it was great. I actually got a blow in."

"On Kaden?" Clayton asked. He was big, built like a grizzly bear, and a lot quieter, but now he turned his warm brown eyes upon me with surprise.

"Well, it was more like a graze," I said with a shrug.

"That counts," Jack said. "Own it."

I grinned a little as we kept walking through the town. "He invited me to come on a hunt tonight too."

"He did?" Clayton stroked his beard. "Are you certain?"

My grin fell. "I think so. His words were pretty clear."

Clayton gave me a long look as if seeing me in a different light. "He's never invited an outsider on a hunt before. Not even ones who wanted to join our pack."

"Is that a good thing?" I asked, suddenly unsure of myself.

Jack shrugged. "I guess we'll find out."

CHAPTER EIGHTEEN

THAT AFTERNOON, Stella canceled our usual training exercises and told me to get some rest. She said I'd need it for tonight while tossing me a bag of chips. Resting was hard though because I was a jittery bundle of nerves, too anxious for sunset to arrive to relax. The Cancer pack had never let me join them for anything like this, and I wanted to do a good job, to prove myself to Kaden and the others.

When the time came, I dressed in sweats and a t-shirt—clothes I could shed easily for our shift—and then headed outside. Stella waited for me behind the house and looked almost as excited as I felt, and I grinned at her as I walked up.

"Where is everyone else?" I asked.

"They're with Kaden at the clearing. We'll join them in a minute." She gave me a warm smile. "I thought you might want to shift here instead."

A touch of heat hit my cheeks, but mostly I felt gratitude

for her kindness. Even though I'd never said anything, Stella had recognized I was nervous about being naked around others. I quickly stripped down and let my wolf free, my white paws sinking into the grass and my tail whipping about. *At last*, my wolf seemed to say.

"This is going to be a relatively short hunt," Stella said. "Tonight Kaden and some of the others are teaching the teenagers what to do, and you're going to observe. I'll stick to your side in human form so I can explain how the pack hunting formations work, what they're tracking, and how they communicate to bring down prey. It's all about cooperation and communication, and it's important for you to see and smell the hunt with your wolf senses."

It didn't matter that I wouldn't be joining the actual hunt, I was thrilled to even be included. Besides, I hadn't really given much thought to what place would be the best to sink my teeth into on an animal to bring it down. Truthfully, I wasn't sure I was ready for that.

We headed into the forest to find the rest of the pack. I heard their movements up ahead, and my anticipation only grew. I was determined to prove myself to them, however, I could. Surely this hunt wouldn't be much more difficult than learning to throw a punch or sniff out a correct object in the forest. *If all these pups can do it, so can I,* I thought. Of course, they'd had their wolves long before I did. I'd spent twenty-two years without my wolf, where they got theirs as toddlers. It would take time for me to start thinking like one.

As we approached the clearing, I peered through the branches, trying to catch a glimpse of the pack. I spotted about a dozen wolves, all in different shades of fur, and it wasn't hard to pick Kaden out at the front. He was *huge* and solid black. I'd seen Dad's wolf form several times, and he had nothing on Kaden, who looked equal parts majestic and deadly, an alpha that deserved the respect he received.

When the group was getting ready to go, Kaden circled them, preparing them for what was to come. I remembered Stella saying they could communicate telepathically in wolf form, and wondered if Kaden's wolf's voice was as dominating as he was in human form.

"Okay, we're off," Stella said, as the wolves began to bound into the forest. "Let's follow them. Stay back and don't get in the way. Kaden is teaching them formations."

I nodded as well as I could in wolf form and loped at a comfortable pace beside Stella. She was nimble and quick in her human form, but I could have easily outpaced her. I put my nose to the ground and tracked the group by scent, staying a short distance behind the other wolves so I didn't interfere with their hunt. *Deer.* I pointed my nose in the direction, and Stella smiled her approval.

"Come this way," she said. "We're going to go up onto a ridge so we can see the pack better."

I followed her up a slight incline. From up here, I could see Kaden leading some of the younger wolves, heading around the edge of the slight depression the deer were settling down in. One group flanked the deer, chasing them in the right direction so they would head straight into the ambush waiting for them at the end.

As I watched Kaden and the younger shifters, I longed

to be out there with them, feeling the thrill of the hunt and the surety of having a pack at my back. My wolf wanted nothing more than to be free and run down deer with the rest of the pack. The need to belong, to be a part of something more than myself, burned inside of me.

The Cancer pack had never felt like home, but even in the short time I'd spent here, I could see the Ophiuchus pack being the place where I could finally feel accepted. I could already picture myself down there with the rest of them so easily, and I wanted it so bad it made my chest ache.

I rode the high of the hunt with them, even from many feet away. It was easy to do, my wolf's enhanced senses picking up on the smallest of movements, while Stella watched beside me, sometimes explaining what they were doing.

The pack cornered one deer, a huge buck that was almost as big as Kaden. The rest of the deer split off, and the wolves parted to allow them to pass. Together the wolves took down the deer, Kaden jumping onto its back while one of the younger wolves darting in to bite its throat.

The moment the deer went down, I felt something bubbling in my chest. If I'd been in human form, it would have been a cheer, but as it was, when I opened my mouth, a howl poured out. I didn't even mean to let it loose, and I quickly clamped my jaw shut, but it was too late. My howl was out there, the first time I'd ever heard it.

Stella made a noise next to me. I looked over, trying to see if I'd done something wrong, but she had a hand in front of her mouth as if she was covering a smile. I narrowed my eyes at her. She was trying not to laugh. A moment later, the howl was echoed in the group, one young shifter picking it up, and then the next. Soon the howl went through the entire group, and Stella's shoulders started shaking with silent laughter as a few more howls echoed from the town, just a few miles away.

A single, low howl pierced through everything, the loudest and most haunting one of all. When I look down at the group, Kaden had his head tilted back toward the moon, which danced across his black fur. The rest of the wolves fell silent at his signal.

I swore he looked at me as he ended the howl, and if I could blush as a wolf, I had no doubt I would be doing so. The howl had felt right though, in the moment.

Stella shook her head, smiling. "Are you ready to head down?"

She pulled my clothes out from the bag she carried, and I shifted back to human form to put them on. We walked back down the ridge, and I watched as a group of the younger shifters dragged the deer back to be cleaned and dressed, shoving each other and laughing.

Once we'd made it back to the clearing, Kaden walked up to us. He was shirtless, no surprise there. I grinned at him, unable to keep the joy I felt in check. Even though he didn't smile back, he looked less moody than usual, the harsh lines of his handsome face softening into something more approachable.

"What did you think?" he asked, hands stuck in his

pockets. The question was casual enough, but he watched me closely for the answer.

"It was incredible, the way you all moved in formation together, like you'd been doing it forever. I'd like to learn how to do it too."

Kaden looked at me for a long moment. "Once you're in a pack, you'll be able to communicate thoughts as a wolf with other pack members. That's what made it look so easy."

"I want that," I said in a rush, the words coming out before I'd even realized I'd made up my mind on the matter. "Being part of a pack."

I felt it, deep in my bones. Like all other wolves, I was born to be part of a pack, even with my half-human heritage. Somehow I would find a way to get Kaden to trust me and to prove to him I could be a part of his pack. Even if it meant cleaning every toilet in town.

When I met Kaden's gaze again, he tilted his head at me and the look on his face was almost approval. Then a slow smirk crossed his mouth. "Nice howl, by the way."

I blushed, but his tone was light enough that I didn't feel too bad about it. "It was my first one."

"Not bad. Though I bet you could howl louder under the right circumstances."

I swallowed, my mouth suddenly dry. "Maybe you could show me."

He opened his mouth to reply, but then shook his head and looked away. "Come on. They'll be waiting for me."

As we headed back toward the house, I lifted my head and scented the air, smelling people and food. Stella had gone ahead, leaving me to walk with Kaden, though his company was silent. I didn't mind, since I had a lot to process. The high of the hunt had worn off finally, and I'd never imagined the thrill that would have come with being part of it. I doubted I could sleep tonight, for entirely different reasons than usual.

When we got to the house, I froze. Kaden's normally empty backyard was alight with string lights and full of people talking in groups, with the smaller children and teenagers running around. They must have set this up while we were on the hunt. A grill was set up to one side, and the crowd cheered as Kaden walked over to it and waved.

I paused at the edge of the forest as pieces of meat were brought out and set onto the grill for Kaden to cook. The deer, I realized. Kaden hadn't mentioned a barbecue before, but then again, he seemed to enjoy keeping me on my toes. I wondered if I was invited. There were more shifters from the Ophiuchus here in one place than I had seen yet, and they all seemed to know each other. I felt intensely out of place, unsure if I was allowed to even be here, or if Kaden expected me to go inside.

As I debated, I found myself watching the wolf pups. They wrestled in the grass, growling and baring their teeth at each other. It was still shocking to see them, but they were incredibly cute, and I couldn't help but smile. A group of teens passed close to me, and I heard one of them giving a recount from the hunt. He must have been the one to kill the deer.

The longing to be a part of this, to be one of them, hit me

once again. Everything I'd heard about the thirteenth pack had been wrong. They weren't monsters or bogeymen. They were just another pack and a good one at that. Maybe Kaden was right, and everything I knew about the Sun and Moon Witches was wrong as well.

I turned my head as something caught in my peripheral vision. Clayton was walking toward me holding hands with another male shifter, who was a lot smaller than him. Then again, everyone was smaller than Clayton.

"Come join the party," he said. "You were part of the hunt too, even if you didn't participate."

I ducked my head. "Thanks. I wasn't sure..."

"I remember that feeling, but you'll be one of us soon enough," the other man said.

Clayton gestured to the man beside him. "This is Grant. My mate."

I blinked, my mouth falling open. I'd never seen a gay mated couple before. "You have the mate bond?"

"Of course we do," Clayton said, standing a bit taller. "Why wouldn't we?"

I held my hands up. "I'm sorry. That came out wrong. I just didn't realize it was possible. In the Zodiac Wolves, there aren't any homosexual mate pairs."

Grant gave me a sympathetic smile. "I was originally part of the Libra Pack, but I left when I met Clayton and felt the mate bond. It was right after I turned twenty-two and got my wolf, but luckily I hadn't been mated at the Convergence. I went hiking in the woods on a trip, and everything changed for me when I stumbled onto Clayton by accident while he was on patrol." He squeezed Clayton's hand, and for the first time, I saw Clayton's stoic face soften. They looked as in love as any other couple I'd seen mated. It must be true. "They let me join the pack, and the rest is history."

"That's...that's great," I said, and I meant it, though my mind was working double time. Would Grant have been mated to a female mate if he hadn't left the Zodiac Wolves? Or would he simply not have gotten a mate at all?

A darker thought hit me. Was it possible that the Sun Witches controlled the mate bonds too? They could use it to manipulate the wolves, moving shifters between the packs like chess pawns, if what Kaden had said was true. I didn't know why they'd ban homosexual pairings, but I remembered someone saying that the reason for the mating bond was for procreation, to keep shifters strong and their blood pure. *They'd definitely use it against us,* I thought darkly.

Anger filled me. People should be able to love who they wanted to, not be forced to love whoever the spell chose.

And if this was true, then it meant my bond with Jordan might not be real either.

"There you are!" I was pulled out of my thoughts by Stella, who ran up to me, beaming. "Come sit with us while Kaden grills. It'll take him forever, and you might as well come hang out."

She pulled me by the wrist to a patch of grass where some of the other female shifters were sitting. I recognized a few in passing, but Stella quickly introduced me to the others. They all worked as teachers and quickly made room for me in the circle.

"The hunt went well?" the pretty blonde named Marla asked, and it took me a moment to realize she was asking me.

I cleared my throat, surprised to be included in the conversation so easily. "I think so. It was amazing to watch," I added, letting some of the awe overtake me as I thought about the forest once again, the coordination of the pack, and the way that Kaden had directed them all flawlessly.

"I bet you had fun watching Kaden, as well," said a woman with curly brown hair, who I remembered was named Carly. She grinned at me, waggling her eyebrows. I ducked my head and blushed.

"Ah, I wish the mate bond would activate for me," Marla said, putting a hand to her chest. "I would *kill* to be his mate. He's so strong and handsome."

Stella made a choking noise, her nose wrinkling. "You do realize you're talking about my brother, right?"

"And we'd all very much like to be your sister," Carly said with a laugh.

I grinned as I looked between them, shaking my head. For the first time ever, I didn't feel like an outcast, and this wasn't even my birth pack. But could this feeling last? What if they found out more about me—that half of me was human, or that my mate was a Leo—and changed their minds about me?

Kaden still stood at the grill, a beer in one hand, and flipping the meat with the other. Jack and another male shifter stood next to him, laughing about something. I watched as Kaden's lips twitched up at whatever they were saying. He looked relaxed and almost happy, but even from this far away, I could sense the power radiating off of him. The other shifters looked at him for approval and seemed to gravitate around him. There was no way anyone could doubt that he was the boss.

As I continued watching, he glanced up from the grill and surveyed the backyard with a look of pride and affection. It was obvious he saw the entire pack as his family.

Then his eyes landed on me, and they smoldered. The look he gave me was so intense it made my breath hitch and my heartbeat go erratic. My entire body flushed with heat as he continued staring at me as if he was singling me out as the thing that didn't belong. I almost expected him to walk over and ask me what I was doing there, but then he turned away to say something to Jack.

I went back to chatting with Stella's friends, who were telling me about the school they worked at, but I felt his eyes on me again, as if he was watching me.

The feeling didn't leave for the rest of the night.

CHAPTER NINETEEN

THE WEIGHT of Kaden's gaze seemed to follow me all the way to my room later that evening, and I couldn't shake it no matter how hard I tried. I took a long, hot shower before crawling into bed, and tried to relax. The only saving grace was that the annoying mate bond wasn't bothering me tonight, at least. I was still riding out the rest of the adrenaline from the hunt, and it took what felt like hours for me to fall asleep.

Then I was in his backyard again, but now it was just the two of us standing under the moon. His eyes found mine, pinning me in place like they had before, and I wondered again if he was singling me out as something that didn't belong. But when I looked again, I realized the heat behind his eyes wasn't anger or hatred. It was *hunger*. He looked like he was going to eat me alive. I couldn't tell if he wanted to kill me...or fuck me.

He stalked toward me with the moonlight streaming

down upon us, illuminating his chiseled jawline and broad shoulders. I took an involuntary step back, and my back brushed against a tree trunk. I stopped, unwilling to press myself further against it, but even more unwilling to break eye contact with Kaden.

"You're here," he growled, walking toward me until we were almost touching. He leaned down so his face was only a few inches away from mine. I'd seen that look in men's gazes before but never directed toward me. It went like a shock through my entire body, resonating deep down in my gut.

"I'm here," I responded, completely breathless. No snappy one-liners could save me now.

He reached up and slid his hand behind my neck, his long fingers tangling in my hair. "You're *mine.*"

I gasped at the sheer amount of possessiveness in his voice. Before I could fully comprehend it, he closed the few inches between us, and I was trapped between the tree and the heat of his body. His lips crashed into mine, claiming me, branding me as his. I melted into it, feeling the *rightness* of it. He wasn't my mate, but something about this felt as if it had been destined.

I should have pushed back. I should have demanded to know what made him think he could claim me like this when I wasn't even part of his pack. But I couldn't.

I *needed* him.

Kaden's hands gripped me tightly, his hard body pressing me back against the tree. I reached up, brushing my hands against his face and down his neck. He growled against my lips, kissing me so hard I thought he was trying to break me, before drawing back and looking down at me.

I couldn't catch my breath, so caught up in the moment. His eyes had shifted fully from danger to lust now, but I felt even less at ease than I had when I didn't know his intentions. The possessiveness in his eyes continued to send little electric bolts through me as he looked me up and down.

He slid his hand across my stomach, much as he had in training, but it went exactly where I'd hoped it would, not staying on my hip for propriety. His fingers slid down until he was touching me through my clothes. Not enough pressure for anything but a tease, but my hips bucked against the pressure anyway. His skin was scorching me, even through the fabric.

"I will take care of you," he said.

It awakened something within me, some base, animal instinct that my logical brain should have rebelled against. I trembled with need, and Kaden seemed to chase that tremble with his body, pressing into me. I felt the hot line of his cock through layers of fabric. I drew in a sharp breath at the *want* that went through me, a wild thing I couldn't control.

I bared my throat to him, letting him sink his teeth into the soft flesh. It wasn't hard enough to break skin, let alone truly hurt, but I arched my body against his, trying to get closer. Secretly wishing he would mark me as his mate for real, for everyone in the pack to see. I rubbed myself against him like an animal in heat, trying to get any friction I could. He laved my skin with his lips and tongue and somehow I felt the touch in an entirely different place, at the pounding core of me, and I let out a moan at the sensation. I was so wet, practically dripping, and I wanted more than just friction and teasing.

Kaden's lips curl into a smile at the sound of my moan. *Cocky bastard.* But fuck, I loved it. I wanted to see him smile like that every day.

His hands closed around my shoulders once more, and this time I felt the press of something sharp on each shoulder. He'd partially shifted to give himself claws, and I looked down to find them sinking into the fabric of my shirt. He tore the cloth as easily as a knife through butter, and I let out another sound as the shreds fell to the ground, leaving me bare from the waist up. He stepped back, and the cool air rushed in. My nipples hardened instantly in the night air, and I shivered.

He perused my body as if he was looking at a piece of art, and my breath continued to come in loud gasps. I didn't feel exposed, even though I *should.* I stood up a bit taller, presenting myself to him.

His eyes flicked up to mine, and in them, I could see the blatant ownership. I was unbelievably turned on, more than I had ever been before, and I held my hands out to Kaden once more. "Are you just going to look at me all night, or are you going to do something about it?"

His eyes flared at the challenge, and he was on me once again, this time pulling me toward him instead of shoving me back against the tree. I reached up and sank my hands into Kaden's dark hair, silken smooth under my fingertips, and met his energy. He growled into the kiss, hands roving over my exposed skin. As if he could leave his mark on me, claim me, and truly make me his forever.

In that moment, I wanted him to.

He drew one breast into his hand as he broke the kiss. His fingers were light enough that I shivered again, then he pinched my nipple between thumb and forefinger, a sudden burst of pain in the pleasure. His eyes latched on mine as if he wanted to see the reaction. I moaned again, wanting more of it.

He must have seen the need in my eyes, because he kissed me once again, tongue sliding against mine, stroking it. Then he drew back, and the way he looked at me should have been a sin. I shoved my hands under his shirt, wanting to see more of him, to feel his skin against mine. He let me touch his sculpted muscles for a few moments, and then made a low sound like a groan. It vibrated deep from his chest into my fingertips, and the next thing I knew, he'd shoved my hands off him so he could take his shirt off.

I'd seen Kaden shirtless plenty of times—shit, he was practically running around half-naked every time I saw him —but I let my gaze truly linger this time. He was gorgeously sculpted, and I wanted to run my tongue over every divot in his chest, then dip lower and see what his cock tasted like. It was an urge I'd never felt before, but I had a feeling I could make him come apart with my mouth and wanted to try.

"Whatever you're thinking about is turning you on," he said. "I can smell it."

He reached between us and slid his hands into my

pants. I gasped as his fingers touched my slit for the first time, parting my lips and circling my clit. He teased me for a few moments, letting me arch my hips up into his touch before he slid a finger inside of my body. The sensation was foreign since I'd never had anyone else touch me like this, but I arched into the pleasure it brought, wanting more.

Kaden drew his finger out and *licked* it, eyes fluttering closed as if he was tasting something delicious. When he opened them again, they burned with desire. He pressed me back against the tree once more, claiming my mouth with his own, a demand to let him in. His hands slid down the front of me, sharpening into claws as he hit the fabric of my pants, and he tore them off me.

He tossed my ruined pants somewhere to the left. I didn't bother checking where. What did it matter, when I had Kaden in front of me, taking my clothes off, looking at me like *that*? I'd walk back to the house naked if that was what he wanted.

His mouth latched onto my throat, teeth grazing the pulse point in my neck. I reached up to touch him again, but Kaden growled, pinning my hands above my head with one of his own, pinning me against the tree. I tested the strength of his grip, and it didn't budge. I'd never felt turned on by being restrained, but this was a night for new things.

"Do you want this?" Kaden growled, pressing me harder into the tree behind me. I arched my back, trying to rub any part of my body along him to get the release I needed. I was a pulsing thing of desire, and I'd say anything to get him to touch me again, to put his cock inside of me.

"Yes," I moaned. "Yes, please."

Kaden pulled his cock out of his pants and gave it a few strokes. I looked at him with greedy eyes, eager to see what I'd felt pressed against me earlier. I kept my hands right where they were, even though I wanted to reach out and replace his hands with mine. *Another time,* my brain whispered. *You can make him come apart with your hands and mouth.* I shuddered at the prospect.

He grabbed my hips and lifted me up, wrapping my legs around him, my back still pressed against the tree. He slid his cock along my slit a few times, making me shudder against the friction, and then he pushed himself inside of me. I gasped at the sudden fullness, at the feeling of being complete.

He drew his cock out and pounded it back in, thrusting up into me, making me ride him. This angle caused his head to brush the same spot his fingers had found. It sent sparks up my spine, and I drove myself down harder onto his cock with his next thrust. He seemed surprised, sucking in a deep breath, but let me grasp onto his arms so I could get a better hold. I met him, thrust for thrust, chasing that pleasure. It built, liquid and warm, in the pit of my stomach, and my harsh pants became little moans.

"You look so fucking hot like this, taking my cock so well," he said, teeth grazing the taut cord of muscle in my neck. I slid one hand to Kaden's neck, needing something more solid to hold onto. He growled and his lips crashed into mine once more, demanding entrance.

He bit my lower lip, just hard enough that I knew it

would be swollen for hours, and the pain mixing with the pleasure brought me closer to that edge of desire. I ground down onto his cock, trying to chase it. *Almost there, almost there...*

I drew in a deep breath and—

The door burst open, ripping me out of my dream. I jumped to my feet instantly, ready to escape, too many years of being in Dad's house ingraining me to go on the defense mode immediately.

Kaden barreled in, claws out, looking around wildly. I blinked at him, trying to shift the last of my consciousness to the waking world, and not back in a moon-drenched clearing where Kaden had his cock inside me while I screamed his name.

His eyes finally fell on me. "Are you okay?"

"What?" It was the last thing I expected him to say. I stepped out of the fighting stance I'd fallen into on instinct —*feet wider,* I could almost hear Kaden saying—and crossed my arms over my chest. "What are you doing in my room?"

"I heard noises. I thought someone had broken in and attacked you."

What? *Oh.* Heat rose in my face, and I hunched my shoulders, suddenly realizing that the object of my sex dream was standing right in front of me, and I was wearing just a sports bra and shorts. It was one thing to participate in the casual nudity of a shifter, but it was another thing altogether when my body was aching, my desire still so present.

"It was nothing," I said, trying to put as much bluster into the words as possible. "Just a dream."

As if my own realization at my state of undress had sparked his, Kaden's eyes dropped to my breasts, and then went down further, tracing the lines of my body. For a moment, I wondered if I was still asleep, if this was some weird dream-in-a-dream I hadn't woken up from yet, but then he inhaled and closed his eyes.

"You smell of sex," he said.

I was still so caught up in the dream that his voice saying those words sent another bolt of desire down my spine. I could easily imagine him saying other things next, similar to those I'd just heard in my dream. Gooseflesh popped up as if his words had caressed me.

When he opened his eyes, they were hard and angry. "Dreaming about your Leo mate?"

"What?" I asked, shaking myself out of the hold of his voice. "No, I—"

"Don't do that under my roof. I don't care who you want to fuck, but keep your fantasies of that piece of shit far away from me."

I opened my mouth to correct him, but what exactly would I say? *Actually, I wasn't dreaming about my mate, I was dreaming about you.* How would that help the situation?

Part of me wanted to chase the last moment, to regain that hunger in Kaden's eyes as he'd been looking me over, but that didn't make any sense. He was angry, and an angry Kaden was a familiar Kaden. Him looking at me with lust had been out of the ordinary, and probably hadn't meant anything, anyway. Mentioning it would just create conflict where there didn't need to be any.

"Get out of my room," I said instead, which was much more on par with how we usually interacted.

Kaden's eyes flared again, and he looked like he wanted to argue. Then he simply shook his head and walked out, slamming the door behind him.

I took in a deep, shuddering breath. I tried to calm my racing heart, but I couldn't stop thinking about how hot my dream had been. I'd never had sex before. No one in the Cancer pack would touch me. I'd dated a human while I was in college but my parents forbade me from seeing him because he wasn't my mate. And of course, my mate didn't want me. Not that I wanted him either, but that didn't make the ache for him go away. Now I was going to be tormented by dreams of Kaden too.

Really graphic, detailed dreams. Damn, why couldn't he have waited another few seconds to wake me up?

CHAPTER TWENTY

THE NEXT FEW days passed with no small amount of awkwardness. Kaden hadn't brought up the incident in my room, and I hadn't either. That didn't change the fact that the midnight incident hung between us like a stench in the air. Neither of us went poking at it, but it was there, all the same, and I was just waiting for it to get to a breaking point. We seemed to dedicate extra time to ignoring it, carefully looking away and putting distance between our bodies, and it was driving me up the wall.

Worst of all, it was like we noticed every time we were close and made a big deal of getting past it. It was harder when Kaden was pressed against me in a hold, or pinning me to the ground after bowling me over, but there was no time to spend on physical attraction when I was trying to wiggle out of his grasp or throw a punch. It didn't stop my brain from wandering in the off-moments though, and I found myself having to ask Kaden to repeat a lot of things.

It seemed like training was getting more and more physical, the hand-to-hand combat becoming more of a close-quarters thing as I got better and he actually had to work to take me down. He wasn't getting distracted nearly as much as I was, but I still noticed the odd time or two that he stared at me intensely, almost the same look in his eyes as he'd had in the dream. My brain's ability to conjure up the memory of it was eerie.

It was becoming increasingly obvious that Kaden and I had intense chemistry, and I couldn't deny that he felt it either. Not that it mattered. As if the mating bond could feel that I was thinking about someone else, the sharp tugs drawing me back to Jordan became more intense. Every single time I got caught up in looking at Kaden's muscles or drowning in his eyes, I'd feel it. It would be like an itch that I couldn't quite scratch, something telling me that this was out of place. Reminding me that I should be somewhere else right now. I wondered if the moon goddess was getting a huge kick out of my predicament. Rejected by my true mate, and lusting after another shifter instead.

I scratched at my stomach, trying to rid myself of the odd pull as we walked. I shook my head as if I could clear the thoughts physically from my brain and tried to focus on where Kaden and I were headed. We weren't doing combat training today, which was equal parts a letdown and a relief. Instead, we were walking the perimeter of the Ophiuchus pack territory for some reason he hadn't explained yet.

I glanced over at Kaden, who trudged beside me in a black shirt and jeans. I wished I could have been mated to someone like him, rather than Jordan. At least Kaden had never looked at me with such cruel eyes, and he'd never injured me either.

But he wasn't my mate.

Who was I kidding? I wanted Kaden anyway. He was *hot,* and everything an alpha should be, and I would gladly fuck him just to relieve some of this constant pressure between my thighs. If I didn't do something about it soon, I thought I might implode.

Kaden glanced over as if he felt my stare, and I could have sworn his lips twisted down. Despite the chemistry between us, Kaden was always the first to pull away and made it very clear with his actions that he didn't want me.

"How's cleaning going at the school?" Kaden asked as we continued walking through the forest. It was a warm day in early July, and the sunlight filtered through the trees and warmed my shoulders.

"It's fine," I said, surprised he was bothering with small talk. "I like to see Stella with the pups."

Stella had an amazing gift when it came to the children. That was one of the first things I'd noticed when I'd stepped into her kindergarten classroom. I'd spent too much time simply watching her teach and the children interact with her, before remembering I had to actually *clean* the room I was standing in.

I'd spent days cleaning the place, all except the huge fucking snake they had in one of the rooms. No way was I getting near that thing. I couldn't believe they actually had it at the school, where it could hiss at the children walking past. I suspected it was thinking about eating them, but Stella told me the snake was harmless. Sure.

I was still getting used to seeing wolf pups at the school too. It was incredible to see a child running around, only to have a wolf there a moment later. It seemed to happen mostly when they got upset. I'd never had to deal with upset baby shifters, but the teachers had a good handle on it. They seemed used to the extra work of running down a small wolf that could outpace even the fastest adult in human form.

"What are we doing out here?" I asked.

"I want to show you the different routes we use for patrols and show you what sorts of thing to watch out for when you're on duty."

My eyebrows shot up. "Wow, that almost sounds like you might actually trust me a tiny bit."

"Don't get your hopes up. This is as much a test as anything else."

Of course. Everything was a test, and no one would tell me what my grade was.

As we got further into the forest, Kaden said, "Most of the packs have no idea where we live, and I'd like to keep it that way. The mystery surrounding us has kept us safe for all this time, but we need to be prepared for an attack, now more than ever. After the most recent Convergence, we might be targeted now, especially with the upheaval." He paused and rested that heavy gaze upon me. "And with you here."

I met his eyes with a hard look of my own. "You did want to use me as bait."

He grunted. "And we will, once we're ready."

We kept walking, trudging uphill and through some mud, and I couldn't help but think this would be a lot easier as wolves. When I'd hiked before, I'd always had my camera, or at least my phone, to make the journey more fun, but now I had neither of those. Maybe if I was a good girl, Kaden would let me have a phone again. I let out a heavy sigh and he shot me a glance.

"What is it?" he asked.

"Nothing. It's just... I wish I had my camera." There wasn't any response, so I just shook my head and continued. "I majored in photography in college, and I loved taking photos of nature. This forest is so beautiful I'd like to capture it too, but, well, no camera."

"What happened to it?" Kaden asked, surprising me. "Was it left back at the Convergence?"

"No, it was smashed before that. I got on the bad side of the Cancer beta's son, and he and his mate decided it would be a fun way to torment me. I had some photos on my phone as well, but...well, I guess I lost that too."

His hard blue eyes raked up and down my body. "Are they the ones who gave you those scars on your body?"

I flushed at the unexpected question, embarrassed he had seen so much of me, including all the things about my body that brought me shame. "A few of them, yeah."

"And the others?"

The anger in his voice shocked me. I swallowed and said, "Most of them were from my father."

Kaden growled, a low and terrifying sound that raised

the hair on my arms. "If he wasn't already dead, I'd kill him myself for that."

I froze, his words echoing through me. "I...you would?"

He kept walking, falling into silence once more. I stared after him for a moment, trying to wrap my head around what he'd just said, before chasing after him. Did he...care for me? Or was he just pissed off that an alpha would treat their pack member—their *daughter*—that way?

I caught up with him and felt a connection between us, one I wanted to explore more. I found myself babbling, unable to stop. "I was lucky he let me go to college at all. The only reason he agreed was because my brother pressured him. Did you go to college?"

"No, I didn't have the chance. I became alpha at eighteen." He'd gone back to being his normal, surly self, and I didn't expect him to continue, but then he surprised me by speaking up again. "I planned to go to college, even applied and everything, and then my parents were killed. I had to drop everything to take care of Stella and the pack."

"That must have been tough," I said. "What would you have studied?"

"I don't know. Maybe astronomy. I still have my telescope. It's set up on the roof, and I like to go up there to relax sometimes. It helps get my mind off of things."

I smiled at the image of him under the stars and opened my mouth to ask him more about it, but Kaden stopped suddenly, his face turning hard. He turned his head up to the sky and inhaled sharply.

I paused next to him. "What is it?"

He swore under his breath. "We walked too far outside of the pack borders. We need to head back."

He turned around and started heading back, and I hurried after him, wondering what the big deal was. Or how he could even tell we'd left the pack lands. But mostly I was disappointed we'd been interrupted—Kaden had finally started opening up to me, but now that was over.

Kaden suddenly jerked his head toward me and commanded, "Ayla, shift right now."

I complied without questioning the order, without even stopping to take off my clothes. I'd been practicing with Stella to get the timing down in case I needed to shift in an emergency, and I could do it as fast as any seasoned wolf now. Except an alpha, of course. Kaden was already in his wolf form as I stepped forward to meet him, my shredded clothes in a pile behind me. He wasn't looking at me, and I noted that our paws were completely different sizes. My pure white wolf felt small next to his black one.

I wouldn't have picked up the sounds of people approaching if I'd been in human form, but I heard them clearly now and followed Kaden's gaze to the tree line ahead of us. Three males walked out of the trees, and they were close enough for me to see the ram symbols on their arms.

Aries.

They fanned out, coming straight for us, and the middle one said, "Take the female alive."

A low growl emanated from Kaden's wolf beside me. A warning. The three Aries males ignored it completely, stepping right up to us and shifting into their wolves. Their pack was allied with the Leos, and there could only be one reason why they would want me.

What the hell do I do? I'd worked so hard on fighting in human form and shifting into wolf form with Stella. I could smell something that belonged to the Ophiuchus pack from miles away, but what use would that be to me right now? I'd never fought anything in my wolf form—we hadn't gotten to that part of my training yet.

Kaden looked over at me, his black ears twitching, and jerked his head back toward the direction of Coronis. If I'd been in human form, I would have frowned, but I just cocked my head at him. He repeated the motion, this time with a soft growl. I swore I saw some sort of desperation in his eyes.

He wants me to run, I thought. No way. I shook my head at him as best as I could. I wasn't going to leave him. It was a stupid idea, anyway. I could lead the Aries pack directly to the town if they decided to give chase, and the moon wasn't out to give me an advantage. No, there wasn't any option except to stay and fight.

Kaden and the Aries wolves circled each other, growling and snapping. I hadn't felt this kind of tension, or the threat of serious violence, in quite some time. I'd almost forgotten how terrifying it could be.

Their growls became deeper, more threatening, and I backed away a few steps, still trying to figure out what exactly to do. Another wolf emerged from the shadows, a bit to the left, and neither the Aries wolves nor Kaden saw it. I watched in horror as the wolf lunged toward Kaden.

I opened my mouth to warn him—no good. I couldn't do more than bark or howl, and who knew if he'd understand it. No, there was no time to think. I threw myself into the wolf's path, knocking it off course. We both tumbled to the side, and I rolled to my feet instantly, crouched and ready to fight. I bared my teeth at the wolf, who shook its head, like shaking off water. Then, it jumped at me, too fast for me to follow, and suddenly we were fighting.

The moves that Kaden had taught me were useful for my wolf body, at least to an extent, and with my enhanced senses, it was a lot easier to react to the attacks and counteract them. We tussled for a bit before I got my jaws wrapped around the shifter's hind leg. I bit down hard, squeezing my eyes shut as I broke skin and blood spurted out. The shifter howled and fought to get free. With a great wrench of his leg, he finally got out of my grasp and sprinted away.

I sunk back down into a crouch, half-expecting him to turn around and bowl me over. I was so focused on the fleeing wolf, that the next attack took me completely by surprise. Faster than anything I'd ever seen move, a blur of gray fur raced toward me. Just as I turned to face the new shifter, he rammed into my side. It felt like a freight train. I went airborne, flying several feet back before hitting the ground hard enough that my breath left me in a huge w*huff.* For a moment, I laid there, my brain trying to catch up with the sudden shift in environment, and then the pain came in.

I'd gotten good at dealing with pain over the years. It came with dealing with Dad and Jackie's punishments, of being beaten up by other Cancer pack members. It was easy to breathe through the pain eventually, but what could I do when I couldn't even *breathe?*

I felt the pull of my bones as they started reshaping into my human form. *No, not now!* I thought desperately, trying to hold onto my wolf form, but it was like trying to hold onto water. It slipped through my fingers and I found myself settling back into my human form.

That was exactly what I *shouldn't* do. I stood no chance against fully trained shifters in human form. I was barely holding my own in my untrained wolf form. It didn't do any good. I tried to move, to push myself up, but it was useless. My human body was weak and injured, and there was no way I'd be standing on my own any time soon.

From where I lay, I could barely see Kaden fighting the other wolves. They moved so fast, all I saw were flashes of teeth, claws, and clumps of fur flying into the air, and heard the occasional growl and yelp to punctuate the silence. I tried to get up to help him, to draw in a deep breath to brace myself for the pain, but I couldn't seem to catch my breath. My head swam when I tried to push myself up, my arm collapsing underneath me.

"Kaden," I tried to say, but there was no sound, just me shaping my lips around his name. Was I going to die here, like this? After everything I'd been through?

Very suddenly, it was silent. I held myself perfectly still, body tensed for one of the Aries wolves to come and end it all, but a moment later, Kaden stood over me in human form. The relief that flowed through me was so strong I actually let out a sob. He was alive, and the Aries wolves weren't. Thank the gods.

He was completely nude, and at first, I tried to keep my gaze on his face. If I wasn't in so much pain, I'd take a peek at the rest of him. Then again, if I was going to die, I might as well peek a little bit. What was he going to do, kill me? I let my eyes drop to his chest, where the hints of muscle I'd seen all through training were on full display, all in one unbroken line of perfection. Then lower, to the tiny trail of dark hair moving down his abs, down, down, down to his...

"We have to get you back to pack lands," Kaden said, and my eyes snapped back to his face. "It isn't safe here. There might be more of them out there."

I nodded, or tried to. Nothing seemed to want to move. I wished my shifter healing would kick in already, but maybe I was too injured.

Kaden leaned over and picked me up. His hands were gentle, gentler than I'd felt them yet, and I wished I could appreciate it. When he jostled me, it made everything hurt worse, and I let out a groan.

"Sorry," Kaden said, and I frowned. That wasn't like him at all. "Hold on tight, we'll be there in a minute."

Then he took off in a run.

CHAPTER TWENTY-ONE

THE FOREST BLURRED BY, dense trees cast in deep enough shadows that even if we'd been moving at a slower pace, I'd still be hard-pressed to notice any details. I couldn't catch my breath, no matter how hard I tried. I'd thought that the agony would fade as we went on, but the sharp pains wouldn't let me get a solid breath in. It took my lungs a few extra inhales to realize they weren't getting the oxygen they needed, and a few moments more to finally pinpoint what was causing it. My ribs.

"I can't breathe," I wheezed out, trying to catch Kaden's attention. He was intent on running, eyes focused ahead. He didn't even seem to hear me. I was astounded by his speed. *I* could run this fast, but only in wolf form, but maybe this was another benefit of being the alpha. I tried to get his attention again, pounding my fist feebly against his chest, and repeated what I'd said.

Kaden finally looked down at me and shook his head once. "We're not safe here. We have to keep going."

Ah. We were still outside our pack lands. I still didn't know how they marked them, or why we would be safe there, since Kaden hadn't shared that secret just yet. Just as I opened my mouth to ask, he slowed to a trot, nostrils flaring as he caught scent of something different. I could smell the difference as well, but it didn't smell like home to me. Not yet.

"I'm setting you down," Kaden said, and I braced against the jostle. He'd held me so tight on the run that I'd hardly felt it, but *this* would hurt just as much as when he picked me up. I clenched my teeth and tried to hold in the groan, but it was no use.

Kaden crouched at my side and glanced up at my face with concern. It was the first time I'd seen the look on his face directed toward me, and I was taken aback. When he'd kidnapped me, my well-being had been the last thing on his mind, and when he continually beat my ass in training he didn't seem to care how scraped up I got. I struggled to sit up, uncomfortable with the look he was giving me. I needed him to be gruff and uncaring as usual, or else it would signal I was really in trouble.

Kaden put a hand on my shoulder, exerting just enough pressure to stop me from rising further. The injury in my side burned as I pushed against him for a few moments, before it became too much and I collapsed back on the ground, panting.

"Stay down, or I'll make you." The commanding alpha tone in his voice let me know that he meant it.

I huffed out a breath, but couldn't do much more than that. He began poking at my ribs, and I used the time to observe him. I took in the proud nose, hard blue eyes, and the stubborn set of his jaw. My gaze trailed down his neck to where the blood started. I wondered whose it was. He didn't appear injured, so it must have been from the other wolves. He'd taken down all of them as if it had been nothing.

I sucked in a deep breath as he prodded my ribs, pain chasing away that train of thought. I'd lost count of the number of times I'd been hurt, but that didn't make it any easier. Once the adrenaline faded, there was nothing to protect me from the pain. Getting through the beating was easy, but the aftermath hadn't ever been. On top of that, the feeling of not being able to breathe was about to send me into a panic, and I tried desperately to hang onto any semblance of control.

"The Aries' ram charge broke several of your ribs," Kaden said.

"No shit," I muttered, but the sharp edge of sarcasm I'd meant to color my words with was lost in the pain.

Kaden shot me a dark look. "Your ribs almost punctured your lungs when you shifted back. I need to put your ribs back into place before I can move you."

I nodded, tilting my head back to catch the barest hint of sunlight streaming through the branches high above. Kaden had been kind enough to set me down on a patch of moss, and there weren't any stray sticks to dig into my back as I did my best to relax and wait for the impending pain.

When it came, I closed my eyes, breath hissing out.

"Good," Kaden said, his voice low and soothing.

I reached out, hand scrabbling against his tattooed arm, and he let me grab onto it without question.

"Look at me," Kaden said, and I shook my head. I'd start crying if I looked at him, and I was trying extremely hard not to cry from the pain alone. "Look at me," he repeated, and I forced my eyes open. His eyes were intense, the color of the sky just after sunset, and I felt myself falling into them.

"I don't know if I can get through this," I wheezed finally because Kaden seemed to be waiting for me to say something. Kaden had taken his hand off my side for a few moments, probably so I wouldn't scream and alert the entire Aries pack to our location.

"You can." Kaden's words held an easy confidence that I didn't share. "Ready?"

"No," I groaned. "But you're going to go ahead anyway, so just get it over with."

He continued shifting my ribs around, and I did my best to hold still. Kaden kept up a low stream of words, the most I'd heard him say in one sitting, but I had no idea what he was saying. The words all seemed jumbled together in my brain, but I latched onto that voice, trying to make it the only thing I paid attention to, not the forest around us, not his fingers on my skin, and not the panic growing inside me as I struggled to breathe.

Then Kaden's hand was on my jaw, tilting it back down. I hadn't even realized that I'd looked away from him. *Overbearing alpha,* I thought but didn't pull my chin away.

"Ayla," he said, my name sounding just as unusual on his tongue as it always did. He called me by it so infrequently, but today seemed to be the day he was saying it the most. "I need to tend to you now. We won't make it back to Coronis without fixing you up out here, and if I move you, I'll just throw the ribs out of place again." He paused as if considering his next words, chewing on them before he spat them out. "This is going to be a bit strange, but I need you to trust me."

I hesitated only a moment. He'd been the only one to jump to my aid so readily in years. During the attack, he'd tried to get me to run, even though that had been a stupid idea, and showed that he hadn't been thinking straight. He'd shown me more loyalty in the few weeks I'd been here than I'd seen in twenty-two years in the Cancer pack. If he wanted me dead, he could have let the Aries pack have me. Every single thing he'd done for me, from the moment I'd been captured, made me realize just how much I trusted him.

"I do trust you," I said, with complete sincerity.

He nodded and settled more comfortably on his haunches at my injured side. He leaned down, and I assumed at first that it was to look at the wound. His breath ghosted over my side and I shivered, battered flesh flinching at the added sensation. Kaden opened his mouth and I felt my jaw drop as he *licked* me.

His tongue was hot, wet, and not entirely unpleasant. It started at the crest of my hip and dragged up the oversensitive flesh. I wanted to shove him away, to demand to know what kind of game he was playing. Before I could gather the right words, his eyes flicked up to meet mine, and I snapped my mouth shut.

He slid his tongue back down across my injury, just as slow, and it didn't feel...awful. In fact, my mind flashed back to the dream I'd had, when Kaden had been very resourceful with his tongue in a different way. I held very still, avoiding Kaden's eyes as he continued licking up and down my side, tongue scorching hot and almost soothing.

As he continued, a blush began staining my cheeks, and I was beyond grateful for the blood covering me, so maybe he wouldn't notice if he looked up. The pain was fading and something else began pulling at me. It felt as if it was going in time with Kaden's tongue, a low *throb-throb* that I didn't want to examine too closely. It was too close to desire for comfort, and I'd have no explanation this time for the scent of my lust if Kaden happened to notice.

As he continued, I started noticing less of the pain and more of the feeling of his tongue, flattened against my bare flesh and stroking up and down. I drew in a deeper breath experimentally, muscles tensed for the inevitable rush of pain. It didn't come.

I blinked, trying to reconcile Kaden's tongue with my lessening pain. Was he *healing* me? I should push him away, or tell him that I was fine now, but I didn't. I'd never admit it to him, but I didn't want him to stop.

Kaden deemed it necessary to continue licking me for a few minutes longer, and my heart raced as the pain faded to nothing. I flattened my palms on the moss below me to stop myself from doing something incredibly stupid, like pull him closer and see if his tongue felt just as good on other parts of my skin, like I'd imagined it in the dream.

Finally, Kaden drew back, licking his lips like he'd tasted something delicious. I watched him, breath caught in my throat as I waited for his next move. His gaze tracked over the skin he'd laved his tongue over for several minutes, and then drifted across the rest of my body.

His nostrils flared slightly as he took in my bare flesh, and then he cleared his throat and looked away as if he just realized I was naked. That we were *both* naked. The sexual tension that had disappeared in the heat of the fight and the rush to get me back to Ophiuchus pack lands returned with a vengeance.

"Better?" he asked, but his voice was rough. Like speaking was difficult.

I swiped a hand over the unmarred skin experimentally. My injury was completely gone as if I'd never been attacked at all. Incredible.

"I didn't know you had healing powers," I said because I didn't think *better* would be an adequate way to describe how I was feeling right now. I desperately hoped he couldn't smell it, and wouldn't remark on it like he had the other night.

Kaden shot me a smirk, back to being the cocky alpha I knew. "All of the Ophiuchus pack have healing saliva. It's our pack power." He bared his teeth. "We also have a poison bite."

"I'll remember that," I said dryly. "I thought only the Virgo pack could heal."

"They're even better at it than we are, but since I'm the alpha my healing is stronger than anyone else in the pack."

"Really?" I asked, trying to keep my tone neutral.

"Who do you think healed you when you first got here?"

My eyes widened at the thought of him stripping me naked and healing me when I'd first been captured. Had those oversized clothes been his too? That led me to other thoughts of those days, things I'd avoided thinking about. One of his wolves had bit me, and I'd passed out. "The poison bite...is that how you knocked me out?"

"Yes, a small amount of our poison works well as a tranquilizer. Stella made sure not to bite you for long enough to kill you."

"*Stella* poisoned me?" I asked. "And here I thought we were friends."

Kaden stood, brushing off his bare thighs before holding a hand out to me. "Can you walk?"

"Maybe." I took his hand, almost smiling as I remembered the first time I'd taken his hand like this. He didn't try to launch me over his shoulder this time, either. He pulled me up, and I huffed out a breath as I was almost catapulted upright—and straight against his chest.

I put my hands out, my instincts from Kaden's training kicking in before my logical brain could interfere, and touched bare skin. His hands were on my arms, gripped tight enough that I couldn't slip free easily, my hands flat against his naked chest. Under my palms, his heart was beating just as quickly as my own.

He was close enough to smell, that odd, musky scent that reminded me of dense forests and moonlight. *Home,* I thought. His breath ghosted across my lips and neck. The receding blush made a reappearance, and there would be no hiding it from this close, under this much scrutiny. He inhaled, scenting me, and I leaned in, almost involuntarily. I felt a strong pull to him, much like the constant pull of the mate bond to Jordan. But where Jordan's compulsion felt like a hand always crushing my stomach and yanking it backward, this felt natural, like it was meant to be.

Kaden's eyes dropped to my lips. I licked them compulsively, and for a moment, I could have sworn I felt the vibration of a low growl sing through the air between us. Then he shoved me away from him without ceremony.

"You should have listened to me," Kaden said, turning away.

I felt something suspiciously similar to disappointment curl in my gut. I'd *wanted* him to breach the distance, no matter how much fallout it would cause.

"I told you to run," he said. "You could have gotten yourself killed back there. You're still in training, and your Moon Touched gift wouldn't help you here. It's daylight now, in case you didn't notice."

"Running would have only brought them back to the pack," I snapped, unable to hold back. *Fuck,* he was so infuriating. Hot one minute and cold the next, and always bossing me around like he was my alpha—which he wasn't. "I only stayed to keep you from getting killed."

"I don't need your help," he snarled, turning back to me.

I crossed my arms over my breasts. "You've made that *abundantly* clear."

His eyes dropped to the spot I was covering, and he ran a hand through his hair and let out a breath. "Come on, we need to get back. I need to let the others know that other packs are starting to sniff around our borders, looking for you. They'll be back in greater numbers, and I want us to be prepared for that."

He began walking without waiting to see if I'd follow. A thought struck me, something that had been niggling in the back of my mind. It was shaken loose at the idea of them looking for me. Had my bond with Jordan led the Aries pack right to us? Was that how they'd found us so easily?

I shook my head. That was a problem for later. Preferably when I had clothes. I followed Kaden back toward the town, mulling over the events in my head, trying to make sense of them. Unfortunately, the only thing I got was more questions and too few answers.

CHAPTER TWENTY-TWO

I WAS surprised by how normal everything was over the next few days. Almost dying didn't get me out of my cleaning duties, unfortunately, and Kaden didn't seem to think I needed any days off either. I woke up the next morning to a note saying to continue cleaning the school. No Kaden in sight.

"All right, then," I'd muttered at the note, and tore it off the fridge. That afternoon, I asked Stella if she could spend a little extra time with me to show me how to fight as a wolf. I explained what had happened, probably unnecessarily, since Kaden seemed to share everything with her and had probably informed her of what had happened, blow-by-blow. Except for the part when he'd licked my naked body. I had a feeling that was something he wouldn't share with anyone.

"I guess it's too late to tell you to take it slow since we have a new problem on our hands," Stella said. "I'll have to get it approved, of course, but I can show you some basic stuff today."

"Good luck," I said. "I can't seem to pin Kaden down long enough to exchange a word with him. He even has Clayton doing my combat training now. If I didn't know any better, I'd say he's avoiding me."

"He's just preparing," she said. "There's a lot to get ready now that we know the Aries pack is hunting us. Two shifters got away, the one who charged you, and the one you injured. I'm sure they're telling the Leo pack our general location as we speak."

I sighed. That was my fault. And maybe Stella was right, and Kaden was too busy with 'alpha things' to keep training someone who wasn't even part of his pack, who'd put everyone in it in danger. But I couldn't ignore that his disappearance coincided very helpfully with the fact that we'd almost kissed—and that he'd likely smelled the same desire from me, but this time directed toward him.

Over the next few days, I avoided thinking about it as much as possible. Stella taught me ways to fight as a wolf, and I spent time practicing moving between patches of moonlight every evening. I wanted to make sure I would never find myself helpless or powerless again. I was evolving, and some primal part of me was fiercely proud of the rapid changes I was going through. I would never be at anyone's mercy again.

Clayton was a much better teacher than Kaden, objectively. He gave out praise and didn't borderline insult me, but I missed Kaden's training anyway. It wasn't that I had anything against Clayton, quite the opposite. Since the barbecue, he'd almost been like a friend. But he wasn't Kaden, and I missed the physical proximity our training had brought us.

Changes started happening around town, as well. All entrances and exits of the town were guarded twenty-four seven. Everyone seemed to be on high alert, gazes focused on the forest, and all of the children were accompanied by adults everywhere they went. I was also on guard and kept telling myself that when I was scanning the crowds, it wasn't for Kaden, but for threats.

Really, the disappearing act he'd done was impressive. If I ever found him, I'd ask him how he learned to do it just so I could use that trick myself. The only plus side was that I wasn't having any inappropriate dreams about Kaden anymore.

Now it was the night of the full moon, which Stella had been hyping up for days beforehand. I could feel it, the change in the air, and felt the same thrill of excitement that filled Stella's voice whenever she talked about it. This was the first full moon I'd experience after having my wolf unlocked, and I wasn't sure what to expect. Would I finally see Kaden again tonight?

I headed downstairs at sunset and found Stella already waiting for me. She wore a sexy little red dress that showed off her long legs, and her eyes were especially bright. She'd told me to wear something cute too, and I'd opted for a light, breezy sundress that brushed against my skin as I walked.

"All ready for the full moon party?" she asked. "I have to warn you, it can get pretty rowdy."

I glanced down at my dress, wondering if I was under-dressed...or overdressed. "How so?"

"Emotions run high during a full moon and there's always a lot of fighting at these things...and a lot of sex."

I grinned at her. "Is that why you're dressed up? Hoping to get lucky?"

She grinned back and gave me a wink. "Hey, just because I haven't found my mate yet doesn't mean I can't have a little fun, right?"

"Should I be worried? Is it like a full-out orgy all over the forest?"

"No, not really," she said with a laugh. "Not this time, anyway. Nine months before the Ophiuchus sign is in power is when our females go into heat, so around mid-March. Now that's like one big orgy, but it's not the right time of year, thank goodness."

"The Cancer pack used to have full moon events. I was never invited, though. I'm not sure I'm welcome tonight either." Since I still wasn't part of the pack, I didn't know if I was even *allowed* to attend. I frowned as I grabbed a bottle of water out of the fridge and downed it. I was so eager to prove myself to the pack, but this would probably be one of the things Kaden wouldn't allow.

"Of course you're welcome," Stella said. "Right, Kaden?"

If I'd had any more water in my mouth, I probably would have spit it out. I hadn't even heard Kaden come in, but when I turned toward the back doorway, Kaden was looming in it. My heart rate soared as I looked him over. He looked incredibly delectable for some reason I couldn't put a finger on, and I wanted to lick his jawline, to see if he tasted as good too. I sucked in a breath and glanced away quickly before I had any more of those thoughts.

"Fine," Kaden said. "As long as you behave yourself." He walked back outside, and I wondered why he'd even come to the kitchen in the first place. Maybe he *was* avoiding me.

I grinned at Stella, shoving those thoughts away. No matter what was going on with him, at least I'd get to spend more time around the pack. "Looks like I'll get to go."

Stella clapped her hands, bouncing on her heels. "I can't wait. I bet we can find you someone to hook up with too."

I laughed and shook my head at that, knowing that wasn't going to happen. Even if I wanted it, which I didn't really—my brain was already scrambled enough with thoughts of Kaden and Jordan—I doubted anyone would want to hook up with the outcast wolf still mated to someone in the Leo pack.

As night fell we made our way into the forest. Despite Kaden okaying my presence, I felt a twinge of uneasiness. Would I truly be accepted? I wished I could be a member of the pack, but I kept hearing things like *wait until we know you're trustworthy.* The uneasiness mixed with impatience simmered unpleasantly in my gut.

Kaden melted from the trees, almost like a ghost, and I found my gaze glued to him as we walked. He didn't have a shirt on—*shocker*—and my eyes immediately gravitated toward the muscles moving under his skin as he walked. No matter how many times I yanked my gaze away, I found it back, just a few seconds later. I wanted to tackle him, to press my body against him, to devour him. *What the hell is wrong with me?* I thought. I could usually contain these inappropriate thoughts better.

It got even worse when Kaden started looking back at me, a frown on his face as if he was trying to puzzle something out. What was his deal? And why was he so fucking sexy? I wanted to lick every inch of his body like a popsicle.

Stella walked between us, blissfully unaware of the sexual tension so thick I could have taken a bite out of it. I was uncomfortably aware of Kaden's body as he moved— every breath, every rustle of fabric, every soft footfall against the ground. By the time we joined the rest of the pack in the clearing, I was bordering on uncomfortably horny, and even breathing was torture. I tried desperately to control it, and I spent so much energy doing that, that I didn't notice that many of the male shifters we passed stared at me. At first, I thought it was because I was acting strangely, but no. There was a hunger in their gazes, all the same.

Jack took a few steps toward me with one of his charming smiles, except there was a naughty gleam in his eye that told me exactly what he wanted. "Ayla. You look positively ravishing tonight. Care to join for the evening?"

Before I could answer, Kaden pushed between us, his

growl resonating through the air. "Get the fuck away from her," he said.

As I stared at the alpha in shock, Jack backed down immediately, dipping his head and walking away. If he were in wolf form, I was sure his tail would be between his legs.

"Rude much?" I asked Kaden. "Maybe I wanted to go with him, did you ever think of that?"

He turned murderous eyes upon me. "Not happening."

"What's going on?" Stella asked, concern written all over her face.

"Keep everyone here," Kaden told her. At the same time, Kaden picked me up and hauled me over his shoulder, while I let out a shriek.

"Let me go!" I said, pounding against his back as he carried me away from the group, back toward the house. "What the fuck do you think you're doing?"

He didn't answer, just kept trudging through leaves and branches while carrying me like I was a naughty child. I tried to break free but gave up as his fingers tightened each time until it was almost painful. He was too damn strong.

Kaden stopped once we were away from the pack and dumped me on the grass. "What's going on with you? Every single unmated male is giving you eyes tonight."

"I don't know," I said, glaring up at him. "I wish I did."

Kaden's frown deepened and then he leaned in closer, inhaling. I jerked away, but Kaden's eyes flared with something that looked almost like panic. "Fuck," he growled, and I thought *yes, that's what I'd like* before I realized that the tone was more urgent than amorous. "We have to get you out of here right now."

"What's going on?" I asked, but Kaden ignored me, twisting around as if he was looking for someone.

"Clayton," he barked, and the beta of the pack trudged over. "You'll be leading the hunt tonight." Kaden didn't even wait for an acknowledgment before he picked me up again.

"What are you doing?" I asked, trying to push down the intense desire I felt at his touch. "I'm not going anywhere with you until I get answers."

I managed to squirm enough that I broke free, but thanks to Kaden's training, I landed gracefully and managed to dart away. Kaden lunged toward me and I evaded him, despite a part of me wanting to let him capture me. It was incredibly hard to think, with *want, want, want* pounding through my brain like a second heartbeat. Finally, he caught me by the arm and dragged me the remaining few yards to the house. He didn't say a single thing until we were inside, and then he slammed the door, throwing the deadbolt.

"You're going into heat," he said.

Shock washed over me like a cool bucket of water, temporarily dousing the desire I was feeling. "How is that possible?"

"You're mated now, so you're fertile. And you're packless, so you're going to go into heat during every full moon. Every unmated male is going to want to fuck you." He pinched the bridge of his nose between his fingers. "I brought you back here for your own protection."

I crossed my arms, covering my nipples, which had

become so hard and sensitive that even the slight brush of my dress against them was driving me wild. "This is insane. Are you planning to guard me all night?"

"I don't know," Kaden said, sounding as frustrated as he looked. "I just knew I had to get you out of there before someone tore off your clothes." He turned away and let out a long, colorful string of curses. If I'd been in a better state of mind, I would have quipped something back at him, but as it was, all I felt was the rising desire. He turned back to me, his face under control once more. "Sit down. I'll get you some water."

I complied, sitting on one of the sofas in the living room. My entire body felt like it was overheating, and I closed my eyes, trying to suppress my reactions. It was as if I didn't have any control over anything. "You know," I said, eyes still closed, "I really don't like this."

"That makes two of us," Kaden said dryly.

I jumped at the sound of his voice. He'd moved silently again, or maybe I was just so out of it I hadn't heard him approach. He leaned over me, a glass of water in one hand, and my body *ached* for him to be mine. After he handed me the water, whatever he saw in my gaze had him backing off quickly. He took a seat across the coffee table, carefully out of touching range. The perfect spot for my eyes to soak him up, and I found myself licking my lips and squirming in my seat. He drank from his own glass of water, and I stared at his throat as it moved. Then I watched his forearms as he set the water down on the table. Damn, I had no idea forearms could be so fucking sexy. Every inch of him was driving me wild. At the very least he could do me a favor and put on a damn shirt already.

"You should get away from me too," I said, my voice low and breathless. "You're also an unmated male."

"I can't do that."

"Why not?"

"If I leave, you'll be unprotected during your heat. Someone has to keep you safe."

"But if you stay..." I let the words trail off.

He shook his head. "Unlike the others, I can control myself."

How disappointing. I sipped at the water and stared outside, hoping the sight of the moon and the stars would give me some comfort. "So, what now? We just sit here?"

"Oh, no," Kaden said, leaning forward. "Now, it gets much worse."

CHAPTER TWENTY-THREE

THE MOON ROSE, and with it, my heat became almost unbearable. I tried to sit, my pride keeping me in place for a few minutes longer, but by the time the moon was above the trees, I was practically panting. I'd never experienced anything like this before. I felt out of control, a wild thing that couldn't be contained in my own skin. I was pretty sure I would die if I didn't have someone touching me, taking away this need in my body. I was so fucking horny I thought I might explode.

I set the water glass down and balled my hands into fists, trying to keep them in my lap so I wouldn't try to take my clothes off. The urge was unbearable. The heat between my legs felt hot and heavy, and I carefully didn't rub against anything. What would Kaden think if I just stripped my clothes off and rubbed myself along his couch to try to get rid of this *awful* need? I could never look him in the face again.

But even worse than that was the urge to cross the distance between us. It grew and grew until I had to stand up, or I felt like I'd die right there. "I'm going insane," I said, pacing back and forth, trying to get the energy out. It didn't do a damn bit of good.

"You can't get to your mate," Kaden said with a frown. "That must be why."

I threw my hands up in the air as I paced behind the couch, trying to get further away from him before I made a very bad decision. "I don't even want my mate!"

Kaden's eyes narrowed at me. "You say that, but your body says otherwise. I can *smell* it."

Anger burst through the desire at his words. This was just like the other night with my dream. I wanted *nothing* to do with Jordan. How could I get that through his thick skull?

"It's not him I want, it's—"

As soon as the words were out, I slapped a hand over my mouth. Kaden's eyes widened at my admission. Shit, I hadn't meant to say that out loud. I turned away, wishing I had never admitted how much I wanted him, feeling vulnerable as hell, and still so turned on I thought I might die.

"Ayla..." The sound of my name on his lips was so sensual it made me tremble with need. I turned back to see his fingers curling around the armchair edges, nostrils flared wide as if he was taking in my scent again. He let out a shuddering breath and closed his eyes, his knuckles going white as he clutched the chair. "We can't."

I could hear the edge of lust in his voice, and that's what really set me over the edge. "Why not?"

His jaw moved as he swallowed. "You should go to your room. Watch TV. Read a book. Try to distract yourself."

"We both know that won't help." There would be no way to get through this alone. I ground my teeth, trying one last time to take control over my traitorous body, but it didn't do any good. I needed release. I needed *him*.

I crossed the space between us as if drawn to him. This pull didn't feel the same as the mating bond with Jordan, but it was just as strong. I dropped to my knees beside his chair, ready to beg, to debase myself, whatever it took. If I'd been any saner, I would've had too much pride to do such a thing, but the need in my body was so strong I didn't care.

"Ayla," he said, a warning in his voice. A warning I chose to ignore.

"Please," I whispered. "Please help me."

I watched his resolve shatter, like a glass ceiling falling. The careful control he had over his body unwound, and he let go of his death grip on the chair and pulled me into his lap. His touch ignited the fire inside me and I moved to kiss him, but he stopped me with a hand on my lips.

"I can offer you some relief with my fingers," he said. "But nothing more."

"Thank you," I said with a whimper. Anything to get this awful heat out of me, and the feeling that I was literally coming apart at the seams from lust.

He shifted me on the chair for better access, and then he yanked my dress up to my thighs. Low, animal noises escaped my throat as his strong fingers gripped my knees and spread my legs. I reached for my panties, trying to get them off quickly, but Kaden's hands pushed mine aside.

"You're soaked," he murmured, and that only made me whimper even more. His knuckles brushed against the pounding heat of me, and I sucked in a shuddering breath.

"Please," I said. "Just keep going."

His jaw tightened, and he pressed a hand down onto my pelvis, holding me still.

"Let me get these off," he said, tugging at the soaked underwear.

I nodded, trying to think past the pounding need, and how that single brush of his knuckles across my sex had felt like so much more. I lifted my hips slightly to let him slide off my underwear and closed my eyes against the feeling of the air against my bare skin. It was just this side of *not enough* that I groaned in frustration. I reached for Kaden, putting my hand on his chest. I needed him to touch me, *now*.

He grabbed my hands and pushed them down to my sides. "Don't touch me. I touch you, not the other way around."

His eyes were cold, detached, as if he was telling me about the weather, not working to help me get off. I nodded and quivered beneath him, so slick that it felt like I was dripping onto the chair beneath us.

Even through the haze of desire, I paused as his words registered. "Do you not want to do this?"

"I want it too much. Being around you right now is difficult. All I *want*," he said, as his fingers tightened around my wrists, "is to rip your clothes off and fuck you senseless."

The words sent another bolt of desire through me, and I moaned as if he'd just licked down my body. *I* wanted that too, and it was such a relief to know my lust wasn't one-sided. For a second, I'd worried he was only doing this out of some sense of duty or pity.

"Then touch me," I said.

With a growl, he released my wrists and slid one hand down to the throbbing ache between my thighs. Then he dragged his fingers lightly across my slit, finger dipping inside just enough to cause my breath to sharpen. I shuddered, body quivering with the need to move, to chase that touch, make it more concrete.

"Stop fucking teasing me," I ground out.

Kaden made a low rumbling sound that was almost a laugh, and I looked up to glare at him, but just then he stroked his thumb along my clit in a delicious, torturous slide. He followed it up with another stroke, and then slid two of his fingers inside of me, while keeping his thumb on my clit. I shut my eyes so tight that little spots of light danced at the edge of my vision, while he worked his fingers in and out of me, giving me exactly what I'd needed all this time. His other hand found my breast, touching my rock-hard nipples, and I couldn't hold myself still any longer. I ground myself on his hand, chasing that feeling, wanting even more.

"How the hell are you so good at this?" I gasped out.

"I'm unmated, not celibate."

Kaden increased the tempo, circling my clit with his thumb and crooking his fingers inside of me, pistoning them in and out as if it was his cock instead. He was almost brutal, too quick, and too skilled to bring me to a gentle orgasm. No, this one was going to tear through me with something I'd never experienced before. I'd certainly never been able to bring myself this much pleasure with my own fingers.

I shuddered around him, hands clenching into fists, nails digging into my skin with the effort to not touch him. Then the need that was pounding through my body all seemed to gather in my pussy, laser-focused into a single point of desire, before exploding to the rest of me. My eyes rolled back with the intensity of my orgasm, and I let out a low moan. Kaden's fingers continued their rhythm, working me through the orgasm while I twitched against him. Finally, he released me, fingers leaving my body, and I leaned against his chest, breathless and trembling.

He rested his hands on the arms of the chair again, gripping them like it was all he could do not to touch me further. I opened my mouth to thank Kaden, when the next wave of desire poured over me, as subtle as a train. My back arched, my nipples straining against the fabric of my dress, and I moaned.

"That didn't work," I said, my voice desperate as I tried to get a handle on the wave of need. I gripped Kaden's shoulders, and when our eyes met, I found a well of lust waiting, deep and untamed. He could probably smell just how unsatisfied I was. He'd just made me come, but it had seemed to make things *worse,* not better. "I feel like I'm going to burn up. Kaden, please..."

"Damn," he said, his brow creased in frustration. "You need sex. Nothing else will do."

"Don't sound so enthusiastic, you might ruin the mood," I gasped out, trying desperately to hold onto whatever semblance of my sanity I had with the sarcasm. It didn't work, and I found myself grinding my wet pussy against Kaden's lap, where I felt his hard length under his pants. He wanted me too, so why weren't we fucking already?

He grabbed my hips to still me, but that only turned me on even more. "Do you realize what you're asking for?"

"Yes!" Of course I knew. I'd been begging for it for what seemed like hours now. "If you don't help me, I'll have to find someone else who can."

"No fucking way." His hands cupped my breasts through my thin dress and squeezed, and it was enough to make me moan and stop squirming against him. "The only man who will touch you tonight is me."

"Then get on with it already," I said, but then paused as a tiny bit of common sense returned to my brain for a split second. "Wait. Will I get pregnant?"

He shook his head. "I don't think so. I'm not your mate."

My mind must have really been gone because I thought I heard bitterness in his voice. I wasn't sure though, because I was too hung up on the idea of having Kaden's wolf pups. *It's a shame he won't get me pregnant,* I thought, and then shook my head violently, shoving the crazy thought away.

"Then what's the problem?" I asked.

He pinched my breasts almost painfully, sending a bolt of pleasure straight through me. "The problem is it can never be more than one night. Do you understand?"

"I understand." I leaned closer to him, breathing in his musky scent, while my animal instincts fought for control. I'd wanted him in my dream, and I wanted him even more now. If it was only for one night, I'd take it. "Kaden, please fuck me."

The words seemed to break down some wall inside of him as if he'd been holding back before. Kaden bared his teeth, the burn of desire clear in his gaze. In that look, I saw the alpha wolf in him, the dangerous male who had kidnapped me and threatened to kill me if I hurt anyone he loved. He grabbed my dress and yanked it over my head in one smooth flourish. I wasn't wearing a bra underneath, and now I was completely exposed to his hungry, roaming eyes. He pulled me close and pressed his nose to my neck, breathing me in, but not kissing me. Never kissing me.

"As you wish, little wolf."

CHAPTER TWENTY-FOUR

KADEN TOSSED me on the couch without ceremony and looked down at me like a king gazing at his domain. His eyes traced every line of my naked body. My legs. My breasts. My scars. It was all on display for him, and though I was tempted to cover myself, I didn't. Maybe the heat madness made me braver, or maybe I felt more comfortable with Kaden than anyone else in my life, but for once I wanted him to see me. All of me.

"Fuck, you're beautiful," he said, and his praise struck through the lust haze and made my stomach flip-flop. No man had ever said such a thing to me before.

He reached down to his jeans, unzipping them. I could see the bulge there, and I had to hold my hands down before I sat up and offered to do it myself. I doubted my help would be welcome. He hadn't wanted me to touch him before, and just because we were going to have sex didn't mean that had changed anything. He was only doing this because he had to, because we were out of options.

He stripped off his jeans, leaving him completely nude. I'd seen him in various states of undress since I'd known him, but this was different. Knowing why he was naked now held a different kind of weight. All the other times I'd tried— and failed—to avoid staring at his magnificent body, but this time I let my gaze trace down his abs, to the sharp vee of his hips, and then lower. This time I could really take a good, long look.

His cock was a thing of art, perfectly proportioned to his large size, rock hard and jutting toward me. I swallowed audibly at the sight. I wanted to sink myself down onto it until he was so deep inside of me, I'd feel full enough to sate this overwhelming need. I wanted to slide my tongue along the vein on the underside, just to see if I could get him to lose a bit of his control. I was almost overwhelmed with the possibilities, and the irony was I had no idea how to do any of them. My body seemed to have its own ideas though, but I was still a bit nervous at my lack of experience. No amount of lust could override the fact that I'd never had sex before.

Kaden stalked toward me like the predator he was, and I drew in a sharp breath. He sank to his knees in front of where I lay, presented like an offering, and drew his cock into his hand. His eyes roamed over my legs, spread wide, and I watched his nostrils flare as he looked at my sex. A spark of *something* passed through his gaze, and his grip tightened around his cock.

"If we had more time, I'd make you come with my

mouth," he said. "But I don't think that's what you need right now."

I let out a little whimper and arched my hips up at that. Honestly, that sounded amazing, but he was right. I needed him inside me. Nothing else would do.

When he looked back up at me, his eyes were dark, darker than I'd ever seen them, just a thin ring of blue around pupils blown huge. He wanted this as much as I did. The knowledge flooded me with desire and I nearly dragged him on top of me. But then he frowned slightly as he looked at my face, and he must have seen something hidden under the pure, base *want,* because he said, "You've never done this before, have you?"

I shook my head but wasn't able to find any words, feeling frustrating beyond measure. My body screamed for me to pull him closer, to reach down and be the one to put his cock inside, but my mind was stuck on the mechanics of it. Apprehension twisted in my gut, but it was overpowered by the need to have Kaden pounding the heat out of me with his cock. "No, it's my first time," I managed to say.

He grimaced, and he looked like he was forcibly holding himself back. "You do realize that the moment I'm inside you, I won't be able to help myself, right? I'll try to be gentle, but the heat frenzy makes it difficult."

I hadn't realized my heat was affecting him so much too, but now I saw it in the crinkles around his eyes, the straining of his shoulders, and the tightness of his mouth. He was doing everything in his power not to fuck me senseless. The thought that he wanted me so badly turned me on even more, and I moaned and arched my hips. He wouldn't hurt me, that much I knew. "Please, just hurry."

Kaden slid his hands along my waist and exhaled as if he'd been holding his breath for a long time. He looked into my eyes as he parted the lips of my pussy with his cock, sliding alongside my entrance a few times before actually pushing into the wet heat of me. It was agonizingly slow, and I felt him holding himself back by the way his muscles trembled and the tight press of his hands against my hips, almost painful. I kept my eyes on his face, watching his reaction as he entered me, though I was torn. I wanted to look down, to see his flesh disappearing into mine, but his face seemed more important right now. When he bottomed out, he was practically vibrating. I shifted slightly, trying to let myself settle around him.

"Are you good?" His voice was so rugged it hardly sounded like words.

"Yes. Don't stop." I shifted again, and his hands clenched around my hips. It wasn't painful like I'd expected, I just felt incredibly full.

Kaden growled, and drew himself out, and thrust back in. I let out a noise, unable to help it, my hands flying to his arms. I wanted something to hang onto. He thrust again, slowly, surely, and I felt that slight tremor running through him, even as his cock nudged at a spot of pure pleasure, dragging along it on both the up and downstroke. What remained of the discomfort faded, and my hips tried to lift to encourage him to move. I needed so much *more* to sate the ravenous beast inside me.

"Come on," I gasped out as he drew himself almost completely out of me. "Fuck me like you mean it. You won't hurt me. You couldn't."

"Is this what you want?" His eyes met mine, his own need smoldering inside of them. Then he slammed into me hard, all the way to the hilt.

"Yes!" I gasped and raised my hips up against his hands, but he pushed me back down, holding me in place. *That* felt good, too.

Kaden bottomed out, and when he drew out again, he plunged his cock back inside of me faster. He picked up the tempo and set a punishing pace, never letting my hips up to match him. He had complete control of the situation, and I *loved* it.

Flesh slapped against flesh every time he pounded into me, as our animal instincts took over and drove us into a frenzy. It built with each thrust until I was riding the high of it, wishing it would never end. Kaden was laser-focused on fucking me, breathing hard as he plunged his cock inside of me again and again, bringing me closer to pleasure.

"Fuck, you feel so good," he said. "Like you were made to take my cock."

"More," I said, gasping the word. "I'm close."

By the way his breathing hitched, I knew he was close to coming as well. I had to plant my feet to keep my position, and finally, he let me thrust my hips back into him, hands sliding down to grasp my ass. He lifted me up to stroke new parts of me with his cock, and my pleasure reached new heights.

He let out a moan, the first one I'd heard from him, and it was what sent me over the edge. My legs wrapped around him, pulling him in as deep as he could go, and I ground myself on his cock, riding the waves of pleasure. Through the blur of it, I could feel his length pulsing with his own orgasm, thrusting as deep as he could go. His release was hot inside of me, another added sensation that prolonged my own orgasm.

When I came down off my high, I felt like jelly, and let myself fall back against the sofa. Kaden let me slide through his fingers, cock slipping out of me. I winced, the feeling new and fresh, but good, nonetheless. I was panting hard as if I'd just run a mile. I had to lay there for a few moments before I could string enough words together to make a sentence.

"Thank you," was all I could say, my voice husky as if I'd been screaming. I probably had, at the end there. I could hardly remember. I wanted to say *that was amazing,* but I knew that wouldn't be received well. When I glanced at Kaden, still looming above me, his eyes were emotionless.

"I'm just doing my duty," he said.

I frowned at that and realized he'd never kissed me, not even once. It really was just sex, wasn't it—nothing more, nothing less.

I didn't have time to think about that though, because another wave of blinding desire came over me. I groaned and found myself arching my hips toward him again, my nipples hard as stone. I couldn't help but slide my hands between my legs, desperate for more relief.

"Why isn't it going away?" I asked when I was able to form words again. It didn't seem to be getting better, each wave of desire turning me more and more into a mindless animal, unable to keep track of my train of thought.

"Get on your hands and knees," he commanded.

I obeyed immediately, arching my back and presenting myself to him. He ran a hand down my spine, and I shivered, gooseflesh popping up in wake of his touch. I backed up, trying to seek out his cock without looking. I bumped into him, into his hard flesh—he hadn't gone soft, either. He was right, the heat was affecting him just as much as me. He was better at controlling it, but I felt his cock pulse as I rubbed against him, trying to encourage him to put it in me. His hips twitched forward, and I couldn't help the triumphant smile that crossed my face.

He slid the hand up my back and wrapped my hair around his hands. I closed my eyes, trying to think past the need, but it was no use. He tugged slightly, and I whimpered at how good it felt. I wanted him to use me, own me, defile me. Anything, as long as he did it now.

He pushed his cock into me roughly, no gentleness this time, and leaned over my back. "We're going to be here all night," he growled in my ear. "Fucking until the sun rises. I'm going to have you every way, every position. This is what you signed up for when you asked for my help, Ayla."

I shuddered at the way he said my name, which sent another bolt of desire through me. He thrust into me hard, as if to prove his point, and pulled my hair so that my neck was exposed. The first time we fucked he hadn't touched me outside of his hands on my hips and his dick inside of me, but now that had changed. His resolve had crumbled, and now the flood gates had been opened.

He draped himself over me, pressing our bodies flush together. His breath was hot on my neck as he thrust into me, hard enough to send me forward a bit. I braced myself better on the arm of the sofa and pushed back against him. His hand slid from my waist to my front, gliding across my stomach before dipping lower, parting the lips of my sex.

His fingers found my clit, and I threw my head back, fully baring my throat to him. He bit into the juncture between shoulder and neck as he continued pounding into me brutally from behind, each slap of flesh against flesh sending a shockwave of movement through me. Pain and pleasure mixed, and then his tongue laved at the area, bringing an entirely new kind of sensation into the mix.

"Not thinking of your Leo mate now, are you?" he purred into my ear, and I shuddered, back arching as another teeth-achingly good orgasm rolled over me. Jordan was the absolute last thing on my mind. I was only aware that Kaden was here now, taking care of me in the best way possible.

My arms and legs gave out, and Kaden kept me propped up and thrust into me over and over again through my orgasm, a low noise that sounded almost like a growl building in his throat. The new angle pounded into my g-spot with every thrust, and my body came alive again, chasing that desire like there was no tomorrow. I came again on his cock, not moments later, and I *screamed*. It felt as if my flesh was melting off my bones. This much desire shouldn't have been possible.

He let my hips go and I slumped on the couch, unable to comprehend anything except that my thighs were shaking. When he nudged at me with his knee, I turned onto my side. His eyes looked down at me, hungry, angry, *hot*.

I opened my mouth to ask him something, but again, another wave of desire rolled over me, and this time, I didn't even bother holding back my groan. I reached for him, and he let me pull him close, wrap my hands around his dick. He stiffened against me, eyes flaring wide, and I climbed on top of him and slid his cock inside of me, and then I was lost to the world. I rode him like an animal, bucking and moaning, taking my pleasure from him, while he looked up at me. He gripped my breasts and squeezed, while his eyes carried a fire inside of them that let me know the need wasn't one-sided. Then I came all over him, milking his cock with my pussy as I bounced up and down and yelled his name.

Every time I thought that the heat would clear and we'd have a few moments to rest, another wave would overtake me, and Kaden would fuck me again, finding new positions each time. At some point, we moved to the floor and he fucked me from the back, front, side, and everything in between. His heavy weight was reassuring on top of me, harsh pants punctuating each rough thrust. Every time I looked up and my eyes said, *more,* he complied. Even when we took a short break to get some water from the kitchen, he ended up bending me over the counter and thrusting into me from behind, while fingering my back entrance, sending a whole new level of pleasure through me. On our way back to the couch he picked me up and plunged his cock inside of me again, lifting me so we were clinging to each other as he claimed me.

It was incredible, rough, and wild. We fucked like animals, overcome by our basest instincts, unable to stop ourselves. I had no doubt we'd be ridiculously sore in the morning, but that didn't stop us. I knew I'd have vivid memories of this night for years to come, but all I could do was live in the moment, drowning in Kaden's eyes and body as he took me again and again, always ready for another round, always willing to bring me to orgasm. And each time the need for each other only returned.

It seemed to go on forever, until finally, *finally*, the moon set and the faint traces of predawn began to appear in the sky. I rolled off of Kaden and fell to the floor, so bone-deep tired that I didn't think I could move for hours. I knew we'd have to eventually get up—we were still in the living room where anyone could walk in on us, but right now all I wanted to do was sleep.

My body felt sore, but in the best way, and it took several minutes for me to realize what we'd done. I'd just spent the entire night having hot, wild sex with Kaden, and I'd enjoyed it. A lot. He had too if the number of orgasms we'd shared was anything to go by.

Kaden picked me up and carried me to my room, kicking open the door. I wondered how he still had the strength to walk, let alone carry me too, as he set me on the bed. I looked up at him with a tentative smile, but he wouldn't meet my eyes. His face was hard again, his eyes shuttered. Something sank in my stomach. So this was how it would be.

He'd only fucked me out of duty, and now that the all-consuming lust had left us, he didn't want me anymore. He'd made it very clear the sex was only for one night because I would literally die otherwise. And during all that sex, he hadn't kissed me, not even once.

"This can't happen ever again," he said. Then he left without another word. The slam of the door was so loud it vibrated through me.

I closed my eyes, the mortification filling me. Once again, I'd been rejected by a man I thought might actually care about me. How the hell was I supposed to live in this house with him now?

CHAPTER TWENTY-FIVE

I WANTED TO SHOWER, but I didn't think I could move. I was tired, yes, but underneath that was only shame as I came back to myself more solidly and realized the full gravity of the situation. The heat had passed, the mating frenzy over, and I couldn't believe I'd really done and said all those things.

I'll never leave my room again, I thought and shoved my face into the pillow. I considered screaming into it, but I was too tired to even do that. There was no way I could face Kaden again, let alone any of the pack. Nope, this room was my home now.

I managed to drift to sleep for a while and was grateful for the reprieve from my own spinning thoughts. My body ached as if I'd done ten trainings with Kaden in a row, as if he'd had me punch the bag for hours on end, instead of the twenty-odd minutes he usually had me do. *Well, you certainly went several rounds with him,* my brain quipped at me. *Shut up*, I told it, and turned over in bed, wincing at the way my muscles twinged.

A knock came at my door at about midday. "Are you all right?" Stella asked through the door, and I winced again. "Did Kaden do something?"

Why, yes. He did a lot of things, in all different positions, I thought, and almost laughed out loud at the thought of Stella's face if I'd said that. "I'm fine," I called back and hoped that she couldn't hear the blatant lie. If I opened that door I was sure she would see a big sign with I JUST HAD SEX WITH YOUR BROTHER ALL NIGHT emblazoned on my forehead.

"Okay." She paused for way too long. "Let me know if you need anything."

I wondered if she could smell it. Shit, I wondered if the entire town had heard me last night. They'd probably figured out what was wrong with me, much like Kaden had. He hadn't gotten me out of there in time, and I wondered if they all knew what exactly went down in Kaden's house. It wouldn't take much imagination. Which meant I could never face any of them again either.

I could never live down this embarrassment. I punched my pillow into a better shape, mostly just to punch something. I'd hated feeling so out of control of my body. I'd felt more animal than human, as if I had no control, no judgment. Last night, in the middle of the heat with Kaden draped over me, doing his best to answer the overwhelming desire in my body, I wouldn't have cared if the entire pack had been watching us.

I groaned and tried to find a more comfortable position. I'd do anything to get rid of this mate bond. I *hated* it. It had turned me into a beast, unable to control myself, and even worse, it would happen again and again because I was never going to be with Jordan. Not even if he showed up out of the blue with flowers and candy and begged me to be his mate. *Yeah right, and the sky is falling,* I thought bitterly. Which meant I was doomed to spend every full moon in this state.

I managed to avoid leaving my room all day, sleeping on and off, and letting my body rest. I got up to shower eventually, and Stella, bless her kind heart, left me some food outside my door. I devoured it as if I'd never eaten before, then chugged a ton of water. My body needed it all to recover.

Another knock sounded at my door just after night fell. I sighed, wondering if Stella was going to come in and question me after all. "I'm fine, Stella. Just tired."

"It's me," Kaden's voice said, and I sat up straighter, any drowsiness gone. What could he want? "Can I come in?"

I paused, unable to stop the wild thought that he might be coming back to apologize and tell me how much last night had meant to him, but then I shook that fantasy away. "Yeah."

I tried to figure out what the hell to do with my limbs as he came in. I finally settled onto the bed, legs crossed and hands in my lap. Not that it would have mattered.

Kaden glanced around the room, carefully avoided looking at me. "Are you willing to go on a supply run tomorrow to get some things?"

Wow, so we weren't going to talk about last night at all. Just move on, back to business, as if it had never happened. Like I didn't know the sound he made when he came inside me. "Sure."

"Be ready at 7. Don't be late."

I crossed my arms. "It won't be a problem."

Kaden opened his mouth as if he wanted to say something else, but then nodded and walked back out, closing the door behind him. I let out a long breath, my shoulders sinking. I hadn't expected anything different from him, but it was still disappointing. I almost wished he'd been mad at me or something. At least if he'd exploded at me, we could have addressed what had happened. But no, we'd let this sit and fester between us until the end of time, which I was certain Kaden could do.

I WOKE ALMOST EXACTLY at dawn, feeling much more aware and alert, and I sprung out of bed to get ready. I showered and dressed, but skipped breakfast, still too guilty to face Stella. There was no avoiding Kaden though. He stood at the door of the van that was parked in his driveway, talking with Clayton in a low tone. I swallowed, realizing there were other people in the van too. Would they say anything about the other night? Maybe we could all just pretend it never happened and move on like Kaden had done. I was starting to think that was the best move.

When Kaden saw me approaching, he fell silent and let

his eyes roam over me, although not in a sensual way. More like a dad who was checking to make sure my outfit wasn't too sexy for a date. "Be careful today," he said. "With the other packs looking for us, it's dangerous to even be leaving in a vehicle. They could easily track you back here."

"You're not going?" I asked.

Kaden shook his head. His eyes were back to being completely emotionless as he held my gaze. "Are you willing to put your life on the line to help a pack that isn't even yours?"

I nodded and steeled myself, lifting my chin as I stared back into Kaden's eyes. "I'd give my life for this pack if need be."

I meant every word too. He'd made sure to make the distinction that this wasn't my pack, but this felt like the place where I *belonged*. Even with my mortification over the mating frenzy, I wanted to be one of them, and I'd spend as much time as Kaden needed to prove myself a worthy member.

Kaden's eyes held mine for a beat longer, as if testing my sincerity. I let it all show in my face and eventually, he nodded. "Get in the van."

He walked away without another word. *Back to normal,* I thought and climbed into the van. There were six wolves total, most of them Kaden's friends. Clayton was driving, and I was sharing an aisle of seats with Jack and another guy I'd seen around town, who was about the size as Kaden, aka big and muscular, except his hair was long and blond, almost like a surfer. When I glanced behind me to the back row, I noted two pack members I'd only seen once or twice. They looked like warrior twins, both with caramel-colored hair and bright green eyes.

The female gave me a smile, and there was nothing soft in it. "Welcome aboard. I'm Harper. This is my brother, Dane."

"Ayla," I said, inclining my head.

"Oh, I know who you are, trust me," Harper said, grinning like she knew a private joke. "After the other night, everyone knows who you are."

Jack cleared his throat. "Yeah, about that. I'm really sorry, Ayla. I didn't realize..."

My cheeks burned with mortification. "It's okay. Really."

He rubbed the back of his neck. "Right. But seriously, I had no idea you were in heat, or that you were Kaden's woman."

"I'm definitely not *his* woman," I sputtered.

"That bite mark on your neck says otherwise," the guy next to Jack said. "I'm Tanner, by the way. I'd shake your hand but I don't want Kaden to bite mine off."

Everyone else in the van rumbled with laughter, except for me. I wanted to sink down through the floor of the car and melt into the ground. They had no idea of the truth—that Kaden didn't really want me. Not like that.

Clayton got in the van and snapped his head around. "Are these pups bothering you, Ayla? Should I make them get out and run alongside the van?"

I ducked my head with a small smile. Good old Clayton, always looking out for me like a big brother. And to think I'd once been annoyed at having him always watching my back. "No, it's fine."

He shrugged his big, broad shoulders as he turned back to the front. "Okay, but just say the word and they're out."

"Aw, we're just having a bit of fun." Harper patted me on the shoulder. "I'm just happy we have another girl in the group, anyway."

"Especially one that puts Kaden in his place," Tanner added with a grin.

I relaxed a little then, realizing they weren't teasing me to embarrass me, but more as a show of camaraderie. I'd spent so much of my life being bullied, I hadn't noticed the difference at first. This was what it felt like to have friends. To be part of a real pack.

"Everyone buckled up?" Clayton asked, eyes meeting ours in the rearview mirror, and the corners of his brown eyes crinkled with a smile. No one bothered to answer him, and he pulled out of Kaden's driveway.

"What kind of supplies do we need?" I asked, once we were on the road. Excitement thrummed through me now that I realized we were actually leaving pack territory—my first time since being brought here. I might actually get some answers, for once.

"Anything we can't get easily in the town," Tanner said and looked as if he expected me to be satisfied with that answer. *Duh, that much was obvious.*

"We have safe house drop sites all over the province," Jack added. "Our supplies are dropped off by people we work for or buy from, and once or twice a month we do a supply run."

Province. I didn't know if Jack meant to let that slip, but I clung onto it like a lifeline. It was the first real hint I'd gotten of where we were. Province meant that we were in Canada, not the US. "Which province?"

Jack shot me a sharp look. *Busted.*

Harper laughed from the backseat. "They really haven't told you much, have they? We're in Manitoba. Have you ever heard of the Narcisse Snake Dens?"

I frowned. "No."

Harper leaned forward, putting her arms on the back of my seat. "It's full of red-sided garter snakes. Gotta love them. They hide in these dens in the winter and reappear in spring. We have the largest number of red-sided garter snakes in the world in one place. You should visit sometime. It's a big conservation now since they're lower in numbers, and it's a cool place to visit."

"What happened?" I asked. Garter snakes were everywhere, why would they be concerned about conservation? "To the snakes, I mean. Why do they need conservation?" I added when Harper cocked her head at me in a silent question.

"Big frost killed a bunch of them before they could winter down a couple of decades ago, and some ecologists got worried. Highway 17 cuts right across their path to the dens, and nearly ten thousand were hit by cars every year until we made tunnels for the snakes to go under. Now it's a bad year if even a thousand are hit." She sounded proud of the fact like it was something she'd helped with.

"How do you know all of this?" I knew the Ophiuchus pack was called the "snake bearers," and Kaden had that snake tattoo on his arm, but I didn't know much more than that.

"The Narcisse Snake Dens are part of Ophiuchus pack lands, along with the other wildlife areas around it," Harper said. "One of the tasks we give teen pack members is to run maintenance on the fences to stop the snakes from getting hit."

I supposed that made sense. The Cancer pack protected its lands too, including the wildlife—especially the crabs—in the area. "Even Kaden?"

"Oh yeah, he was the best at it," Jack said with a grin.

I could hardly imagine a young Kaden stopping traffic to help a snake cross a highway. Then again, he was the same person who had a telescope up on the roof of his house to look at the stars. There was so much more to him below the grumpy surface, and I desperately wished I could get to know that side of him. *Not that you'll get a chance now*, my brain made sure to supply. I shoved the thought away and made an awkward joke instead. "And here I thought there was another reason they called you snake charmers."

Harper waggled her eyebrows at me. "From what I heard, you're the one charming snakes. Kaden's snake, anyway."

The entire van chuckled at that and I grinned and shook

my head. The laughter died down when Clayton called out, "Be on the lookout. We're leaving pack lands."

I peered out of the windows, but all I saw was forest on either side of the road. Everyone seemed to have a sixth sense about it, and I had no clue how they could tell. There weren't any visible markers, and I didn't see any of the other shifters looking for visible clues. They all just nodded, and Tanner clenched his hand into a fist.

"How do you know?" I asked.

"It's a pack thing," Tanner said. Wasn't he just being Mr. Forthcoming with his information today?

"The alpha marks the territory," Jack added.

"You mean marks like...he pees?" I asked. All six of them laughed, and I looked around at them, waiting for them to tell me.

Jack shook his head and his elbow found my side. "Do they do that in the Cancer pack? I know the Zodiac Wolves are backward, but I didn't think they were *that* backward."

I huffed out a breath and shook my head. *Fine, let them keep their secrets.* It was probably just another thing that only pack members knew about.

We idly chatted as we drove and I was surprised by how easy it was to talk to them. They didn't exclude me from the conversation. If I'd been with my old pack, it would have been a silent, long drive and it would have been made extremely clear that I wasn't supposed to talk to anyone, and no one would talk to me.

We arrived at a city after about an hour, and Clayton pulled into a storage facility area. It was huge, rows upon rows of metal buildings. I'd never think that a storage facility could take up an entire block, but I'd never spent much time in a city either.

Clayton backed the van up to a storage unit. We'd taken so many turns I had no doubt I would get lost trying to get out on my own. When he parked, everyone jumped into motion.

"Up and at 'em," Jack said, as I took my seatbelt off. "We don't have all day."

We all quickly unloaded from the van. Clayton unlocked the storage unit and pulled it open, while Dane, the quiet one, opened the back of the van. The unit was stuffed with boxes, and they started piling them into the back of the van. I went to help, but then the hairs stood up at the back of my neck, and I looked around. That usually only happened when someone was watching, but I couldn't see anyone. The other shifters seemed immune to it, and I shook the feeling off.

I grabbed a box, but a hand on my shoulder stopped me. Harper motioned me a few feet away. I frowned at her. "What is it?"

The joking air that seemed to surround the female shifter had all but evaporated. She looked at me, and her eyes suddenly seemed much older than her years. I didn't know how old she was, but with those eyes alone, I would have said at least forty, though she didn't look a day over her mid-twenties. "If you want to leave, now would be the best time."

I stared at her, mouth wide open. Her words didn't quite compute.

"None of us will try to stop you," she added. "We don't think it's right that Kaden's forcing you to stay with us like a prisoner. He's a good alpha but he gets ideas in his head about the Leo pack, and he won't see reason when it comes to them."

It hit me all at once. I'd been so caught up in training and everything else that I'd managed to forget I'd spent the first few days with the Ophiuchus pack in a cell. "You mean, run away?" I asked. "How would you even explain it to Kaden?"

"We've all agreed that we'll say you slipped past us at a gas station after asking to go to the bathroom. By the time we thought to check on you, you were long gone."

"You've really thought about this, haven't you?" I cocked my head at her, surprised and also pleased by her kindness. It was comforting to know they'd thought about me long enough to realize I might not be comfortable being held captive in their pack lands.

I couldn't deny that the idea of going somewhere else was tempting. I'd be free from Kaden and his moods, free from being the town's janitor, free from working so hard to prove myself worthy. But then I thought about leaving Coronis and my chest clenched. The small town had grown on me, and all of its occupants had as well. I'd take it all, even if it included being bait for the Leo pack.

Even if it meant putting up with Kaden's rejection.

I shook my head and smiled at Harper. "Thank you for

the offer, I really appreciate it. But I think I've finally found my place, and it's with the Ophiuchus pack. I hope one day I'll be allowed to join you as a full member."

"I hope so too." Harper patted me on the shoulder before turning to go help with the rest of the boxes.

As I went to join her, movement caught at the corner of my eye. I swiveled my head around to catch the sight—and scent—of new shifters. There were six of them, and they weren't from the Ophiuchus pack.

I had a feeling they were here for me.

CHAPTER TWENTY-SIX

ADRENALINE COURSED through my body as the six wolves began stalking toward us. As they got closer, I saw that several had Aries symbols like the shifters in the woods, but there were a few that had Taurus symbols as well. A spike of anger followed hot on the adrenaline. Still no Leos. Jordan wouldn't send any of his own pack after me, just his grunts. I wasn't worth his own time either, that much was clear.

When I glanced around, I realized that everyone but me had shifted. I let my wolf unfurl, bones reforming, fur covering my skin, teeth turning to fangs. It happened quickly now, my clothes tearing and falling off me as my body changed. When I was standing on four legs instead of two, I let off a long, menacing growl at the wolves surrounding us.

Everyone suddenly jumped into action, leaping forward, teeth bared. The air filled with the sounds of fighting, growling, and snapping. Harper burst out from the storage container, and I watched as she snarled and threw herself directly into the path of the attacking Aries shifters. I was in the thick of it too, ready to defend myself and the people I'd endangered by being with me. As members of the same pack, they could communicate telepathically, all except for me. But I wouldn't let that stop me.

Kaden should never have let me out of the pack lands, I thought, as I chomped on the leg of a Taurus wolf.

Out of the corner of my eye, I saw an Aries shifter preparing to charge right for Harper, and I felt the ghost of the pain from when I'd been hit by that same move in the woods. Harper would be knocked head-on with it.

No! I leaped forward before I could think to do anything else, and slammed into Harper just as the ram charge hit, knocking her out of the way. For a moment, I didn't feel anything as we fell in a tangle of fur and limbs. I braced for the overwhelming pain of before, but it felt mild in comparison. The charge must have just clipped me, the rest of it hitting dead air.

I nuzzled Harper with my nose, smelling her for injury, checking to see if she was all right. She nudged her head against me, her caramel-colored tail swishing, and in her eyes, I saw gratitude. We both turned back, preparing to join the fight again.

I had one thing going for me: they wanted me alive. I had the best chance of surviving out of anyone here, and even though I wasn't an official pack member yet, I felt a strong sense of loyalty to the others.

The wolf that had charged us had already joined the fight again, going against Clayton with another Aries wolf. *No, you don't,* I thought. *You're not hurting anyone else.*

I watched, enhanced senses picking up the perfect time to duck in. *There.* An opening. I lunged forward and bit into the neck of the Aries that had attacked Harper. He was so focused on fighting Clayton that he didn't notice that he'd left himself wide open for a side attack. There was a crunch and the soft give of flesh beneath my jaws, along with the taste of hot blood coating my tongue. The Aries shifter yelped and ripped himself out of my grip in a feeble attempt to escape. It did nothing but hasten the shifter's death, and I didn't even have time to watch him fall to the ground before I joined the fighting once more.

My contribution seemed to have done something because the Ophiuchus wolves were winning, I saw two more of the wolves on the ground, unmoving. The rest of the Taurus and Aries wolves stepped back as we swelled together, growling and snapping at the wolves, and they turned tail and ran. I watched them go, satisfaction thrumming through my veins alongside the rush of adrenaline.

Everyone around me began to shift back, and I followed suit. I scanned over everyone, trying to see if anyone was hurt. No one seemed to be mortally wounded. Just a few scrapes and bruises. Jack and Clayton both were bleeding, but nothing that a shifter couldn't heal.

"Let's get out of here," Clayton said. "We don't have much time before they come back with reinforcements."

We all voiced agreement before getting the rest of the

supplies loaded up. We were all buck naked, but that didn't matter—what mattered was getting this done as quickly as possible. Once finished, Clayton passed out spare jackets and blankets to all of us, and we piled back into the van.

As we drove away, a thought struck me. "Will they be able to track us back to Coronis?"

"Nope," Harper said. She was sitting beside me in the van this time, with Tanner in the back. "They won't be able to track us once we get back into pack territory." She cocked her head, studying me with an odd expression on her face.

"What?" I asked.

"You saved my life. I thought I was going to be hit with the Aries' ram charge for sure, but you knocked me out of the way. It was a damn fool thing to do. You almost got hit yourself."

"I've been hit with it before, and I walked away." *Not without Kaden's help,* my mind helpfully reminded me, but I shoved that thought out of the way. I didn't need to be thinking anything at all about Kaden right now. He wasn't even here. "No one else should have to go through that pain."

Harper observed me for a few moments longer, and then turned to look out the window. She didn't say another thing for the rest of the drive, and I found that I already missed her tough smile. Everyone was pretty subdued, in fact. I wanted to talk with them to help the jitter of the fight fade, or to apologize for putting everyone in danger, but I didn't want to interrupt their thoughts.

We got back to Coronis on a return trip that seemed to

take twice as long as the one to the storage facility, and Clayton pulled right back up into Kaden's driveway. Where Kaden stood with his arms crossed, his muscles bulging, and his jaw clenched.

As we began piling out, I watched Kaden's face. His frown deepened as he took in our half-dressed states and the blood all over us—and then he charged forward. He grabbed my arm and dragged me to the side, his gaze raking down my body, which I'd wrapped up as best I could in a small blanket.

"What happened?" he growled. "Are you injured?"

I yanked my arm away from him and adjusted the blanket, covering myself better. "We were attacked, but I'm fine. I don't need you to heal me, if that's what you're worried about."

His lips pressed into a tight line, and then he asked, "Aries again?"

"And some Taurus too."

He swore under his breath and turned to Harper, who watched us with wide eyes. "Did you ask her?"

Harper stood a little taller under her alpha's scrutiny and nodded. "I did, but she refused. She said she wants to remain with the pack."

What? I blinked between them, my brain still struggling to catch up. Surely, *surely*, this wasn't what it sounded like.

"How did she perform in a fight?" Kaden asked.

Harper grinned. "Good. Better than good, actually. She saved my life and even killed one of the Aries wolves."

"What are you talking about?" I asked, getting right up in Kaden's face. "Was this some kind of test?"

Kaden looked down at me with no emotion on his perfect face. I could hardly believe that only hours earlier we'd been naked together. "Yes, a loyalty test for potential recruits. Everyone has to go through it. The way is cleared for the recruit to leave and even betray the pack if they wanted to, so we can see their true loyalties and motivations."

"And the attack?" I practically spat at him. "Was that part of the test too?"

"No, the attack wasn't part of it, but now no one will doubt you."

"No one will doubt me? Who would be left to doubt me if they'd all been killed?" I shoved my finger into his chest. "You put *everyone* in danger just to prove my loyalty. Your stupid test could have cost all of them their lives!"

"Careful," Kaden growled deep in his chest. "Remember who you're talking to."

Part of me wanted to back down in the face of that power. He'd threatened to kill me for less before, but now I didn't care. Besides, I knew he would never really hurt me. Not physically anyway. And I was exhausted, covered in blood, and really sick of his fucking attitude.

I put my hands on my hips. "Oh, I remember, alpha. I just watched members of *your* pack fight for their lives, all to defend me in a battle that didn't need to happen. You should never have let me leave the pack lands, or at the very least you could have had the balls to come with us since you knew what might happen. So you can shove your authority up your ass."

His eyebrows darted up at that, and all the other shifters gaped at me like I'd lost my damn mind. Fuck it, I was pretty sure my mind was long gone at this point, and I was beyond caring. I just didn't want anyone else to die for me.

I was pretty sure Kaden was about to snap and go off on me, and I knew his anger would be terrifying. But he just crossed those meaty arms and stared at me so long I thought he wasn't going to answer at all.

"You're right," he said, and my mouth fell open. Was the sky falling, or had Kaden just admitted I was *right*? "I shouldn't have put you or the others in danger," he continued, while his hand reached up like he was going to touch my face before he dropped it again. "At the very least, I should have been there to protect you. But I had to be sure you were loyal before I could invite you to join the pack."

I took a step back. "You...what?"

Kaden's eyes had a certain gleam to them, one I hadn't seen before. It looked almost like satisfaction. "You've proven your loyalty, and passed all of our tests. I'm inviting you to become a true member of the Ophiuchus pack, if you so desire."

I stared at him for a few moments, elation running through my veins. This was all I had wanted for so long, ever since Stella had taken me on a tour of Coronis. My anger faded and a grin broke across my face as I took in the sincerity in Kaden's voice. He was really offering this to me.

Me, who had always been rejected and unwanted. Until now.

Before I could think better of it, I lunged forward and wrapped my arms around Kaden. "Thank you."

He huffed out a breath, caught off guard, standing as stiff as a board as I hugged him. "What the hell are you doing?"

"We call them hugs, Kaden," I said. "They're used to show gratitude among people who aren't emotionally stunted."

"You're insufferable," Kaden said, but he didn't push me away either.

I pulled back and the other shifters came forward to congratulate me, welcoming me to the pack. Kaden watched us with a look on his face that I thought might actually be pride. *My alpha*, I thought as warmth spread through me. But I couldn't stop the heartbreaking thought that followed it.

He should be my mate too.

CHAPTER TWENTY-SEVEN

MEET us in town at dusk, the note said. I'd read over it so many times, the words had all blurred together into a nonsensical mess in my head. After returning from our supply run, I'd had a quick lunch and taken a shower, then found the note waiting for me on my bed. It looked like Stella's handwriting, not Kaden's, and I wasn't sure what to make of it.

Once the sun dipped below the horizon, I finally left the house. As I stepped outside, I heard distant music, which sounded like it was coming from the center of town. I'd heard similar noise during the night of the full moon, but there wasn't anything to celebrate today.

I stopped at the edge of the town square and stared. Every Ophiuchus shifter who lived in Coronis seemed to be there on the grass. Tables had been set up, laden with food and drinks, and I watched for a few moments as everyone milled around, chatting and smiling. The atmosphere was completely relaxed as if the entire day had been a bad dream.

Stella broke away from the crowd and began walking toward me with a huge smile. "Come on," she said, motioning me toward the group of people.

I followed her toward the tables, and several shifters looked up at me. An older woman walked up to me, someone I'd never met before. "Ayla," she said, grinning at me as if we were long-lost friends instead of complete strangers. "Welcome to the pack!"

"Thank you," I said, and hurried after Stella toward the food table. If I was going to talk to everyone in the Ophiuchus pack, I at least wanted to eat while I was doing it. A few more shifters stopped me on the way, offering their congratulations, and it was all very kind but overwhelming too.

"Ayla!"

I turned to find Stella coming toward me with two plates of food and let out a relieved sigh.

She pushed one into my hands with a grin. "You look like you need this."

"What's going on?" I gestured around the park with my fork. "What's this for?"

Stella laughed. "It's for you, silly. Your 'welcome to the pack' feast."

I stared at her for a few moments, unable to speak past the sudden tightness in my throat. I'd never so much as had a birthday party in my life. At most, Wesley and Mira would give me gifts and wish me happy birthday, but Dad had never seen much point in celebrating something that he saw as a mistake. No one else had bothered to take the time, either.

"This..." I paused, a sudden wave of emotion overwhelming me. It was too much. I'd never *belonged* to this extent before. I still could hardly believe it. I was part of the Ophiuchus pack, and I had a family now.

Stella seemed to understand what I was feeling, because she locked arms with me and led me over to a quieter part of the park, away from most of the people. "I'm sorry I wasn't able to tell you about the test. I felt so bad, just sending you into that without any warning. And then you were attacked... I should have been there."

"It's all right." Now that the anger had faded, I understood Kaden's actions a little better. Kaden's priority was the pack, and he had to make sure I was loyal before he could completely trust me to be a part of it. He'd given me the option to run away, and I suspected he'd remained behind during the test so I wouldn't be swayed in any way by him being there. "I'm just glad no one got injured."

"Usually there would have been even more tests, you know," she said. "It usually takes a year or two to get an invite to the pack. But since you defended the others and saved Harper's life, Kaden told the pack elders that no further tests were required."

I tilted my head as I considered what she'd said. The Cancer pack had elders too, which were supposed to advise my father, though he usually ignored them. It sounded like the Ophiuchus elders might have more sway here. But the more pressing question was, had Kaden known we might be attacked? Had he planned it this way all along so I'd get accepted into the pack faster?

"I'm so happy you get to join us," Stella said, reaching forward and squeezing my hand.

"Me too."

Another group of shifters came forward, and I recognized Clayton's mate, Grant, among them. "Welcome to the pack," he said and shook my hand as if this was a job interview. "I knew you'd pass the tests too."

I remembered that he'd been an outsider too, and wondered how long it had taken him. Before I could ask about his own tests, other shifters came forward to say hello to me, and I flashed big smiles at all of them, trying to remember everyone's names.

I could get used to this, I decided after a few more people came up to introduce themselves. Their enthusiasm was a bit overwhelming, but it was so nice feeling like I belonged somewhere. Somewhere where no one had ever even mentioned my half-human side, or my red hair, or treated me like dirt. Yes, I could definitely get used to this.

"So am I an official member, just like that?" I asked once we had a moment alone again.

"Not yet. You need to go through the initiation ritual. Then you'll be a true member of the pack."

"What is the ritual?" I asked, my heartbeat picking up at the thought. How did they do it, with no Sun Witches to perform the spell?

Stella just gave me a mysterious smile. "You'll see. It's nothing bad, don't worry."

Anytime someone told me not to worry it only made me worry more. I sighed and finished up my food, but this time when I looked up I found Kaden staring at me. I hadn't seen him up until now, and when he turned away to talk to Clayton, I let my eyes linger on his profile. Need fluttered inside my stomach, but it was different from the other night. There was no heat forcing it this time. It was all me.

He looked back and I held his gaze, even as I felt my cheeks color at getting caught staring. Even from this distance, sparks flew between us, and I suddenly found it harder to breathe. Or sit still. I forced myself to look away again, even as I felt his gaze on the back of my neck. Heart pounding, I found myself glancing back, my eyes drawn back to him without fail, even as I conversed with several other shifters.

We were drawn to each other, there was no question about it. I wanted to go to him, to figure out exactly what he was thinking as he stared at me like that, but there wasn't time in between all of the conversations. Stella thankfully stayed by my side and helped me not get overwhelmed. I glanced over at Kaden as Stella finished introducing me to the mother of one of her students.

Too bad he isn't my true mate, I thought again, and a wave of sadness rolled through me at the realization. He was everything an alpha should be, and I couldn't deny the way I felt about him. But no, I'd gotten that psychopath Jordan instead. *The world really isn't fair, is it?* I thought with a sigh and then turned back when a small hand tugged at my own.

I grinned down at the little shifter beaming up at me and shoved the sadness away. Now wasn't the time to be thinking about that. I'd gotten everything else I wanted—a family, a home, and a pack where I could feel accepted and safe. I should be celebrating, not pining for the one thing I didn't get.

Finally, after what seemed like hours of endless introductions and a wash of faces that all blended into one, Kaden called for silence. The moon was high in the night sky, still almost full, and it cast enough light over everyone gathered. He held something in his hands, a long object that looked kind of like a staff. The pack gathered around, and Kaden stopped in front of me.

"Ayla Beros, do you wish to become a true member of the Ophiuchus pack?" he asked.

I took a closer look at the staff. It was made of metal and there was a strange ridge on it, spiraling all the way down. *A snake,* I realized as he tilted it up. I swallowed hard and said, "Yes, I do."

At my words, the bronze began *shifting,* and I took an involuntary step back as the snake came alive. I could tell it wasn't real, something born of magic, but I didn't want it coming anywhere near me.

"What's that?" I asked as Kaden brought it closer to me. "No, thank you. I don't do snakes."

Kaden gave me a hard look. "Don't be a chicken. Hold out your arm."

I grimaced and held my arm out. He touched the staff to my palm and the snake slithered onto it. It felt cool, like the metal it was made from. He guided the snake to wrap around my arm, and then let the tail end of it coil around his own arm. It was almost like the ritual with the Sun Witches, where they tied the mated pairs together. I doubted the cloth felt like cold snakeskin, though. I shuddered, and then Kaden began speaking. I forgot my discomfort as he began the oath.

"Do you swear to uphold loyalty to the Ophiuchus Pack until your last breath?" he asked. "To become one with the pack and its members, giving up your birth pack, never to look back to them for guidance or support?"

Not a problem, I thought, before I said, "I do."

Kaden's voice was low as he continued the ritual. "Repeat after me: I, Ayla Beros, accept the offering of the snake."

I repeated his words, and the snake tightened its hold around me, pressing Kaden's fingers into my arm almost hard enough to bruise. The snake looked up at me, eyes dull and clearly not alive, but I had the sense that *something* in there was giving me an appraising look. Then, faster than I could think to pull away, it struck, sinking its fangs into my upper arm. I jumped and let out a surprised, "Ow!"

Kaden's fingers tightened against my arm, him this time, not the snake. "Hold still." A moment later, the snake drew back and flicked a tongue out at me before sliding back down my arm. "You're a part of the pack now."

Kaden released me, and I watched as the twin bites

faded into a glowing Ophiuchus symbol, the same mark that adorned every other shifter in the pack. At the same time, I felt the poison from the snake's bite seeping into my veins, and I had a moment of panic before I realized it didn't hurt. I could feel it merging into my bloodstream, making me stronger.

I twisted my arm to look at the pack mark better. I glanced up to meet Kaden's eyes, and there was nothing but satisfaction in his gaze.

I was one of the snake bearers now.

CHAPTER TWENTY-EIGHT

IT WAS late into the night when the party finally began to wind down. Shifters loved to party at night under the moon, but eventually, most people headed to bed, and now it was our turn.

"Let's go home," Stella said, covering her mouth with a yawn. "I feel like my feet might fall off after all that dancing."

Home. It certainly felt like it now. Although things would change now that I was a full member of the pack. I wouldn't need guards trailing after me anymore, and I would probably have to find another place to live at some point. I couldn't imagine Kaden would want me there for much longer.

"I'm so excited you're one of us now," Stella said, as we walked back to the house. "I'll have to show you how your poison bite and healing work."

I blushed as I remembered Kaden's tongue licking my wound closed. "I know a bit about those already."

"Right, of course. I'm sorry I bit you at the Convergence, but I made sure not to give you too much poison. I just wanted to knock you out, not kill you."

I almost opened my mouth to correct her but thought better of it. What had happened between Kaden and me should remain between us. I wasn't sure how much everyone else knew, but I knew that Kaden probably didn't want it all broadcasted.

"Oh, another good thing," Stella continued. "Becoming a pack member will also stop you from going into heat every month. I know you had some issues with that at the last full moon. Now you'll only have to worry about that once a year."

"That's a relief." Once a year was much more manageable. Except... Was that why Kaden had rushed to make me a pack member, to avoid having to deal with me going into heat again? My chest tightened at the thought that this was the real reason he'd fought for me to join so quickly. Not because I deserved it, or because I'd proved myself loyal, but because he didn't want to have to fuck me again next month.

We made it back to the house, and there was no sign of Kaden anywhere, though he'd left the party a while before we did. I wondered where Kaden had gone off to, if he was busy sulking in his room or taking a brooding walk through the forest, doing whatever alphas did to mark the park territory.

I sat on my bed after saying goodnight to Stella and

touched the pack mark on my arm. I'd never carried the Cancer symbol, nor had access to the crab armor, but now I felt power running through my veins from the Ophiuchus healing lick and poison bite. I was really one of them, though I had a feeling I would never like snakes the way some of them did.

But did I truly deserve to be one of them?

A thump on my roof startled me. My mind immediately flew to an attack, and my heart started pounding. It came again, and I ran out of my room to see if either Stella or Kaden had heard it. Neither of their doors was open. I looked at Stella's door and then turned to Kaden's. I walked up to the door and knocked. "Kaden? Are you in there?"

No answer. I tried the handle. I had never been in his room since I was forbidden to even clean it. The door was unlocked, and I held my breath as I opened it just a crack. No one was inside. I looked around, finding it surprisingly clean and spare, without many personal touches like Stella's room had. I did see a picture of what must have been his parents sitting on the desk next to a closed laptop.

"Kaden?" I asked again, just to be sure. The sliding door onto the patio was open, and I peered outside. Why was his door open? I walked out onto the balcony and looked up. It was a cloudless night, the stars glimmering brightly, and the moon still cast a pleasant glow over everything. I stared at it for a few moments before something caught my eye. A ladder. I remembered Kaden saying he had a telescope on the roof, and felt silly for thinking an attacker would be able to make it up there without alerting anyone.

I moved to the other side of the balcony where I could see him sitting on a flatter portion of the roof, his eye pressed to the lens of the telescope. On impulse, I climbed up to join him. I had to ask him about the real reason he'd made me a pack member, or I'd never be able to get any sleep.

He didn't look up at me until I'd settled right beside him, though he must have heard me coming from a mile away. "I told you not to enter my room."

"I heard something and went to investigate." When he only grunted in response, I asked, "What are you looking at?"

"The Ophiuchus constellation is bright tonight." He motioned me forward and leaned away so I could peer through the telescope.

I didn't know exactly what I was looking for and pulled back. It was just a jumble of bright stars to me. "Pretty."

He shook his head with a scowl. "It's right underneath the Hercules constellation, which I'm sure you're more familiar with. Ophiuchus comes from the Greek word that means serpent-bearer. It looks like a man holding a snake."

"Right." I looked back into the telescope, squinting at the stars and trying to see anything that resembled a man. Kaden was close enough that I felt the heat of his body in the few inches of space that separated us, and it was hard for me to focus on anything else. The fact that he was my alpha now should have made me hesitant, but instead, it only made me crave him more.

When I looked at Kaden, his eyes were fixed on me,

their dark depths glittering in the light of the moon. "How does it feel to be one of us now?"

"It feels good," I said. "But Stella told me that now that I'm in the pack I won't go into heat every month."

"That's true."

I lifted my chin and held his gaze. "Kaden, I have to know. Is that the only reason you made me a member of the pack? To stop me from going into heat so often?"

Kaden's jaw clenched as if he hadn't expected me to be that blunt. "Not the only reason. I'd planned to test you from the moment we captured you, but the full moon did bring the timetable up."

I huffed. "I knew it was a little too convenient. Would I even be a member now if not for my heat?"

"I did it to protect you," Kaden growled.

I let out a bitter laugh. "Was it really so bad? What happened between us? Is my body really so repulsive to you?"

Kaden closed his eyes and inhaled sharply. "No. It's not what you think."

"Then *what?*" I reached out and captured Kaden's jaw in my hand, needing him to open his eyes. I wanted to see the truth in them. He flinched as if my touch had hurt him, and I quickly drew my hand back, my heart breaking at the sight.

I stood up, unable to bear being around his rejection for another second. But as I started to walk away, he rose and took a step toward me.

"Ayla." His hand closed around my wrist, and I turned

back to face him. Inside his eyes, I saw my own feelings reflected. Guilt, lust, and no small amount of need. He dragged me closer, and before I even knew what was happening, his lips crashed against mine.

His hand slid up to cup the back of my head, and he pulled me close so our bodies were flush. I groaned into the kiss, melting against him as his lips moved across mine. He held me like I belonged to him, while his tongue stroked my own, an erotic dance that sent heat to my core. Even during our frenzied night of sex, he'd never once kissed me, and now I knew I'd been missing out on something incredible.

I could drown in this forever, I thought as his mouth claimed mine over and over. I couldn't breathe, couldn't think, couldn't move—and couldn't care less. He kissed me like he'd been dying to do this for years, gripping my hair to tilt my head exactly the way he wanted me. He kissed me like he'd fucked me, like he couldn't control himself, like an animal driven by instinct alone—and I kissed him back the same way.

Then Kaden suddenly jerked back, breaking our connection while putting distance between us like he'd been burned. "No. I can't."

I blinked and touched my lips, still tasting him on them. "Can't, or won't?"

"*Won't,*" Kaden said, shaking his head. "I refuse to be with someone who is mated to someone else. I've gone through that once before, and I will never do it again. It nearly killed me the first time."

I sucked in a deep breath at the revelation. "I don't feel

anything for my mate. Please, trust me when I say that. I don't *want* him. I'd rather die than be with him."

"It doesn't matter, the bond will always be there. If Jordan showed up right now and snapped his fingers, you'd run right to his side. It isn't a matter of wanting him or not."

I winced. "I wish you had more faith in me than that."

Kaden pinched the bridge of his nose between his fingers before looking back at me, his face haunted. "I was in love once with a girl named Eileen. We were childhood sweethearts, and everyone expected that we'd be mates when we became adults. But the mate bond never appeared between us." He shook his head. "We decided that it didn't matter. We'd make it work, and she would be the future alpha female.

"One day we went to trade with the Sagittarius pack. They're the only pack who has ever treated us kindly, and I've worked hard to build a good relationship with them. When the beta of their pack shifted, a mating bond appeared between him and Eileen. She fought it for as long as she could because she wanted to be with me, but it didn't matter. Our love wasn't enough, in the end. She had to go to her mate." Kaden looked me dead in the eye, and even though the words were vulnerable, his voice was hard. "It tore us apart, and it got to the point where it hurt for us to even look at each other. She joined the Sagittarius pack and I haven't seen her since. So no, Ayla, it isn't that I don't have faith in you. I've been down this road before and I'm never going down it again."

With those words, he walked past me toward the edge of the roof, while my heart pounded in my throat.

"Kaden, wait—" I said, but he was already gone.

He leaped off the edge of the roof and landed on the grass as if the drop was nothing, then disappeared into the forest behind the house. All I could do was watch him go, while my soul was shattered into a million pieces. What could I have said to him anyway? It was clear he would never believe that I wanted only him. Worst of all, if I was completely honest with myself, I wasn't sure what would happen if I saw Jordan again. The mate bond had faded to a dull hum that I managed to ignore on a daily basis, but I had a feeling if Jordan appeared in front of me it would be a lot harder to resist. I couldn't blame Kaden for not wanting to risk that chance.

Besides, as the alpha, he had to find his own mate. His own alpha female, who would bear his children and lead the pack with him. Someone who wasn't me.

Jealousy tore through me at that thought, along with a deep sadness that brought me to my knees. How was I going to live in this pack while wanting my alpha with every fiber of my being? Or worse, watching him mate with someone else—while knowing I would forever be alone and unwanted?

CHAPTER TWENTY-NINE

IN THE MORNING, I walked downstairs to the kitchen and stopped dead in my tracks. Kaden was the last person I expected to see after he'd left last night, yet there he was, standing in front of the coffee maker in a shirt that clung to his muscles and jeans that hugged his perfect ass. I stared at him for a few seconds, feeling as if I was falling into a bottomless well of longing and loneliness. His dark hair was messy as if he hadn't slept well, and a scowl seemed to live on his face now. I jerked my gaze away before heading toward the fridge to find something to eat for breakfast.

He cleared his throat. "I need you at the community center."

"Good morning to you too," I grumbled. "Janitor duty again?"

Kaden didn't so much as glance at me again as he walked out the door. I threw my hands up as I watched him go. *Looks like everything is back to normal.* It was as if our kiss last night had never happened, except I still remembered the taste of him. With a sigh, I closed the fridge, and headed out after him.

The community center was in the middle of the town, and when I stepped inside I looked around at the clean space with pride. Thanks to me, it was looking more like a gathering place for the town and less like a giant storage shed that hadn't seen the light of day for years. The dust bunnies that had gathered in this place had been legendary. Not to mention the mold in the bathrooms. I shuddered just thinking about it. But the place still looked clean, so why was I here?

Clayton exited from a door, and he waved me over. "Good, you're here. Come inside, the others are waiting."

"Others?" I asked as I followed him into the room. "What's going on?"

Stella sat with Harper, Jack, Dane, and Tanner around a long table, while Kaden paced on the other side of it. Stella motioned for me to come sit by her, and I complied, glancing between everyone's faces. They all looked solemn, and I wondered if someone had died while I'd been asleep.

Once Clayton and I were seated, Kaden stopped pacing and turned to address us. "I've gathered you all here to discuss a plan to draw out the Leos. We can't sit around and let them attack us any time we leave our pack lands. The supply run yesterday taught us that much. But they also don't know exactly where we are, or how to get inside our borders, or they'd be here already."

"What do you plan to do?" Harper asked, from her spot next to her twin. I'd still never actually heard Dane speak.

"I'm going to contact them and ask the Leo alpha, Dixon, to meet us on neutral ground to give them Ayla." Kaden's eyes landed on me. "She'll be our bait."

I bit back my initial reaction, which was to say 'no fucking way.' It *was* what I'd agreed to, way back when Kaden had me in a cell, but that didn't mean I was happy about it. So many things could go wrong, things that would end up with me as a prisoner of the Leo pack. Or dead.

"Are you sure they still want her?" Jack asked.

Kaden crossed his arms, the only one still standing, and he looked every inch the commanding alpha. "The Leo pack keeps sending people to capture her. The alpha heir won't stop searching for her until she's been found. She's his *mate*." He practically spat the last word.

"Yeah, but he rejected her," Stella said.

"And killed most of her pack," Tanner added.

"That won't stop him from needing to find her," Clayton said. "The draw toward a mate is unbearable. He'll want to find her, even if it's to try to break the bond."

"This is a fun trip down memory lane and all," I said, unable to hide the bitterness in my tone, "but can we get back to the part where I'm going to be bait. Are you actually planning to give me up?"

"Of course not," Kaden said as if I was being daft. "You'll just be the lure to get them to meet with us. I plan to challenge the alpha to a duel, and once I win, we'll wipe out the rest of the Leos."

"Are you really powerful enough to do that?" I asked. Fear set me on edge as I remembered the ferocity of the Leo alpha as he killed my father. Or how the Leos had attacked so swiftly, along with their allies, brutally taking down the rest of the pack within minutes. They were trained for battle, and there were a whole lot more of them than in the Ophiuchus pack.

"It won't be a problem," Kaden said.

I rolled my eyes. *Moon goddess save me from the arrogance of alphas,* I thought. "How can you be so sure you'll win?"

"Kaden is Moon Touched," Stella said. "All of the alphas in our pack have been, for as long as we can remember."

I blinked, then turned to look at Kaden again. That explained how he'd been unsurprised by my own strange power, but I was still shocked by the revelation. What sorts of magic did he have? And just how many more secrets was he keeping? "So your pack *does* have Moon Witch blood? That rumor is true?"

"A few of us still do, yes, though it's pretty rare now," Kaden said. "My family has always been the strongest line."

"How am I just finding out about this?" I asked.

"Now that you're a member of the pack, you can know the truth about us," Harper said, as she nudged her twin. "Our family has a little Moon Witch blood too. Dane here can look into a pool of moonlight and see the past sometimes."

My eyebrows darted up as Dane nodded, his lips

pressed into a tight line. I glanced around the rest of the table, wondering what else they could do.

"You asked once about the pack land boundaries," Clayton said. "Kaden's set up magical wards along the borders of our land, which keep us hidden and protect everyone inside. No one can track us back here or enter the area without our permission."

"He can also go invisible," Stella added, and I glanced over at her to see her wearing a mischievous smile. "We both can."

Well, that explained a lot. Kaden seemed to have the ability to eternally sneak up on me, even after I'd gotten my wolf unlocked and had my enhanced senses. And the number of times I'd felt like he was there, watching me... I narrowed my eyes at him, realizing he really had been watching all along.

"That's impressive, but is it enough to stand up against the Leos?" I asked. "I was there, you know. I had a front-row seat as the Leo alpha used his lion roar and made everyone either freeze or flee in panic. I still remember the spray of blood as he tore my father apart in front of me."

"It'll be enough," Kaden said.

"I have to agree with Ayla," Tanner said. "I think we're making a mistake going up against the Leos. We're safe here. They can't get to us as long as we remain inside the pack lands. Why risk all that?"

Kaden grabbed the back of a chair, leaning forward as he addressed us, his eyes intense. "Because we can't stay hidden in the pack lands forever. Even if we forget that Ayla will always be hunted by the Leos, or how they murdered my parents, this is a fight that will come to us, sooner or later. The Leos won't stop until all other packs bend to their rule, including ours."

"We don't know that," Tanner said. "We've hidden from them for centuries. Nothing needs to change now."

Kaden's hands tightened around the back of the chair so hard I thought he might break it. "The future of our pack depends on it. My parents recognized that. They saw that our numbers were dwindling, that we had fewer mates among our own pack, and that our long-term survival depended on rejoining the Zodiac Wolves so we could breed and trade with them. But the other packs don't want us, which is why we will force them to accept us as one of them. Even if it means wiping most of them off the face of the world."

"How does that make you any different from the Leos?" I asked, my spine stiffening at his words.

Kaden's eyes blazed as they landed on me. "Because we're doing it to survive. Not to rule."

I spread my hands wide. "It's all going to feel the same to those that are dead."

Kaden drew himself up a little taller. "Once the Leo pack falls, the others won't put up much resistance. We'll avoid as much unnecessary bloodshed as possible."

He had a point there. The Leo pack had always been one of the two pillars of the Zodiac Wolves, with the Cancer pack being the other one. But I still felt like the Ophiuchus pack was vastly outnumbered.

"What about the Moon Witches?" I asked. "Can't they help us against the other packs, like the Sun Witches are helping the other Leos?"

"We haven't seen them for decades," Stella said, shaking her head. "They must be in hiding from the Sun Witches and the other Zodiac Wolves. We have no idea how to even contact them."

Damn. I swallowed, my stomach twisting as my anxiety spiked high. I didn't like anything about this plan. There were so many things that could go wrong. But at the same time, I also understood Kaden's point that we couldn't hide here until the Leos eventually found us and wiped us out. Like they'd done to my former pack.

Everyone seemed to be waiting for me to say something. I was the crux of their plan, I realized, but they wouldn't force me to do anything I wasn't comfortable with either.

"Fine, use me as bait." I sat up straighter and met Kaden's eyes with resolve hardening my own. "All I want is vengeance against the Leo pack for killing Wesley—and I want Jordan dead. I can't do it myself because of the bond, but I will do whatever I can to help you end his life."

Clayton cleared his throat. "Ayla, there's something you need to know. If we kill the Leo alpha heir, the shock of it to your newly formed bond might kill you too."

I sucked in a deep breath. Fucking mating bond. It never ceased to give me problems. I considered what he said for only a second, but the choice was easy. "It's worth the risk. I can't live like this. I'd rather be dead than tied to that asshole forever."

Kaden's face darkened, until he looked almost murderous. "I'll make the arrangements."

We all glanced around at each other, the grim determination I felt echoing in everyone else's eyes. This really was it, the turning point we couldn't go back from. I was ready for it, more ready than I had ever been before.

Let the Leo pack try to take me. I'd go down kicking and screaming if I had to, and I'd take as many of those fuckers with me as I could.

* * *

THAT NIGHT, I couldn't sleep. I threw on some of my training sweats and headed outside, then did a quick lap of the town under the soft moonlight. I ran past all the places that had come to feel like home over the last few weeks and my throat tightened with emotion. I'd only just become a true member of the pack, and now I was about to put all of that at risk. I had no other choice though. I would never truly be free of the Leos until their pack was defeated—and my mate bond with Jordan was severed.

I stopped at the edge of town and closed my eyes, reaching for the bond I so often tried to ignore. It was there, always, like a chain wrapped around my waist, trying to drag me back to the Leos. *South*, it told me, urging me to head in the direction where Jordan must be. My mouth went dry as

I forcibly shook the feeling off, pushing the thought of my mate to the back of my mind.

How strong would the bond be once we faced each other in person again? Could I bear it, or would I throw myself at Jordan like some lovesick puppy? The thought terrified me more than anything else about this upcoming meeting. I had to harden my heart in preparation and make sure I could escape again if I had to.

For the next hour, I practiced teleporting between patches of moonlight, moving through the town so fast the buildings and trees were a blur. Over the last few weeks, I'd practiced this any chance I could, and I'd gotten so good I could land and instantly vanish again as long as I had a clear notion of where I wanted to go. I could also use my power for longer without getting tired. I wasn't sure I would have had the discipline to keep doing it without Kaden's combat training to remind me that even if it was hard, if you kept it up, you'd see results.

I stopped in a patch of moonlight to catch my breath, finally feeling the exhaustion set in. Maybe now I'd be able to sleep.

"I often wonder if he regrets it," Kaden said from behind me, making me jump.

I spun around, heart pounding in my throat. "Don't ever fucking sneak up on me again! How long have you been there?"

He gave me a one-shouldered shrug from where he stood, leaning against a tree with his arms crossed. "I like to watch you practice."

"Invisibility is not my favorite look on you," I muttered, then thought about what he'd said. "If who regrets what?"

"Your mate. The Leo alpha heir." Kaden cocked his head. "Does he lie in bed at night wishing he'd never rejected you?"

I snorted. "I doubt it. He only saw me as a half-human mutt, barely worthy of his notice."

"Then he's a fool. From the moment we met, I knew there was so much more to you."

His words turned me to mush inside. I'm sure he had no idea how much his praise meant to me. I'd received so little of it in my life that I clung to each word tightly. I took a step toward him, unable to stop myself.

"You're the only one who's ever really seen me," I said, my voice barely above a whisper. "Even when I came to you as a broken wolf who didn't truly know herself."

He reached up and took a piece of my red hair, then tucked it back behind my ear. "Little wolf, you were never broken, only beaten and bruised. All you needed was someone to believe in you."

Emotions welled up inside me, especially as I thought of what we were about to face. "Kaden, if I get captured..."

"You won't. You're Moon Touched, and I doubt the Leos know that. You can use your power to escape, along with your new Ophiuchus powers."

"I'm eager to learn to use them." I lifted my chin, trying to summon my bravery. "And maybe next time, I'll be the one healing *you*."

"Are you really so eager to lick me?" he asked, his voice turning low and sensual.

"Do you really want me to answer that?" I replied, suddenly breathless.

His gaze dropped to my mouth as if he was strongly considering it. Then he tore his eyes away and raked a hand through his hair. "No."

I was pretty sure we both knew the answer anyway. If it were up to me, we'd be rolling on the forest floor already, while I traced my tongue down his neck, along his snake tattoo, and finally around his thick cock. Was he thinking about the same thing?

"Kaden." I had to say something or I would regret it forever. "No matter what happens when we meet the Leos, I need you to know this. You're the one I want. Not him."

His brow furrowed and something like pain flashed across his face. "I know you think that now, but that will change when you're face to face with him."

"It won't." The rightness of my words gave me strength. "You believed in me before, please believe in me now."

"I wish I could, but there are some things we can't fight. I hope you prove me wrong." He shook his head. "You should head home."

"By myself?"

"I'm going to do a quick patrol of the wards."

"Right," I said, my hopes sinking faster than the Titanic. "I'll see you later."

I turned away and headed toward the house, feeling more raw than before. I'd put myself out there, telling Kaden how I felt about him, and been rejected once again. I couldn't really blame him either. If I knew he was mated to someone else, I'd guard my heart too.

As long as I was tied to Jordan, I could never be with Kaden. I had to break this mate bond—or risk forever losing the person I'd come to care about most.

CHAPTER THIRTY

THE LEO PACK agreed to meet with us in a week's time. Their pack lands were in Arizona, which was pretty far from the Ophiuchus territory in Manitoba, but they agreed to fly up to Canada for this meeting. On a private jet, naturally. The Leos would never settle for anything less.

The meeting was set at a small airstrip a few hours away, which was far enough for it to be neutral territory. Kaden convinced them to meet us at night, so I could use my power if needed to escape. The Sun Witches would also be weaker then, while those of us who were Moon Touched would be stronger. I prayed it would be enough, especially as the week passed and the hour of the meeting drew near.

With only hours to go, my stomach was all tangled up in knots. The whole pack seemed to be on edge, and who could blame them? It didn't help that I'd barely seen Kaden all week either. He'd been busy getting everything ready, while Stella and I had doubled down on training. She'd taught me to use both the healing lick and the poison bite, including how to regulate the amount of poison released from my fangs. I was as ready as I would ever be to face the Leos.

Then it was time to leave. I packed a bag, mostly to make it look like I really planned to go with the Leos. As I closed it up, I had the strangest feeling of nostalgia. The last time I'd gone to my room to pack my bags, my life had changed completely. I wondered if that would happen again, and prayed that if anything were to happen I would be able to stay with my new pack.

When I met Stella in the yard, there were several vehicles parked outside, but no sign of Kaden.

"He went early to scout the location and make sure the Leo pack doesn't have any traps in place. We'll make sure we have the upper hand this time." Her eyes blazed, and I knew she was thinking about her parent's deaths. The Leo alpha had a lot to pay for.

Stella climbed into an SUV and motioned for me to follow her. She sat in the back, and I wasn't surprised to find Clayton in the driver's seat. The van was packed with warriors, and there was another one just like it right behind us.

The drive was long, tense, and silent. Even Stella remained quiet. My hands were so sweaty I had to keep rubbing them on my jeans. I tried to focus on the view out the window, but I barely saw any of it. The last time I'd seen the Leos, I'd been running from them in terror. Now I was on my way to meet them head-on, and though I was still terrified, I wasn't the same girl I'd been then. I was stronger, and I wasn't alone. I had a pack that would protect me.

When we arrived, I saw Kaden standing with Harper and Dane. They all turned toward the vans as we parked in an empty field alongside the airstrip. Night had fallen, and there was very little here other than a small building with a tower and the runway, which had definitely seen better days, and beyond that, a dark forest.

We got out of the van, and Kaden walked over to us. "Are you ready?" He was asking both me and Stella, but his eyes were only on me.

"As ready as we can be," I said.

He nodded. "The Leos should be arriving in the next half hour. We have scouts patrolling the forest in case they try to approach that way instead. All we can do now is wait."

Stella took my hand. "Just remember, whatever happens, you're one of us now."

I gave her a warm smile, blinking back sudden tears. "Thank you."

The other shifters got into position around us, and we waited in silence as the waning moon rose behind clouds. Would there be enough moonlight for me to use my power? I hoped I wouldn't have to find out the hard way.

A gray wolf emerged from the forest and trotted over to Kaden, tongue lolling out the side of its mouth. It shifted back into a very naked Jack, who had zero shame as he let it all hang out. He was hot, no doubt about it, but he didn't make my heart race like Kaden did.

"There's no trace of the Leos or any other packs being

here in the last day or two," he told Kaden.

"Good," our alpha said. He checked his phone with a frown. "They should have been here by now."

"They must be running late," Stella said.

"Maybe." Kaden didn't sound convinced. The other shifters all looked grim too like they were expecting the worst.

We decided to keep waiting. Jack shifted back into wolf form to go snoop around some more, and some of the other warriors grew restless after more time passed. Kaden looked up into the night sky every few minutes, though none of us could hear the roar of a jet.

After about thirty minutes, Stella tugged on my arm and jerked her head back to the van. She grabbed a bag of chips and some water from inside it, and then we sat in the grass.

"Do you think they aren't coming?" I asked.

Stella's mouth twisted with disgust. "I think that the Leos have no honor, and we shouldn't have tried to bother with this. They're probably scheming something right now."

Hours passed, and there was still no sign of the Leos. At one point, Stella and I dozed in the grass, but Kaden walked over to us, his jaw clenched.

"They're not coming," he said, and I could hear the frustration in his voice.

"Have you heard anything from them?" Stella asked.

"No, not a peep."

Damn. All of that anticipation and stress for them to not even show up. Assholes.

We bundled back into the cars and prepared to leave.

The drive back was tense. I could feel the anger rolling off Kaden, almost choking me with its intensity.

"We'll find another way to get to the Leos," I eventually said, when Kaden met my eyes in the rearview mirror briefly. He didn't say anything. I didn't know if he believed me or not, and I didn't try to say anything else to convince him.

By the time we got back, it was already dawn. Some of the other shifters went home to get some sleep, while Stella and I followed Kaden into the house. Kaden disappeared into his room without another word, while Stella made a pot of coffee with a yawn. I stared at the sun, wondering if I should try to get more sleep, or accept that it was a lost cause.

"At least we got a nap in," Stella muttered, rubbing weariness from her eyes.

"I'm going to go take a shower," I said. "Maybe it will wake me up."

"Good idea. I'll get one after you."

I headed upstairs and popped into the shower. The warm water instantly helped perk me up, and I felt a lot better after washing my hair. Showers did such a good job of washing away all the shit from the previous day and giving a fresh start. That was exactly what I needed today.

I dropped the soap when an ear-piercing sound blared through the house. I covered my ears, glancing around, and then realized the sound was coming from the town. An alarm, blasting throughout the pack lands—warning us we were in danger.

It was so loud it made every hair on my body stand on end. I went into full panic mode, stopping just to grab a towel on the way out into the hall. I almost ran smack into Kaden, who was coming out of his room.

The second he saw me, he grabbed my arm. "Come on, we have to get out of here."

"What's happening?" I asked, as he practically carried me down the stairs.

"My wards along the pack lands are being broken. It should be impossible, but there's no way I'm wrong about it. I can feel them being torn apart."

"Is it the Leos?" I asked, as my panic rose to new heights.

"It must be. They must have been there all along and somehow followed us back." His face darkened with barely-checked anger. "It should be impossible."

"Where are we going?" I asked, clutching my towel tight to keep it wrapped around my body. Kaden must have noticed because his eyes dropped to my exposed shoulders and then to my legs.

"Get dressed. We're going to the town square to prepare for battle."

I rolled my eyes. It was just like Kaden to drag me down here and then order me to run back up and get dressed. I barely even noticed my state of undress anymore, and I'd probably be in wolf form soon anyway. Back at the Convergence, I'd been so conscious of being naked, but now I was a lot more comfortable with it, after all the shifting I'd done. No one looked twice at someone who was nude and getting ready to shift. But I had a feeling Kaden wanted me dressed for him more than for me. Either he didn't want other guys looking at me, or he found me way too distracting without my clothes on.

I quickly dressed in some of my training clothes, then ran back downstairs. Kaden jerked his head to the door, and I was surprised he'd waited for me. There was no sign of Stella, so she must have already left.

Together we ran toward the center of town, while other shifters did the same, some already in wolf form. The park in the center was packed, much like it had been at my party, but this time there was no laughter and no music. Everyone looked scared, and no one seemed to know quite what was going on.

Kaden let out a howl that shook me to my very core, getting everyone's attention. Pack members drew closer to Kaden, looking up to him for answers. I spotted Stella in the crowd, her eyes wide.

"We're under attack," Kaden said, and a collective murmur went through the crowd. Kaden held his hand up and it stopped. "We've trained for this. You all know what to do. Warriors, take up defensive positions. Everyone else, head for one of the hidden shelters. Follow Clayton and Stella."

Kaden put his hands on Stella's shoulders and they shared a look. He said something to her low, too low for me to make out among the commotion around me. Then Stella hugged her brother tight, before pulling away. She joined Clayton on the other side of the park, where some shifters were gathering, including all the children. I watched her go with a lump in my throat, praying they would all be safe, and then turned to join the fighters.

Kaden grabbed my arm. "Not so fast. You're going with Stella."

I yanked my arm out from his grip. "No, I'm going to fight for my pack."

"They're here for you," he said, his brow furrowing. "But I won't let them have you. You need to hide with Stella and the others."

"I thought I was bait?" I said with a short laugh. "Now you want me to hide? No way."

"Ayla, I don't have time to argue with you." He took my face in his hands, gazing into my eyes. "I need you to hide, and I need you to go now. I care about you too much to lose you."

I gaped at him. "You—what?"

His mouth was on mine then, hot and rough, and he kissed me like he feared it might be the last time. I clung to his shoulders as I opened for him, wanting everything he would give me. His lips, his tongue, his hands. All of it, for as long as I could get it. Even if it was only a few seconds.

"I care about you too," I said, between rushed, frantic kisses. Neither one of us could seem to stop. "But I'm still going to fight. I won't let anyone die for me while I hide away."

That ended the kissing.

Kaden's eyes narrowed. "Don't make me force you."

"Force me?" I scoffed, and then realized what he meant. Now that I was a member of the pack, he could make me do anything he wanted using his alpha command. I'd never seen him use it before on anyone, which said a lot about him as an alpha. Dad had gone around flinging commands at everyone, and I had no doubt the Leo alpha did the same.

"Go with Stella," he commanded, his words sounding like a guttural growl, something halfway between man and beast.

I felt the power in his voice and gritted my teeth, waiting for the compulsion to overtake me, but it never did. Huh. That was new. I lifted my chin. "No."

Kaden stared at me with his brow furrowing. "It didn't work on you. That shouldn't be possible."

Suddenly a howl went through the air, loud and clear as a bell. The hairs rose on my neck, and Kaden swore under his breath, shoving me behind him.

That was all the warning we got before a huge attack force entered the town. Wolves poured in, alongside humans that hadn't shifted yet, bearing Leo, Aries, and Taurus pack marks. Walking behind them was a group of robed women—the Sun Witches. Shit, they were here too? That must be how the attackers got through Kaden's wards.

Then I felt a sudden awareness inside me, and all the feelings I'd kept at the back of my mind since the Convergence suddenly flared to life. *Jordan.* He was here, and my eyes couldn't help but seek him out like I was hungry for the sight of him.

There. Standing beside his father, the Leo alpha, at the edge of the forest.

He'd come for me.

CHAPTER THIRTY-ONE

I HADN'T SEEN Jordan since the night of the Convergence, and the tug at the base of my spine from the bond nearly knocked me over. Damn, he was gorgeous. I'd forgotten how pretty he was while I'd been apart from him, and now I soaked up the sight of his perfect blond hair and chiseled jawline. Heat pulsed inside me, drawing me toward him like a dog on a leash.

As if he'd felt it too, Jordan's eyes met mine and he gave me a cocky smile. He looked at me like I was something he owned, and the bond made me want that too. Everything inside me screamed for me to run to him, and I clenched my fists as I resisted the pull. Fuck. Maybe I should have gone with Stella after all.

I turned back toward Kaden and some of the haze cleared. *He* was the one I wanted. Not Jordan. As long as I focused on that, I'd make it through this fight.

Wolves surrounded us from every side, while our own

warriors charged forth to meet them. Kaden leaped from my side, not even bothering to shift as he knocked into one of the enemy wolves and sent it flying. The shifter yelped and didn't get up again.

A male Leo opened his mouth and used his lion roar to scatter our forces as we met them head-on. I felt the urge to run deep in my bones, muscles tensed to do just that, but I gritted my teeth and weathered it. When I looked up again, Kaden was the only other one who hadn't fled, and he ripped into the Leo with his bare hands with a snarl. Other wolves immediately charged him.

I stepped up to help him, but a movement out of the corner of my eye distracted me. A group of wolves was headed after Stella's group. Aries wolves. Getting ready to do their ram charge.

"Oh, no you don't," I muttered and sprinted after them, stripping my shirt off as I did so. I shifted since I could get to them faster on four legs instead of two, and instantly felt more alert as a wolf. Since it was daytime, there was no way I'd be able to use my moon magic, but I still had the powers of the Ophiuchus pack.

I leaped onto the back of the first wolf and bit into him, deep and hard. Poison seeped from my fangs, and I made sure it was enough to kill. He fell, and I stepped in front of Stella, who was shielding some pups with her body in her wolf form. She was black, like her brother, though not nearly as huge. I snarled at the rest of the wolves. Another one jumped forward, and I took him down, too. I was vicious, just like Stella and Kaden had taught me to be, but I'd sooner die than let these wolves hurt my pack's pups.

Thank you, Stella's voice said in my head. It took me a second to remember that as a member of the pack, I could communicate with them as a wolf now.

Go, I told her, as I snapped at another wolf, daring her to get close enough for me to use my teeth on her. Stella nudged the wolf pups away, and they disappeared into the woods with her.

A wolf I now instinctively recognized as Harper jumped in and helped me defeat the last of the wolves trying to go after the pups. Then we gave each other a quick nuzzle of solidarity with our snouts, before running back to the center of town.

I caught sight of Kaden in the center of the town. He was still in human form and covered in blood, surrounded by dead wolves he must have somehow killed with his bare hands. Pride welled up inside me—that was *my* alpha.

"Dixon!" he shouted over the din of the fight. "Come out, you fucking coward, and fight me. Alpha against alpha, like in the old days. Or are you afraid I'll beat you?"

The fighting paused, wolves dropping their prey and turning to face their respective leaders. Dixon laughed from the edge of the battle, where he'd been watching it all. "I'm not afraid, but you should be."

The Leo alpha shifted with a roar, becoming a huge wolf, his fur a reddish-gold that always seemed to catch the sunlight. He was so large and ferocious he almost looked like a lion himself.

Kaden shifted as he ran to meet the other alpha, becoming a monstrous black beast with poison fangs, like something out of a nightmare. The other packs all thought him a villain, and though he certainly looked the part, I knew better now.

Dixon waited for Kaden to get close to him, and then let out his lion's roar. It was far enough away that I didn't feel its effects, but Kaden stopped mid-stride and shook his head. I saw him tremble as if fighting against his body's urge to run, and then he snarled again and leaped at Dixon, teeth flashing.

They tumbled to the ground, rolling and fighting for dominance. It was dead silent as we all stood frozen, watching them tussle for dominance, the only sounds the snarls and growls as the two alphas fought. Kaden landed a bite on Dixon, but the older wolf shook it off and kept fighting. He chomped down on Kaden's leg, jerking him around, and then tossed him into a tree with a show of strength. I pawed at the ground, whining softly, worried for the man I'd come to care so much about. I desperately wanted to run to him and help however I could, but I knew this wasn't my fight.

It went on for what felt like an eternity, a blur of fur, claws, and fangs that was sometimes hard to follow. I watched Kaden land several more bites on Dixon, and with each one, he seemed to weaken. But Dixon was fierce, fighting back with everything he had, his snout coated with Kaden's blood. He managed to knock Kaden to the ground, standing over him, and my breath caught, fearing the worst.

But then Kaden flipped him over, knocking the other alpha to the ground, and sunk his fangs into Dixon's neck. The Leo alpha twitched a few times and then went still.

Kaden lifted his blood-soaked head and howled, signaling the win. The sound echoed through the entire forest, and I knew every shifter fighting on either side had heard it. I looked around, trying to see what the Leo pack would do without their leader. A growl went through several shifters close to me, and then they turned tail and fled. I chased them down, as did others of my pack, and watched several meet their end as they tucked their tails and ran.

Let them flee, Kaden told us, and a huge sigh of relief went through my entire body at the sound of Kaden's voice in my head. *They're nothing but cowards. The victory is ours.*

Something wasn't quite right though. I hadn't seen Jordan during the fight. I closed my eyes and sought him out through the bond, which wanted nothing more than to lead me to him. Uneasiness roiled through my gut as I realized which direction he was in—the same direction Stella had gone with the pups. I ran toward the woods without waiting to see what Kaden would do next, letting the bond finally pull me to Jordan, as it had been trying to do since we were mated.

Jordan lounged against a black SUV with some of the Leos who had successfully fled, and didn't look surprised at all to see me crash through the underbrush. I was momentarily stunned with a wave of desire for him and had to forcibly hold myself back from leaping on him—either to kiss him or to kill him, I wasn't entirely sure.

"So glad you've decided to join us," he drawled, flashing me a sinister smile. "Now you're going to get in the car and come with me."

I shifted back to human form, not even caring that I was naked. "Like hell I will. This is my pack now and your alpha is dead. Get the fuck off our lands and stay out of my life."

"I can't do that." His eyes raked up and down my body possessively and I shuddered with a mix of lust and hatred. "I'm not leaving without you, but I will make you a deal. The Sun Witches have the weak ones from your pack surrounded, along with the children. At my command, they'll burn them all alive. That is, unless you come with me now."

"I don't believe you."

He pulled out a phone from his pocket and tilted it toward me. On the screen, I could see Sun Witches standing around a hatch door they'd uncovered in the middle of the forest. As I watched, they dragged one of the wolf pups out of it, and then the camera panned to show me Stella and Clayton, both captured, both fighting with everything they had to escape. Fire surrounded them, the flames licking at their tails, and only the Sun Witches' magic kept it from spreading across the entire forest.

"You monster," I whispered. I glared at my mate, a man I hated so much it burned in my veins, making my hands shake. I wanted to jump onto him and tear his throat out, but the fucking bond wouldn't let me.

Jordan looked down at his phone, watching the screen,

then raised his eyebrows at me. "It's your choice. Join me...or watch them all burn."

There was nothing I could do. I couldn't fight Jordan, and even if I managed to reach out to Kaden for help, the Sun Witches could easily burn our entire pack lands within seconds. I wasn't going to let innocent wolf pups die for me —or anyone else in my pack.

Defeat flowed through me, and I bowed my head. There was no way out of this. I had to go with him.

I took a step closer, meeting Jordan's eye. "I'll go willingly if the Sun Witches—along with the Leos and your allies—all leave without harming anyone in my pack. Swear it on our bond, and I'm yours."

"You really are attached to them, aren't you?" He tilted his head and smiled as if this had been his plan all along. "Fine, I swear it on our bond."

I thought he might still be lying, but then he barked orders into his phone, and moments later he showed me that the Sun Witches were leaving. They seemed to go poof, vanishing in a burst of sunlight, but at least they were gone. I caught sight of other wolves rushing through the leaves, heading out of the pack lands. I closed my eyes, thankful it was over.

Jordan held out his hand to me. "It's done. Now come with me."

I wanted to slap his hand away, to tell him to shove it up his ass, but I bit my tongue and took it instead. The instant we touched, the mate bond screamed *yes, yes, yes,* and I wanted to both cry and cheer as it swept through me.

Jordan's presence filled my mind, becoming so big it blocked out every other sound and sight except for him. He was my world. My everything. My mate.

NO, my mind screamed. *Kaden is the one, not him.*

I clung tightly to that small shred of my sanity as Jordan helped me into the backseat of the van, never once letting go of me. He slid in beside me and offered me a blanket to cover myself with. I glared at him as I wrapped it around myself.

As we pulled away, I saw Kaden standing in the trees on a ridge above us, where he must have had a full view of me willingly getting in the car. Dark fury twisted his face, but there was something else there too. Something like heartbreak.

I knew exactly what he was thinking—that I couldn't resist the mate bond and decided to be with Jordan after all. Just like he'd said I would. I reached my hand back toward Kaden, placing it flat against the window, wanting to scream his name and tell him I had to do it to save the pack, but we were already gone. I lost sight of my alpha in the trees as the car drove off.

"It's going to be a long journey back to Leo territory," Jordan said, as he stroked my hand with his thumb in a way that made my body ache for more of his touch, even as I cursed his existence. "I need to make sure you don't try to escape again. You're surprisingly good at that."

"I won't escape," I said, lying between my teeth. As soon as night fell, I'd be out of here. I'd run back to Kaden so I could explain everything. As long as I could get Jordan to stop touching me.

"No, you won't." He opened a small box, pulling out a syringe. His hand moved to my arm, gripping tightly, as I realized what he was doing. "I'll make sure of it."

"No!" I pressed myself against the car door, trying to get as far away from the needle as possible, but Jordan boxed me in, looming over me. I tried to jerk away, but Jordan's hold was strong, and his touch made me weak.

Jordan's cold, arrogant expression didn't change as he lowered the syringe to my arm. I turned away from him, unable to bear looking into his face any longer, while the sharp pinch made my breath catch. I clawed at the door handle, trying to get it to open, but whatever Jordan had injected me with was fast-acting, and my limbs quickly stopped working. *No,* I tried to scream, but I blacked out before I could even get the word out.

CHAPTER THIRTY-TWO

I WOKE SURROUNDED by iron bars. *Fuck, this is becoming a bad habit,* I thought.

I closed my eyes and took a deep breath. Maybe I was dreaming, and when I opened my eyes I'd be in my room, and none of this would have happened.

No such luck. When I opened my eyes again, I was still looking at the interior of a strange cell. Did all the packs have prisons or just the two I'd been captured by? The Cancer pack had never had one, which I was suddenly grateful for. Dad would have locked me up in one at least once out of spite.

I started to take in my surroundings when I felt a tug on the bond. *Shit.* I knew exactly who was coming.

Jordan strolled into the room, a smug smirk on his gorgeous face. "I'm glad to see you're awake."

"I find that hard to believe." I crossed my arms. "Where am I?"

"You're in Leo territory. Welcome home."

"Home?" I glared at him. "Have you forgotten how you rejected me at the Convergence? How your pack killed my family? And how you seemed pretty intent on killing me too?"

"A lot has changed, Ayla." Jordan spread his arms wide, and a ripple of desire went through me at the sight. "Thanks to you, I'm the alpha of the Leo pack now. With the help of the Sun Witches, I'll soon rule over all of the other packs—and you'll rule by my side, as my alpha queen."

I laughed. I couldn't help it. The idea was so ridiculous, it was comical. "I will *never* be with you. I'd rather be dead."

Jordan's face changed, losing the charm and replacing it with something sinister. "The way you look at me says otherwise."

"Why didn't you just have someone kill me?" I asked, focusing on my anger. It helped distract me from the need to throw myself at his feet. "Or why not ask the Sun Witches to remove the bond so you can be free of me?" I snorted. "Me, the half-human mutt. That's what you called me, after all, when you said you wanted me to suffer. Or have you real-ized that the best way to make me suffer is to force me to be with you?"

His eyes gleamed, and I thought he might lunge forward and strike me like he'd done back at the Convergence. "You're mine, Ayla. And like I said, things have changed. I have big, big plans for you."

"Oh great," I said. "Can't wait to hear them."

Jordan's face went even darker, but he just turned away

and left. No offer of food or water. The door slammed behind him without another word, and I was alone once again.

I sank down onto the cot, my anger dispersing, only to be replaced by hopelessness. I was being held captive by my worst enemies, and no one was going to rescue me. Kaden wouldn't come after me. Not after what he'd seen. I was truly on my own.

Kaden, I thought fiercely as I stood up and began looking for ways to escape this prison. *I'm going to prove you wrong. I will fight this, and I'll find my way back to you. Somehow.*

The one thing I had going for me was that Jordan underestimated me. He didn't know that I'd spent my time with the Ophiuchus pack training to fight. He didn't know I was Moon Touched.

I rubbed the pack mark on my arm, finding comfort in the knowledge it was still there. I wasn't the same scared, helpless weakling that Jordan had tortured at the Convergence. I was a fighter now.

I was a member of the lost pack.

AUTHOR'S NOTE

THANK YOU for reading Moon Touched! Will Ayla find her way back to Kaden? Find out in Star Cursed!

No matter what your sign is, please don't be offended by my portrayal here! I'm exactly on the Cancer/Leo cusp (July 23), and though I have some traits from each sign, I've never felt like I fit either one perfectly. That's why I chose to write about a heroine torn between those two packs, and though my portrayal of them may not always be favorable, remember what Ayla said: "There was something wrong with the Zodiac packs, something festering from within..." Something a strong heroine like herself is going to get to the bottom of, perhaps? We'll find out more in the next two books, plus we'll spend some time with the other signs. And if this series does well, I'd love to write books about each of the different signs too!

ABOUT THE AUTHOR

Elizabeth Briggs is the *New York Times* bestselling author of paranormal and fantasy romance. She graduated from UCLA with a degree in Sociology and has worked for an international law firm, mentored teens in writing, and volunteered with dog rescue groups. Now she's a full-time geek who lives in Los Angeles with her family and a pack of fluffy dogs.

Visit Elizabeth's website: www.elizabethbriggs.net

Join Elizabeth's Facebook group for fun book chat and early sneak peeks!

Made in the USA
Columbia, SC
05 March 2023